The Book of Virtues

FOR YOUNG PEOPLE

A TREASURY OF GREAT MORAL STORIES

EDITED, WITH COMMENTARY, BY

William J. Bennett

SIMON & SCHUSTER
BOOKS FOR YOUNG READERS
NEW YORK

SIMON & SCHUSTER BOOKS FOR YOUNG READERS
An imprint of Simon & Schuster Children's Publishing Division
1230 Avenue of the Americas, New York, New York 10020

Book design by Sylvia Frezzolini Severance
The text for this book is set in 12 point Sabon
The illustrations are rendered in cut paper
Printed and bound in the United States of America

FIRST EDITION

10 9 8 7 6 5 4 3 2 1

Library of Congress Cataloging-in-Publication Data
The Book of virtues for young people : a treasury of great moral stories / edited,
with commentary, by William J. Bennett.
p.   cm.
Originally published: Parsippany, NJ ; Silver Burdett Press, 1996.
With new ill.   Includes index.
Partial contents: Self-discipline — Compassion — Responsibility — Friendship — Work —
Courage — Perseverence — Honesty — Loyalty — Faith.
Summary: Well-known works including fables, folklore, fiction, drama, and more, by such
authors as Aesop, Dickens, Tolstoy, Shakespeare, and Baldwin, are presented to teach virtues,
including compassion, courage, honesty, friendship, and faith.
ISBN 0-689-81613-8
1. Literature—Collections. 2. Conduct of life—Literary collections.
[1. Conduct of life—Literary collections.] I. Bennett, William John, 1943–
PN6014.B695 1997
808.8'038—DC21   96-53584

To the families of America
from my family:
Bill, Elayne, John
and Joseph Bennett.

✎ Contents

⟨⟨ Introduction

L ife is full of questions, and most of us spend much of our time thinking about the relatively unimportant ones. What time does the game come on TV? Do these shoes go with these pants? Will I get that new bike for my birthday? These are the questions of daily living, and they are natural enough. There is nothing wrong with them. But we need to spend some time thinking about the truly important questions, too, the ones that lead to *better* living. This book will help you find answers to three of them: What are virtues? Why do you need them? How do you get them?

The dictionary defines *virtue* as "a particular moral excellence" and tells us it comes from the Latin word virtus, meaning "strength" or "worth." Virtues come in several different varieties, and this book focuses on ten of them—self-discipline, compassion, responsibility, friendship, work, courage, perseverance, honesty, loyalty, and faith. The stories, poems, and writings in this book will help you recognize these character traits, both in yourself and in others, in part by showing you examples of virtues *in action*. (Remember, virtues for the most part lie in our actions—good deeds, not just good thoughts and intentions.) The more you witness virtues in action, the better you'll understand them. You need very clear understandings of virtues if you are to get them. And you need equally clear understandings of vices, and their consequences, if you are to steer clear of them.

Why do you need virtues? You'll meet several answers to that question in these pages. There are practical reasons: Your reputation, for example, is largely the sum of your virtues. There are social reasons: The kind and number of friends you have will depend on your own virtues. And there are, of course, purely unselfish reasons: Virtues are the character traits that move us to help family, loved ones, and even perfect strangers. In every area of life, you must constantly make choices about how to act, for your own sake and for others'. Many of those choices involve matters of right and wrong, and you can't choose to do the right thing without possessing some virtues.

So how do you get (and keep) these virtues? The answer is one of those solutions that is easier said than done. You practice. Like anything else worthwhile, attaining virtue requires serious effort and attention. You must set some standards for yourself and then do everything you can to live up to them in your *everyday activities*. Hopefully, you will find models and standards in the stories and other writings in this book. People have been using some of them for centuries as reminders of what is good and what is bad, as moral compasses to right and wrong. If you take these stories to heart and pattern your own actions after the examples they set, you'll begin to find that these notions of honesty and loyalty and self-discipline are becoming habits. That's what you want. That's what we all want. When the virtues are a matter of habit for you, you're well equipped to face life. Remember too that none of us can be virtuous all the time. We are not angels, and we can't become angels, at least not in this life. But we can try to be better, and so we should.

SELF-DISCIPLINE

Self-discipline

Self-discipline is the virtue we use to manage ourselves and the different parts of our lives. It involves controlling our tempers, as in the story of "The King and His Hawk" in this chapter. It involves controlling our wishes, as we see in the story of "The Fisherman and His Wife." It means controlling our appetites, as in the fable "The Flies and the Honey Pot." It means controlling our egos, as in the story of "King Canute," and even controlling our mouths, as the poem "Our Lips and Ears" reminds us. Self-discipline also requires recognizing your limits, not wanting too much too soon, and not reaching so far beyond your abilities that you're asking for trouble, as in the legend "The Boy Who Tried To Be the Sun."

In short, self-discipline means saying yes to the right things and no to the wrong things. It means taking charge of yourself.

Unfortunately, self-discipline is one of the hardest virtues to achieve. In particular, many young people have a great difficulty getting to the point where they are truly in control of themselves. "Get your act together" is a phrase they often hear. It really means, "Get some self-discipline."

How do you get it?

You can start by following the directions of your parents, teachers, coaches, and ministers. Yes, self-discipline involves obedience. George Washington's mother was once asked how she raised such a remarkable son. "I taught him to obey," she answered. Following directions promptly, sticking to the rules cheerfully, and staying within the bounds of the law are all part of self-discipline.

Manners are another good way to develop self-discipline. It's one of the main reasons we have manners. They teach us to control our everyday interactions with others. Take a look at George Washington's "Rules of Civility" in this chapter for a good model of how to treat friends and strangers. You might try writing down some of your own rules of conduct, and every once in a while ask yourself how good you are at following them.

Maintaining a schedule is another way to learn self-discipline. One of the hardest things to get control of is time. If you feel like you waste too much of it (perhaps in front of the television), write down a schedule of better ways to spend your time, and stick to it.

All of this talk about rules and schedules may sound tough. And sometimes it is. That's exactly why so many people have trouble with self-discipline. But the truth is that we feel much better about ourselves when we can control our actions.

The bottom line is that learning self-discipline is very much a do-it-yourself project. Your parents and teachers can help, but in the end, it takes lots of practice, and no one can do that for you. It takes time and it takes patience. Use the virtue of perseverance to learn self-discipline. You'll find yourself a happier, healthier, better person.

Anger

CHARLES AND MARY LAMB

Everyone gets angry at times. But anger is not reason enough to lose control or to become bitter and cruel.

> Anger in its time and place
> May assume a kind of grace.
> It must have some reason in it,
> And not last beyond a minute.
> If to further lengths it go,
> It does into malice grow.
> 'Tis the difference that we see
> 'Twixt the serpent and the bee.
> If the latter you provoke,
> It inflicts a hasty stroke,
> Puts you to some little pain,
> But it *never stings again.*
> Close in tufted bush or brake
> Lurks the poison-swelled snake
> Nursing up his cherished wrath;
> In the purlieus of his path,
> In the cold, or in the warm,
> Mean him good, or mean him harm,
> Wheresoever fate may bring you,
> The vile snake will *always sting you.*

✦ The King and His Hawk

RETOLD BY JAMES BALDWIN

Thomas Jefferson gave us simple but effective advice about controlling our temper: When angry, count to ten before you do anything, and if very angry, count to a hundred. Genghis Khan learned the same lesson 800 years ago. His empire once stretched from eastern Europe to the Sea of Japan.

Genghis Khan was a great king and warrior.

He led his army into China and Persia, and he conquered many lands. In every country, men told about his daring deeds, and they said that since Alexander the Great there had been no king like him.

One morning when he was home from the wars, he rode out into the woods to have a day's sport. Many of his friends were with him. They rode out gayly, carrying their bows and arrows. Behind them came the servants with the hounds.

It was a merry hunting party. The woods rang with their shouts and laughter. They expected to carry much game home in the evening.

On the king's wrist sat his favorite hawk, for in those days hawks were trained to hunt. At a word from their masters they would fly high up into the air, and look around for prey. If they chanced to see a deer or a rabbit, they would swoop down upon it swift as any arrow.

All day long Genghis Khan and his huntsmen rode through the woods. But they did not find as much game as they expected.

Toward evening they started for home. The king had

often ridden through the woods, and he knew all the paths. So while the rest of the party took the nearest way, he went by a longer road through a valley between two mountains.

The day had been warm, and the king was very thirsty. His pet hawk had left his wrist and flown away. It would be sure to find its way home.

The king rode slowly along. He had once seen a spring of clear water near this pathway. If he could only find it now! But the hot days of summer had dried up all the mountain brooks.

At last, to his joy, he saw some water trickling down over the edge of a rock. He knew that there was a spring farther up. In the wet season, a swift stream of water always poured down here; but now it came only one drop at a time.

The king leaped from his horse. He took a little silver cup from his hunting bag. He held it so as to catch the slowly falling drops.

It took a long time to fill the cup; and the king was so thirsty that he could hardly wait. At last it was nearly full. He put the cup to his lips, and was about to drink.

All at once there was a whirring sound in the air, and the cup was knocked from his hands. The water was all spilled upon the ground.

The king looked up to see who had done this thing. It was his pet hawk.

The hawk flew back and forth a few times, and then alighted among the rocks by the spring.

The king picked up the cup, and again held it to catch the trickling drops.

This time he did not wait so long. When the cup was half full, he lifted it toward his mouth. But before it had touched his lips, the hawk swooped down again and knocked it from his hands.

And now the king began to grow angry. He tried again, and for the third time the hawk kept him from drinking.

The king was now very angry indeed.

"How do you dare to act so?" he cried. "If I had you in my hands, I would wring your neck!"

Then he filled the cup again. But before he tried to drink, he drew his sword.

"Now, Sir Hawk," he said, "this is the last time."

He had hardly spoken before the hawk swooped down and knocked the cup from his hand. But the king was looking for this. With a quick sweep of the sword he struck the bird as it passed.

The next moment the poor hawk lay bleeding and dying at its master's feet.

"That is what you get for your pains," said Genghis Khan.

But when he looked for his cup, he found that it had fallen between two rocks, where he could not reach it.

"At any rate, I will have a drink from that spring," he said to himself.

With that he began to climb the steep bank to the place from which the water trickled. It was hard work, and the higher he climbed, the thirstier he became.

At last he reached the place. There indeed was a pool of water; but what was that lying in the pool, and almost filling it? It was a huge, dead snake of the most poisonous kind.

The king stopped. He forgot his thirst. He thought only of the poor dead bird lying on the ground below him.

"The hawk saved my life!" he cried, "and how did I repay him? He was my best friend, and I have killed him."

He clambered down the bank. He took the bird up gently, and laid it in his hunting bag. Then he mounted his horse and rode swiftly home. He said to himself,

"I have learned a sad lesson today, and that is, never to do anything in anger."

George Washington's Rules of Civility

When George Washington was fourteen years old, he kept a notebook in which he copied 110 best ways to act around other people. Here are fifty-four of George Washington's "Rules of Civility."

1. Every action in company ought to be with some sign of respect to those present.

2. In the presence of others sing not to yourself with a humming voice, nor drum with your fingers or feet.

3. Speak not when others speak, sit not when others stand, and walk not when others stop.

4. Turn not your back to others, especially in speaking; jog not the table or desk on which another reads or writes; lean not on anyone.

5. Be no flatterer, neither play with anyone that delights not to be played with.

6. Read no letters, books, or papers in company; but when there is a necessity for doing it, you must ask leave. Come not near the books or writings of anyone so as to read them unasked; also look not nigh when another is writing a letter.

7. Let your countenance be pleasant, but in serious matters somewhat grave.

8. Show not yourself glad at the misfortune of another, though he were your enemy.

9. They that are in dignity or office have in all places precedency, but whilst they are young, they ought to respect those that are their equals in birth or other qualities, though they have no public charge.

10. It is good manners to prefer them to whom we speak before ourselves, especially if they be above us, with whom in no sort we ought to begin.

11. Let your discourse with men of business be short and comprehensive.

12. In visiting the sick do not presently play the physician if you be not knowing therein.

13. In writing or speaking give to every person his due title according to his degree and the custom of the place.

14. Strive not with your superiors in argument, but always submit your judgment to others with modesty.

15. Undertake not to teach your equal in the art he himself professes; it savors of arrogancy.

16. When a man does all he can, though it succeeds not well, blame not him that did it.

17. Being to advise or reprehend anyone, consider whether it ought to be in public or in private, presently or at some other time, also in what terms to do it; and in reproving show no signs of choler, but do it with sweetness and mildness.

18. Mock not nor jest at anything of importance; break no jests that are sharp or biting; and if you deliver anything witty or pleasant, abstain from laughing thereat yourself.

19. Wherein you reprove another be unblamable

yourself, for example is more prevalent than precept.

20. Use no reproachful language against anyone, neither curses nor revilings.

21. Be not hasty to believe flying reports to the disparagement of anyone.

22. In your apparel be modest, and endeavor to accommodate nature rather than procure admiration. Keep to the fashion of your equals, such as are civil and orderly with respect to time and place.

23. Play not the peacock, looking everywhere about you to see if you be well decked, if your shoes fit well, if your stockings set neatly and clothes handsomely.

24. Associate yourself with men of good quality if you esteem your own reputation, for it is better to be alone than in bad company.

25. Let your conversation be without malice or envy, for it is a sign of tractable and commendable nature; and in all causes of passion admit reason to govern.

26. Be not immodest in urging your friend to discover a secret.

27. Utter not base and frivolous things amongst grown and learned men, nor very difficult questions or subjects amongst the ignorant, nor things hard to be believed.

28. Speak not of doleful things in time of mirth nor at the table; speak not of melancholy things, as death and wounds; and if others mention them, change, if you can, the discourse. Tell not your dreams but to your intimate friends.

29. Break not a jest when none take pleasure in mirth. Laugh not aloud, nor at all without occasion. Deride no man's misfortunes, though there seem to be some cause.

30. Speak not injurious words, neither in jest or

earnest. Scoff at none, although they give occasion.

31. Be not forward, but friendly and courteous, the first to salute, hear and answer, and be not pensive when it is time to converse.

32. Detract not from others, but neither be excessive in commending.

33. Go not thither where you know not whether you shall be welcome or not. Give not advice without being asked; and when desired, do it briefly.

34. If two contend together, take not the part of either unconstrained, and be not obstinate in your opinion; in things indifferent be of the major side.

35. Reprehend not the imperfection of others, for that belongs to parents, masters, and superiors.

36. Gaze not on the marks or blemishes of others, and ask not how they came. What you may speak in secret to your friend deliver not before others.

37. Speak not in an unknown tongue in company, but in your own language; and that as those of quality do, and not as the vulgar. Sublime matters treat seriously.

38. Think before you speak; pronounce not imperfectly, nor bring out your words too hastily, but orderly and distinctly.

39. When another speaks, be attentive yourself, and disturb not the audience. If any hesitate in his words, help him not, nor prompt him without being desired; interrupt him not, nor answer him till his speech be ended.

40. Treat with men at fit times about business, and whisper not in the company of others.

41. Make no comparisons; and if any of the company be commended for any brave act of virtue, commend not another for the same.

42. Be not apt to relate news if you know not the truth thereof. In discoursing of things you have heard, name not your author always. A secret discover not.

43. Be not curious to know the affairs of others, neither approach to those that speak in private.

44. Undertake not what you cannot perform; but be careful to keep your promise.

45. When you deliver a matter, do it without passion and indiscretion, however mean the person may be you do it to.

46. When your superiors talk to anybody, hear them; neither speak or laugh.

47. In disputes be not so desirous to overcome as not to give liberty to each one to deliver his opinion, and submit to the judgment of the major part, especially if they are judges of the dispute.

48. Be not tedious in discourse, make not many digressions, nor repeat often the same matter of discourse.

49. Speak no evil of the absent, for it is unjust.

50. Be not angry at table, whatever happens; and if you have reason to be so show it not; put on a cheerful countenance, especially if there be strangers, for good humor makes one dish a feast.

51. Set not yourself at the upper end of the table; but if it be your due, or the master of the house will have it so, contend not, lest you should trouble the company.

52. When you speak of God or his attributes, let it be seriously, in reverence and honor, and obey your natural parents.

53. Let your recreations be manful, not sinful.

54. Labor to keep alive in your breast that little spark of celestial fire called conscience.

❧ King Canute on the Seashore
ADAPTED FROM JAMES BALDWIN

Canute the Second, who reigned during the eleventh century, was the first Danish king of England. In this famous tale, he proves to be a man who knows how to control his pride. It is a good lesson for all who aspire to high office.

Long ago, England was ruled by a king named Canute. Like many leaders and men of power, Canute was surrounded by people who were always praising him. Every time he walked into a room, the flattery began.

"You are the greatest man that ever lived," one would say.

"O king, there can never be another as mighty as you," another would insist.

"Your highness, there is nothing you cannot do," someone would smile.

"Great Canute, you are the monarch of all," another would sing. "Nothing in this world dares to disobey you."

The king was a man of sense, and he grew tired of hearing such foolish speeches.

One day he was walking by the seashore, and his officers and courtiers were with him, praising him as usual. Canute decided to teach them a lesson.

"So you say I am the greatest man in the world?" he asked them.

"O king," they cried, "there never has been anyone as mighty as you, and there never will be anyone so great, ever again!"

"And you say all things obey me?" Canute asked.

"Absolutely!" they said. "The world bows before you, and gives you honor."

"I see," the king answered. "In that case, bring me my chair, and we will go down to the water."

"At once, your majesty!" They scrambled to carry his royal chair over the sands.

"Bring it closer to the sea," Canute called. "Put it right here, right at the water's edge." He sat down and surveyed the ocean before him. "I notice the tide is coming in. Do you thing it will stop if I give the command?"

His officers were puzzled, but they did not dare say no. "Give the order, O great king, and it will obey," one of them assured him.

"Very well. Sea," cried Canute, "I command you to come no further! Waves, stop your rolling! Surf, stop your pounding! Do not dare touch my feet!"

He waited a moment, quietly, and a tiny wave rushed up the sand and lapped at his feet.

"How dare you!" Canute shouted. "Ocean, turn back now! I have ordered you to retreat before me, and now you must obey! Go back!"

And in answer another wave swept forward and curled around the king's feet. The tide came in, just as it always did. The water rose higher and higher. It came up around the king's chair, and wet not only his feet, but also his robe. His officers stood about him, alarmed, and wondering whether he was not mad.

"Well, my friends," Canute said, "it seems I do not have quite so much power as you would have me believe. Perhaps you have learned something today. Perhaps now you will remember there is only one King who is all-powerful, and it is he who rules the sea, and holds the ocean in the hollow of his hand. I suggest you reserve your praises for him."

The royal officers and courtiers hung their heads and looked foolish. And some say Canute took off his crown soon afterward, and never wore it again.

ﾠ Our Lips and Ears

How much we talk, especially how much we talk about ourselves, reveals a lot about ourselves.

> If you your lips would keep from slips,
>   Five things observe with care:
> Of whom you speak, to whom you speak,
>   And how and when and where.
>
> If you your ears would save from jeers,
>   These things keep meekly hid:
> Myself and I, and mine and my,
>   And how I do and did.

ﾠ Seeing Gold

Greed often blinds, this Chinese tale reminds us.

A man who had a great craving for wealth was walking through the thronging market one morning when he happened to pass the gold dealer's stall. His glance fell on the glittering display of rings and bullion and nuggets—and he grabbed as much as he could from the table and began to run down the street.

The police soon caught up with him.

"With so many people in the market, how in the world did you think you could get away?" they asked.

"When I reached, I saw only gold, not the people," he answered.

ᕫ The Boy Who Tried to Be the Sun

This Native American tale about knowing one's limits and abiding by them comes from the Northwest Coast. It is remarkably similar to the Greek myth about Phaeton, who also tried to take the sun's place.

Once upon a time there was a woman who went up to the sky to marry the Sun. They lived happily together, especially after they had a young son. But eventually the woman began to feel homesick for her family and friends far below. Besides, she thought her son ought to get the chance to see her homeland.

The Sun, sensing why his wife was so forlorn, suggested she visit her parents for a while. He opened his eyes wide, and his wife and son slid down to earth on his eyelashes, which were the rays of the Sun.

Before long the other children of the village began to tease the boy, saying he had no father. He went to his mother with tears in his eyes and begged her for a bow and arrow. Then he went alone to the edge of the village and began shooting the arrows straight up into the air. The first arrow struck the roof of the sky and lodged there, the second arrow struck the notch of the first and stuck, and so on until a long chain of arrows dangled to the earth.

The boy climbed the chain to the Sun's house, where he told his father how the children of the village had treated him.

"I want to show them I really am your son," he said. "Let me carry your torches for a day."

The Sun shook his head.

"That is a request I cannot grant," he said. "You see, I carry many torches across the sky. In the early morning, and again in the late evening, I burn only a few small ones—those you might be able to carry. But in the middle of the day, I light the great torches only I can bear."

But the boy begged and pleaded and insisted that, since he was the offspring of the Sun, he could surely handle the flames. At last his father consented.

At dawn the next morning, the boy started out. His father had warned him to light only a few small torches at first, but soon the youth grew impatient. He wanted the children in the village below to see him, so he decided to light all the torches at once, large and small.

Immediately it grew unbearably hot all over the earth. The forests burst into flames, the mountain tops smoked, the valleys turned into fiery furnaces. Some of the animals rushed headlong into the lakes and streams to escape the heat, only to find the water had begun to boil. Others tried to hide under rocks. The ermine tried to bury itself, but it did not dig deep enough, and the top of its tail stuck above the ground. It was scorched by the heat, and to this day the top of the ermine's tail has remained black. The mountain goat, however, was luckier. It ran into a cave and escaped the fire, so its fur stayed white.

The Sun looked down and saw all the people running to hide themselves from the flames, and he knew all things would perish if he did not act quickly. With a heavy heart he struck his own son down, and the boy fell back to earth like a stone.

⤞ The Fisherman and His Wife
RETOLD BY CLIFTON JOHNSON

We should know that too much of anything, even a good thing, may prove to be our undoing, as this old tale shows. We need to recognize when enough is enough.

There was once a fisherman who lived with his wife in a poor little hut close by the sea. One day, as the fisherman sat on the rocks at the water's edge fishing with his rod and line, a fish got caught on his hook that was so big and pulled so stoutly that he captured it with the greatest difficulty. He was feeling much pleased that he had secured so big a fish when he was surprised by hearing it say to him, "Pray let me live. I am not a real fish. I am a magician. Put me in the water and let me go."

"You need not make so many words about the matter," said the man. "I wish to have nothing to do with a fish that can talk."

Then he removed it from his hook and put it back into the water. "Now swim away as soon as you please," said the man, and the fish darted straight down to the bottom.

The fisherman returned to his little hut and told his wife how he had caught a great fish, and how it had told him it was a magician, and how, when he heard it speak, he had let it go.

"Did you not ask it for anything?" said the wife.

"No," replied the man. "What should I ask for?"

"What should you ask for!" exclaimed the wife. "You talk as if we had everything we want, but see how wretchedly we live in this dark little hut. Do go back and tell the fish we want a comfortable house."

The fisherman did not like to undertake such an errand. However, as his wife had bidden him to go, he went; and when he came to the sea the water looked all yellow and green. He stood on the rocks where he had fished and said,

> *"Oh, man of the sea!*
> *Come listen to me;*
> *For Alice my wife,*
> *The plague of my life,*
> *Hath sent me to beg a gift of thee!"*

Then the fish came swimming to him and said, "Well, what does she want?"

"Ah," answered the fisherman, "my wife says that when I had caught you I ought to have asked you for something before I let you go. She does not like living any longer in our little hut. She wants a comfortable house."

"Go home then," said the fish. "She is in the house she wants already."

So the man went home and found his wife standing in the doorway of a comfortable house, and behind the house was a yard with ducks and chickens picking about in it, and beyond the yard was a garden where grew all sorts of flowers and fruits. "How happily we shall live now!" said the fisherman.

Everything went right for a week or two, and then the

wife said, "Husband, there is not enough room in this house, and the yard and garden are a great deal smaller than they ought to be. I would like to have a large stone castle to live in. So go to the fish again and tell him to give us a castle."

"Wife," said the fisherman, "I don't like to go to him again, for perhaps, he will be angry. We ought to be content with a good house like this."

"Nonsense!" said the wife. "He will give us a castle very willingly. Go along and try."

The fisherman went, but his heart was heavy, and when he came to the sea the water was a dark gray color and looked very gloomy. He stood on the rocks at the water's edge and said,

> "Oh, man of the sea!
> Come listen to me;
> For Alice my wife,
> The plague of my life,
> Hath sent me to beg a gift of thee!"

Then the fish came swimming to him and said, "Well, what does she want now?"

"Ah," replied the man very sorrowfully, "my wife wants to live in a stone castle."

"Go home then," said the fish. "She is at the castle already."

So away went the fisherman and found his wife standing before a great castle. "See," said she, "is not this fine?"

They went into the castle, and many servants were there, and the rooms were richly furnished with handsome chairs and tables; and behind the castle was a park half a mile long, full of sheep and goats and rabbits and deer.

"Now," said the man, "we will live contented and

happy in this beautiful castle for the rest of our lives."

"Perhaps so," responded the wife. "But let us consider and sleep on it before we make up our minds." And they went to bed.

The next morning when they awoke it was broad daylight, and the wife jogged the fisherman with her elbow and said, "Get up, husband; bestir yourself, for we must be king and queen of all the land."

"Wife, wife," said the man, "why should we wish to be king and queen? I would not be king even if I could be."

"Well, I will be queen, anyway," said the wife. "Say no more about it; but go to the fish and tell him what I want."

So the man went, but he felt very sad to think that his wife should want to be queen. The sea was muddy and streaked with foam as he cried out,

"Oh, man of the sea!
Come listen to me;
For Alice my wife,
The plague of my life,
Hath sent me to beg a gift of thee!"

Then the fish came swimming to him and said, "Well, what would she have now?"

"Alas!" said the man. "My wife wants to be queen."

"Go home," said the fish. "She is queen already."

So the fisherman turned back and presently he came to a palace, and before it he saw a troop of soldiers, and he heard the sound of drums and trumpets. Then he entered the palace and there he found his wife sitting on a throne, with a golden crown on her head, and on each side of her stood six beautiful maidens.

"Well, wife," said the fisherman, "are you queen?"

"Yes," she replied, "I am queen."

When he had looked at her for a long time he said, "Ah, wife, what a fine thing it is to be queen! Now we shall never have anything more to wish for."

"I don't know how that may be," said she. "Never is a long time. I am queen, 'tis true, but I begin to be tired of it. I think I would like to be pope next."

"Oh, wife, wife!" the man exclaimed. "How can you be pope? There is but one pope at a time in all Christendom."

"Husband," said she, "I will be pope this very day."

"Ah, wife!" responded the fisherman. "The fish cannot make you pope and I would not like to ask for such a thing."

"What nonsense!" said she. "If he can make a queen, he can make a pope. Go and try."

So the fisherman went, and when he came to the shore the wind was raging and the waves were dashing on the rocks most fearfully, and the sky was dark with flying clouds. The fisherman was frightened, but nevertheless he obeyed his wife and called out,

> "Oh, man of the sea!
> Come listen to me;
> For Alice my wife,
> The plague of my life,
> Hath sent me to beg a gift of thee!"

Then the fish came swimming to him and said, "What does she want this time?"

"Ah," said the fisherman, "my wife wants to be pope."

"Go home," commanded the fish. "She is pope already."

So the fisherman went home and found his wife sitting on a throne that was a hundred feet high, and on either side many candles of all sizes were burning, and she had three great crowns on her head one above the other and was surrounded by all the pomp and power of the church.

"Wife," said the fisherman, as he gazed at all this magnificence, "are you pope?"

"Yes," she replied, "I am pope."

"Well, wife," said he, "it is a grand thing to be pope. And now you must be content, for you can be nothing greater."

"We will see about that," she said.

Then they went to bed; but the wife could not sleep because all night long she was trying to think what she should be next. At last morning came and the sun rose. "Ha!" cried she. "I was about to sleep, had not the sun disturbed me with its bright light. Cannot I prevent the sun rising?" and she became very angry and said to her husband, "Go to the fish and tell him I want to be lord of the sun and moon."

"Alas, wife," said he, "can you not be content to be pope?"

"No," said she, "I am very uneasy, and cannot bear to see the sun and moon rise without my leave. Go to the fish at once!"

The man went, and as he approached the shore a dreadful storm arose so that the trees and rocks shook, and the sky grew black, and the lightning flashed, and the thunder rolled, and the sea was covered with vast waves like mountains. The fisherman trembled so that his knees knocked together, and he had hardly strength to stand in the gale while he called to the fish:

"Oh, man of the sea!
Come listen to me;
For Alice my wife,

The plague of my life,
Hath sent me to beg a gift of thee!"

Then the fish came swimming to him and said, "What more does she want?"

"Ah," said the fisherman, "she wants to be lord of the sun and moon."

"Go home to your hut again," said the fish.

So the man returned and the palace was gone, and in its place he found the dark little hut that had formerly been his dwelling, and he and his wife have lived in that little hut to this very day.

The Flies and the Honey Pot
AESOP

Grabbing for too much can lead to big trouble.

A jar of honey chanced to spill
Its contents on the windowsill
In many a viscous pool and rill.

The flies, attracted by the sweet,
Began so greedily to eat,
They smeared their fragile wings and feet.
With many a twitch and pull in vain
They gasped to get away again,
And died in aromatic pain.

Moral

O foolish creatures that destroy
Themselves for transitory joy.

The Fox and the Crow

AESOP

If you "crow" about yourself, you may regret it.

A coal-black crow once stole a piece of meat. She flew to a tree and held the meat in her beak.

A fox, who saw her wanted the meat for himself, so he looked up into the tree and said, "How beautiful you are, my friend! Your feathers are fairer than the dove's."

"Is your voice as sweet as your form is beautiful? If so, you must be the queen of birds."

The crow was so happy in hearing the fox's praise that she opened her mouth to show how she could sing. Down fell the piece of meat.

The fox seized upon it and ran away.

The Frogs and the Well

AESOP

The prudent person looks before leaping.

Two frogs lived together in a marsh. But one hot summer the marsh dried up, and they left it to look for another place to live in, for frogs like damp places if they can get them. By and by they came to a deep well, and one of them looked down into it, and said to the other, "This looks a nice cool place. Let us jump in and settle here." But the other, who had a wiser head on his shoulders, replied, "Not so fast, my friend. Supposing this well dried up like the marsh, how should we get out again?"

Think twice before you act.

☙ Boy Wanted
FRANK CRANE

This "want ad" appeared in the early part of this century.

Wanted—A boy that stands straight, sits straight, acts straight, and talks straight;

A boy whose fingernails are not in mourning, whose ears are clean, whose shoes are polished, whose clothes are brushed, whose hair is combed, and whose teeth are well cared for;

A boy who listens carefully when he is spoken to, who asks questions when he does not understand, and does not ask questions about things that are none of his business;

A boy that moves quickly and makes as little noise about it as possible;

A boy who whistles in the street, but does not whistle where he ought to keep still;

A boy who looks cheerful, has a ready smile for everybody, and never sulks;

A boy who is polite to every man and respectful to every woman and girl;

A boy who does not smoke cigarettes and has no desire to learn how;

A boy who is more eager to know how to speak good English than to talk slang;

A boy that never bullies other boys nor allows other boys to bully him;

A boy who, when he does not know a thing, says, "I don't know," and when he has made a mistake says, "I'm sorry," and when he is asked to do a thing says, "I'll try";

A boy who looks you right in the eye and tells the truth every time;

A boy who is eager to read good books;

A boy who would rather put in his spare time at the YMCA gymnasium than to gamble for pennies in a back room;

A boy who does not want to be "smart" nor in any wise to attract attention;

A boy who would rather lose his job or be expelled from school than to tell a lie or be a cad;

A boy whom other boys like;

A boy who is at ease in the company of girls;

A boy who is not sorry for himself, and not forever thinking and talking about himself;

A boy who is friendly with his mother, and more intimate with her than anyone else;

A boy who makes you feel good when he is around;

A boy who is not goody-goody, a prig, or a little pharisee, but just healthy, happy, and full of life.

This boy is wanted everywhere. The family wants him, the school wants him, the office wants him, the boys want him, the girls want him, all creation wants him.

The Vulture

HILAIRE BELLOC

This one belongs on the refrigerator door.

The Vulture eats between his meals,
　　And that's the reason why
He very, very rarely feels
　　As well as you or I.
His eye is dull, his head is bald,
　　His neck is growing thinner.
Oh, what a lesson for us all
　　To only eat at dinner.

COMPASSION

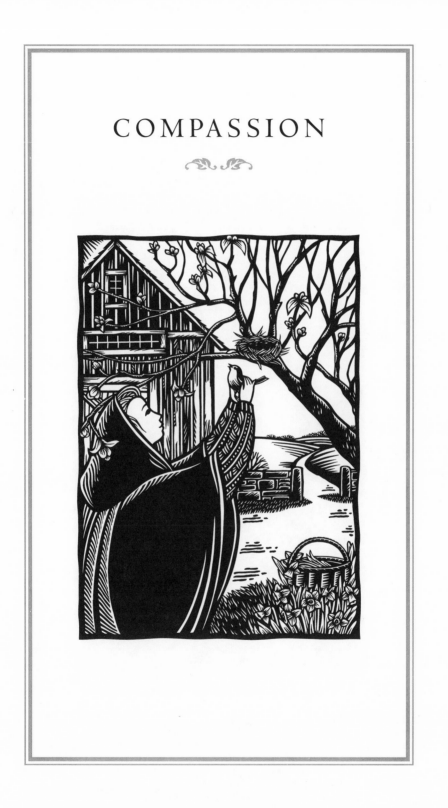

Compassion

In Harper Lee's famous novel, *To Kill a Mockingbird,* Atticus Finch gives his daughter some invaluable advice. "If you can learn a simple trick," he says, "you'll get along a lot better with all kinds of folks. You never really understand a person until you consider things from his point of view . . . . until you climb into his skin and walk around in it."

This is the starting point of compassion: understanding how another person feels by putting yourself in his or her place. It's the best way to appreciate another's difficulties. If you can get in the habit of asking yourself, "How would I feel if I were in his shoes?" you'll soon find yourself able to share in that person's pain and grief.

Why in the world would you want to do that—share someone else's pain?

The answer lies in the fact that true compassion is less about emotion than it is about action. When you have compassion, you don't just feel bad when a friend is sad. You don't just cry. You do something to help. Compassion is active. You show it not so much through your tears as through your aid. It may be a simple act, such as sharing your company, as in the story "Where Love Is, God Is." It may involve some self-sacrifice, as in the story "The Gift of the Magi." The point is that true compassion means showing you care by *doing something*.

A common problem of many young people is loneliness. Fortunately, your compassion for others is one of the best cures for your own loneliness. As we learn this virtue, we find ourselves becoming less self-centered and self-conscious. (See the story about Narcissus in this chapter to learn just how isolating self-centeredness can make us.) We begin to think less about ourselves and more about others. Then we begin to do more for others, and our own sense of being alone disappears. We also find that compassion is often returned to us after we've first given it to others.

All lives have times of unhappiness. We can't avoid it. We can only help each other deal with unhappiness and, hopefully, overcome it. Like all the virtues, compassion takes practice. We have to get in the habit of standing with others in their distress. It's not only a mark of growing up, it's a mark of being a decent human being.

As Rich as Croesus

RETOLD BY JAMES BALDWIN

This story comes from the Greek historian Herodotus. Croesus (560–546 B.C.), king of Lydia in Asia Minor, was a ruler of great wealth. How Cyrus spared his life is a legendary example of mercy. The story also offers important lessons about how money and power don't bring happiness.

Some thousands of years ago there lived in Asia a king whose name was Croesus. The country over which he ruled was not very large, but its people were prosperous and famed for their wealth. Croesus himself was said to be the richest man in the world, and so well known is his name that, to this day, it is not uncommon to say of a very wealthy person that he is "as rich as Croesus."

King Croesus had everything that could make him happy—lands and houses and slaves, fine clothing to wear, and beautiful things to look at. He could not think of anything that he needed to make him more comfortable or contented. "I am the happiest man in the world," he said.

It happened one summer that a great man from across the sea was traveling in Asia. The name of this man was Solon, and he was the lawmaker of Athens in Greece. He was noted for his wisdom and, centuries after his death, the highest praise that could be given to a learned man was to say, "He is as wise as Solon."

Solon had heard of Croesus, and so one day he visited him in his beautiful palace. Croesus was now happier and prouder than ever before, for the wisest man in the world was his guest. He led Solon through his palace and showed him the grand rooms, the fine carpets, the soft couches, the rich furniture, the pictures, the books. Then he invited him out to see his gardens and his orchards and his stables, and he showed him thousands of rare and beautiful things that he had collected from all parts of the world.

In the evening as the wisest of men and the richest of men were dining together, the king said to his guest, "Tell me now, O Solon, who do you think is the happiest of all men?" He expected that Solon would say, "Croesus."

The wise man was silent for a minute, and then he said, "I have in mind a poor man who once lived in Athens and whose name was Tellus. He, I doubt not, was the happiest of all men."

This was not the answer that Croesus wanted, but he hid his disappointment and asked, "Why do you think so?"

"Because," answered his guest, "Tellus was an honest man who labored hard for many years to bring up his children and to give them a good education. And when they were grown and able to do for themselves, he joined the Athenian army and gave his life bravely in the defense of his country. Can you think of anyone who is more deserving of happiness?"

"Perhaps not," answered Croesus, half-choking with disappointment. "But who do you think ranks next to Tellus in happiness?" He was quite sure now that Solon would say, "Croesus."

"I have in mind," said Solon, "two young men whom I knew in Greece. Their father died when they were mere children, and they were very poor. But they worked manfully to keep the house together and to support their mother, who was in feeble health. Year after year they toiled, nor thought of anything but their mother's comfort. When at length she died, they gave all their love to Athens, their native city, and nobly served her as long as they lived."

Then Croesus was angry. "Why is it," he asked, "that you make me of no account and think that my wealth and power are nothing? Why is it that you place these poor working people above the richest king in the world?"

"O king," said Solon, "no man can say whether you are happy or not until you die. For no man knows what misfortunes may overtake you, or what misery may be yours in place of all this splendor."

Many years after this there arose in Asia a powerful king whose name was Cyrus. At the head of a great army he marched from one country to another, overthrowing many a kingdom and attaching it to his great empire of Babylon. King Croesus with all his wealth was not able to stand against this mighty warrior. He resisted as long as he could. Then his city was taken, his beautiful palace was burned, his orchards and gardens were destroyed, his treasures were carried away, and he himself was made prisoner.

"The stubbornness of this man Croesus," said King Cyrus, "has caused us much trouble and the loss of many good soldiers. Take him and make an example of him for other petty kings who may dare to stand in our way."

Thereupon the soldiers seized Croesus and dragged him to the marketplace, handling him pretty roughly all the time. Then they built up a great pile of dry sticks and timber taken from the ruins of his once-beautiful palace. When this was finished they tied the unhappy king in the midst of it, and one ran for a torch to set it on fire.

"Now we shall have a merry blaze," said the savage fellows. "What good can all his wealth do him now?"

As poor Croesus, bruised and bleeding, lay upon the

pyre without a friend to soothe his misery, he thought of the words that Solon had spoken to him years before: "No man can say whether you are happy or not until you die," and he moaned, "O Solon! O Solon! Solon!"

It so happened that Cyrus was riding by at that very moment and heard his moans. "What does he say?" he asked of the soldiers.

"He says, 'Solon, Solon, Solon!'" answered one. Then the king rode nearer and asked Croesus, "Why do you call on the name of Solon?"

Croseus was silent at first. But after Cyrus had repeated his question kindly, he told all about Solon's visit at his palace and what he had said.

The story affected Cyrus deeply. He thought of the words, "No man knows what misfortunes may overtake you, or what misery may be yours in place of all this splendor." And he wondered if sometime he, too, would lose all his power and be helpless in the hands of his enemies.

"After all," said he, "ought not men to be merciful and kind to those who are in distress? I will do to Croesus as I would have others do to me." And he caused Croesus to be given his freedom, and afterward treated him as one of his most honored friends.

Beautiful

The Greek philosopher Socrates believed beauty is a thing that "slips in and permeates our souls."

> Beautiful faces are they that wear
> The light of a pleasant spirit there;
> Beautiful hands are they that do
> Deeds that are noble, good and true;
> Beautiful feet are they that go
> Swiftly to lighten another's woe.

The Rich Man's Feast
HAN-SHAN

The more some people have, the less they feel they can give away. This poem by the ancient Chinese poet Han-shan shows us a lack of compassion almost beyond belief.

> The rich man feasted in his high hall,
> Bright torches shining everywhere,
> When a man too poor to own a lamp
> Crept to the side to share in the glow.
> Who would think they would drive him away,
> Back again to his place in the dark?
> "Will one more person detract from your light?
> Strange, to begrudge me a leftover beam!"

⚛ Echo and Narcissus

RETOLD BY THOMAS BULFINCH

In Greek mythology, Narcissus was a beautiful youth, the son of the river god Cephisus and the nymph Leiriope. His vanity and heartlessness have linked his name with intense self-infatuation. As we see here, people who are stuck on themselves often end up alone.

Echo was a beautiful nymph, fond of the woods and hills, where she devoted herself to woodland sports. She was a favorite of Diana, and attended her in the chase. But Echo had one failing; she was fond of talking, and whether in chat or argument, would have the last word. One day Juno was seeking her husband, who, she had reason to fear, was amusing himself among the nymphs. Echo by her talk contrived to detain the goddess till the nymphs made their escape. When Juno discovered it, she passed sentence upon Echo in these words: "You shall forfeit the use of that tongue with which you have cheated me, except for that one purpose you are so fond of—*reply*. You shall still have the last word, but no power to speak first."

This nymph saw Narcissus, a beautiful youth, as he pursued the chase upon the mountains. She loved him and followed his footsteps. O how she longed to address him in the softest accents, and win him to converse! But it was not in her power. She waited with impatience for him to speak first, and had her answer ready. One day the youth, being separated from his companions, shouted aloud, "Who's here?" Echo replied, "Here." Narcissus looked around, but seeing no one, called out, "Come." Echo answered,

"Come." As no one came, Narcissus called again, "Why do you shun me?" Echo asked the same question. "Let us join one another," said the youth. The maid answered with all her heart in the same words, and hastened to the spot, ready to throw her arms about his neck. He started back, exclaiming, "Hands off! I would rather die than you should have me!" "Have me," said she; but it was all in vain. He left her, and she went to hide her blushes in the recesses of the woods. From that time forth she lived in caves and among mountain cliffs. Her form faded with grief, till at last all her flesh shrank away. Her bones were changed into rocks and there was nothing left of her but her voice. With that she is still ready to reply to anyone who calls her, and keeps up her old habit of having the last word.

Narcissus's cruelty in this case was not the only instance. He shunned all the rest of the nymphs, as he had done poor Echo. One day a maiden who had in vain endeavored to attract him uttered a prayer that he might sometime or other feel what it was to love and meet no return of affection. The avenging goddess heard and granted the prayer.

There was a clear fountain, with water like silver, to which the shepherds never drove their flocks, nor the mountain goats resorted, nor any of the beasts of the forests; neither was it defaced with fallen leaves or branches; but the grass grew fresh around it, and the rocks sheltered it from the sun. Hither came one day the youth, fatigued with hunting, heated and thirsty. He stooped down to drink, and saw his own image in the water; he thought it was some beautiful water spirit living in the fountain. He stood gazing with admiration at those bright eyes, those locks curled like the locks of Bacchus or Apollo, the rounded cheeks, the ivory neck, the parted lips, and the glow of health and exercise over all. He fell in love with himself. He brought his lips near to take a kiss; he plunged his arms in to embrace the beloved object. It fled at the touch, but returned again after a moment and renewed the fascination. He could not tear himself away. He lost all thought of food or rest, while he hovered over the brink of the fountain gazing upon his own image. He talked with the supposed spirit. "Why, beautiful being, do you shun me? Surely my face is not one to repel you. The nymphs love me, and you yourself look not indifferent upon me. When I stretch forth my arms you do the same; and you smile upon me and answer my beckonings with the like." His tears fell into the water and disturbed the image. As he saw it depart, he exclaimed, "Stay, I entreat you! Let me at least gaze upon you, if I may not touch you." With this, and much more of the same kind, he cherished the flame that consumed him, so that by degrees he lost his color, his vigor, and the beauty that formerly had so charmed the nymph Echo. She kept near him, however, and when he exclaimed, "Alas! Alas!" she answered him with the same words. He pined away and died; and when his shade passed the Stygian river, it leaned over the boat to catch a look of itself in the waters. The nymphs mourned for him, especially the water nymphs; and when they smote their breasts Echo smote hers also. They prepared a funeral pyre and would have burned the body, but was nowhere to be found; but in its place a flower, purple within, and surrounded with white leaves, which bears the name and preserves the memory of Narcissus.

If I Can Stop One Heart From Breaking

EMILY DICKINSON

Emily Dickinson (1830–1886) reminds us that acts of compassion add meaning to our lives.

> If I can stop one heart from breaking,
> I shall not live in vain;
> If I can ease one life the aching,
> Or cool one pain,
> Or help one fainting robin
> Unto his nest again,
> I shall not live in vain.

O Captain! My Captain!

WALT WHITMAN

This is Walt Whitman's famous poem in which he mourns Abraham Lincoln, the fallen president. To the poet, Lincoln's assassination was a terrible blow to the American democratic comradeship he celebrated in so much of his verse.

O Captain! my Captain! our fearful trip is done;
The ship has weather'd every rack, the prize we sought
   is won;
The port is near, the bells I hear, the people all exulting,
While follow eyes the steady keel, the vessel grim and
   daring:

But O heart! heart! heart!
    O the bleeding drops of red,
        Where on the deck my Captain lies,
        Fallen cold and dead.
O Captain! my Captain! rise up and hear the bells;
Rise up—for you the flag is flung—for you the bugle trills;
For you bouquets and ribbon'd wreaths—for you the
        shores a-crowding;
For you they call, the swaying mass, their eager faces
        turning:
    Here Captain! dear father!
        This arm beneath your head!
          It is some dream that on the deck,
           You've fallen cold and dead.
My Captain does not answer, his lips are pale and still;
My father does not feel my arm, he has no pulse nor will;
The ship is anchor'd safe and sound, its voyage closed
        and done;
From fearful trip, the victor ship comes in with object
        won:
    Exult, O shores, and ring, O bells!
        But I, with mournful tread,
          Walk the deck my Captain lies,
          Fallen cold and dead.

⚘ Song of Life

CHARLES MACKAY

The Roman statesman Seneca wrote that wherever there is a human being, there is an opportunity for kindness. No selfless act is insignificant.

A traveler on a dusty road
    Strewed acorns on the lea;
And one took root and sprouted up,
    And grew into a tree.
Love sought its shade at evening time,
    To breathe its early vows;
And Age was pleased, in heights of noon,
    To bask beneath its boughs.
The dormouse loved its dangling twigs,
    The birds sweet music bore—
It stood a glory in its place,
    A blessing evermore.

A little spring had lost its way
    Amid the grass and fern;
A passing stranger scooped a well
    Where weary men might turn.
He walled it in, and hung with care
    A ladle on the brink;
He thought not of the deed he did,
    But judged that Toil might drink.
He passed again; and lo! the well,
    By summer never dried,
Had cooled ten thousand parched tongues,
    And saved a life beside.

A nameless man, amid the crowd
    That thronged the daily mart,
Let fall a word of hope and love,
    Unstudied from the heart,
A whisper of the tumult thrown,
    A transitory breath,

It raised a brother from the dust,
    It saved a soul from death.
O germ! O fount! O word of love!
    O thought at random cast!
Ye were but little at the first,
    But mighty at the last.

❧ The Angel of the Battlefield

JOANNA STRONG AND TOM B. LEONARD

*Clara Barton (1821–1912) was known as the Angel
of the Battlefield for her work among the wounded
during the Civil War. As the founder of the
American Red Cross, she holds a place among our
greatest pioneers of philanthropy.*

When the agonizing pain receded a bit, Jack Gibbs was
able to think again. "I'll never make it home," he groaned.
"Not in one piece, anyway."

He sighed and tried to shift his body to a more comfortable position on the cold, rocky ground. But the movement caused another warm gush, and he knew that if he
were to live at all, he must lie still.

"By the time they cart me back to the hospital behind the
lines," he thought, "I'll either have bled to death or I'll be in
such rotten shape they'll have to take my leg off. And what
kind of husband would I be for Sue? A man with one leg!"

A black cloud swept over him, and he lay unconscious.

When he opened his eyes again, Jack was sure he had
died and gone to heaven. A woman was bending over him.
That just couldn't happen on a battlefield of the Civil War.

No woman ever came on the field. No woman would want to! *No woman would be allowed to!*

But there *was* a woman on the battlefield. Her name was Clara Barton.

With the help of two soldiers, she lifted Jack onto a cot that the men removed from a horse-drawn van. She took some bandages out of her kit and bound up his leg. Then she gave him a pain-killing draft. Jack weakly sipped it down, and the men put him in a crude-looking ambulance.

Clara Barton had been doing this kind of work all day long. She had succored hundreds of the wounded, allayed their fears, relieved their pain, cleansed their wounds.

Ever since the dreadful war had begun, Clara Barton had been worried about the men fighting at the front. She knew that wounded men were left lying on the field until the battle was over. She knew that only then were they collected and taken to hospitals—hospitals far behind the lines. She knew that if they survived this delay, the rough jolting of the wagons might well cause their unbound wounds to open. She knew that they often bled to death before they reached the hospital.

Heartsick at this state of affairs, she determined to bring aid to the men *right on the field.* First, she procured a van. Then she equipped it with medicine and first-aid supplies. And then she went to see the general.

She was a slender little woman. To the commanding officer, she didn't look exactly like battlefield material. In fact, her pet idea horrified him. "Miss Barton," he said, "what you are asking is absolutely impossible.

"But General," she insisted, "why is it impossible? I myself will drive the van and give the soldiers what relief I can."

The general shook his head. "The battlefield is no place

for a woman. You couldn't stand the rough life. Anyway, we are now doing everything that can be done for our soldiers. No one could do more."

"*I* could," Clara Barton declared. And then, as if she had just entered the room for the first time, she described all over again to the general her plans for first aid on the field.

This interview was repeated again and again, but constant refusal did not deter her. Finally, the commanding officer gave in. Clara Barton received a pass that would let her through the lines.

During the entire course of the Civil War, she ministered to all she could reach. She labored unceasingly. Once she worked with scant rest for five days and nights in a row. Her name became a byword in the army, spoken of with love and gratitude.

As the government saw what she was actually accomplishing, it gradually afforded her more and more cooperation. The army supplied more vans and more men to drive them. More medical supplies were made available. But it was nevertheless an uphill battle all the way for the courageous Miss Barton.

When the war ended, Clara Barton might have been expected to take a well-earned rest. Instead, she was haunted by the thought of the agony of those unfortunate folks who did not know for sure what had happened to their husbands, their fathers, their brothers. She determined to learn the fates of these missing soldiers and to send the information to their families. She worked at this task for a long time.

Now she knew war at firsthand. She knew what it did to men on the battlefield, and she knew what it did to the families they left behind. When she heard that there was a man in Switzerland by the name of Jean Henry Dunant who had a plan to help soldiers in wartime, she immediately went to Switzerland to lend her aid. Dunant formed an organization called the Red Cross. Workers of this organization were to wear a red cross on a white background so that they could easily be identified. They were to be allowed free access to battlefields so that they might help *all* soldiers, no matter what their nationality, race, or religion.

Here was an idea that fired Clara Barton. She came back to America and convinced the United States government that it should join with the twenty-two other member nations to give money and supplies to an International Red Cross, organized to help soldiers in wartime.

But Clara Barton added another idea to this great Red Cross plan. It was called the American Amendment.

"There are many other calamities that befall mankind," she said. "Earthquakes, floods, forest fires, epidemics, tornadoes. These disasters strike suddenly, killing and wounding many, leaving others homeless and starving. The Red Cross should stretch out a hand of help to all such victims, no matter where such disasters befall."

Today, the International Red Cross brings succor to millions of people all over the world. This was Clara Barton's wonderful idea. Her great courage, great love, and great charity will ever be revered.

The Gift of the Magi

O. HENRY

*William Sydney Porter (1862–1910), better known
as O. Henry, showed us that loving compassion
sometimes makes us act foolishly. But what is foolish for the head may be wise for the heart. O. Henry
wrote "The Gift of the Magi" in 1905.*

One dollar and eighty-seven cents. That was all. And
sixty cents of it was in pennies. Pennies saved one and two
at a time by bulldozing the grocer and the vegetable man
and the butcher until one's cheeks burned with the silent
imputation of parsimony that such close dealing implied.
Three times Della counted it. One dollar and eighty-seven
cents. And the next day would be Christmas.

There was clearly nothing to do but flop down on the
shabby little couch and howl. So Della did it. Which insti-
gates the moral reflection that life is made up of sobs, sniffles, and smiles, with sniffles predominating.

While the mistress of the home is gradually subsiding
from the first stage to the second, take a look at the home.
A furnished flat at $8 per week. It did not exactly beggar
description, but it certainly had that word on the lookout
for the mendicancy squad.

In the vestibule below was a letter box into which no
letter would go, and an electric button from which no mortal finger could coax a ring. Also appertaining thereunto
was a card bearing the name "Mr. James Dillingham Young."

The "Dillingham" had been flung to the breeze during a
former period of prosperity when its possessor was being
paid $30 per week. Now, when the income was shrunk to

$20, the letters of "Dillingham" looked blurred, as though they were thinking seriously of contracting to a modest and unassuming D. But whenever Mr. James Dillingham Young came home and reached his flat above he was called "Jim" and greatly hugged by Mrs. James Dillingham Young, already introduced to you as Della. Which is all very good.

Della finished her cry and attended to her cheeks with the powder rag. She stood by the window and looked out dully at a gray cat walking a gray fence in a gray backyard. Tomorrow would be Christmas Day and she had only $1.87 with which to buy Jim a present. She had been saving every penny she could for months, with this result. Twenty dollars a week doesn't go far. Expenses had been greater than she had calculated. They always are. Only $1.87 to buy a present for Jim. Her Jim. Many a happy hour she had spent planning for something nice for him. Something fine and rare and sterling—something just a little bit near to being worthy of the honor of being owned by Jim.

There was a pier glass between the windows of the room. Perhaps you have seen a pier glass in an $8 flat. A very thin and very agile person may, by observing his reflection in a rapid sequence of longitudinal strips, obtain a fairly accurate conception of his looks. Della, being slender, had mastered the art.

Suddenly she whirled from the window and stood before the glass. Her eyes were shining brilliantly, but her face had lost its color within twenty seconds. Rapidly she pulled down her hair and let it fall to its full length.

Now, there were two possessions of the James Dillingham Youngs in which they both took a mighty pride. One was Jim's gold watch that had been his father's and his grandfather's. The other was Della's hair. Had the

Queen of Sheba lived in the flat across the airshaft, Della would have let her hair hang out the window someday to dry just to depreciate Her Majesty's jewels and gifts. Had King Solomon been the janitor, with all his treasures piled up in the basement, Jim would have pulled out his watch every time he passed, just to see him pluck at his beard from envy.

So now Della's beautiful hair fell about her, rippling and shining like a cascade of brown waters. It reached below her knee and made itself almost a garment for her. And then she did it up again nervously and quickly. Once she faltered for a minute and stood still while a tear or two splashed on the worn red carpet.

On went her old brown jacket; on went her old brown hat. With a whirl of skirts and with the brilliant sparkle still in her eyes, she fluttered out the door and down the stairs to the street.

Where she stopped the sign read: "Mme. Sofronie. Hair Goods of All Kinds." One flight up Della ran, and collected herself, panting. Madame, large, too white, chilly, hardly looked the "Sofronie."

"Will you buy my hair?" asked Della.

"I buy hair," said Madame. "Take yer hat off and let's have a sight at the looks of it."

Down rippled the brown cascade.

"Twenty dollars," said Madame, lifting the mass with a practiced hand.

"Give it to me quick," said Della.

Oh, and the next two hours tripped by on rosy wings. Forget the hashed metaphor. She was ransacking the stores for Jim's present.

She found it at last. It surely had been made for Jim and no one else. There was no other like it in any of the stores, and she had turned all of them inside out. It was a platinum fob chain simple and chaste in design, properly proclaiming its value by substance alone and not by meretricious ornamentation—as all good things should do. It was even worthy of The Watch. As soon as she saw it she knew that it must be Jim's. It was like him. Quietness and value—the description applied to both. Twenty-one dollars they took from her for it, and she hurried home with the 87 cents. With that chain on his watch Jim might be properly anxious about the time in any company. Grand as the watch was, he sometimes looked at it on the sly on account of the old leather strap that he used in place of a chain.

When Della reached home her intoxication gave way a little to prudence and reason. She got out her curling irons and lighted the gas and went to work repairing the ravages made by generosity added to love. Which is always a tremendous task, dear friends—a mammoth task.

Within forty minutes her head was covered with tiny, close-lying curls that made her look wonderfully like a truant schoolboy. She looked at her reflection in the mirror long, carefully, and critically.

"If Jim doesn't kill me," she said to herself, "before he takes a second look at me, he'll say I look like a Coney Island chorus girl. But what could I do—oh! what could I do with a dollar and eighty-seven cents?"

At 7 o'clock the coffee was made and the frying pan was on the back of the stove hot and ready to cook the chops.

Jim was never late. Della doubled the fob chain in her hand and sat on the corner of the table near the door that he always entered. Then she heard his step on the stair away down on the first flight, and she turned white for just a moment. She had a habit of saying silent prayers about the simplest everyday things, and now she whispered: "Please God, make him think I am still pretty."

The door opened and Jim stepped in and closed it. He looked thin and very serious. Poor fellow, he was only twenty-two—and to be burdened with a family! He needed a new overcoat and was without gloves.

Jim stepped inside the door, as immovable as a setter at the scent of a quail. His eyes were fixed upon Della, and there was an expression in them that she could not read, and it terrified her. It was not anger, nor surprise, nor disapproval, nor horror, nor any of the sentiments that she had been prepared for. He simply stared at her fixedly with that peculiar expression on his face.

Della wriggled off the table and went for him.

"Jim, darling," she cried, "don't look at me that way. I had cut my hair off and sold it because I couldn't have lived through Christmas without giving you a present. It'll grow out again—you won't mind, will you? I just had to do it. My hair grows awfully fast. Say 'Merry Christmas!' Jim, and let's be happy. You don't know what a nice—what a beautiful, nice gift I've got for you."

"You've cut off your hair?" asked Jim, laboriously, as if he had not arrived at that patent fact yet even after the hardest mental labor.

"Cut it off and sold it," said Della. "Don't you like me just as well, anyhow? I'm me without my hair, ain't I?"

Jim looked about the room curiously.

"You say your hair is gone?" he said, with an air almost of idiocy.

"You needn't look for it," said Della. "It's sold, I tell you—sold and gone, too. It's Christmas Eve, boy. Be good to me, for it went for you. Maybe the hairs on my head were numbered," she went on with a sudden serious sweetness, "but nobody could ever count my love for you. Shall I put the chops on, Jim?"

Out of his trance Jim seemed quickly to wake. He enfolded his Della. For ten seconds let us regard with discreet scrutiny some inconsequential object in the other direction. Eight dollars a week or a million a year—what is the difference? A mathematician or a wit would give you the wrong answer. The magi brought valuable gifts, but that was not among them. This dark assertion will be illuminated later on.

Jim drew a package from his overcoat pocket and threw it upon the table.

"Don't make any mistake, Dell," he said, "about me. I don't think there's anything in the way of a haircut or a shave or a shampoo that could make me like my girl any less. But if you'll unwrap that package you may see why you had me going a while at first."

White fingers and nimble tore at the string and paper. And then an ecstatic scream of joy; and then, alas! a quick feminine change to hysterical tears and wails, necessitating immediate employment of all the comforting powers of the lord of the flat.

For there lay The Combs—the set of combs, side and back, that Della had worshipped for long in a Broadway window. Beautiful combs, pure tortoiseshell, with jeweled rims—just the shade to wear in the beautiful vanished hair. They were expensive combs, she knew, and her heart had simply craved and yearned over them without the least hope of possession. And now they were hers, but the tresses that should have adorned the coveted adornments were gone.

But she hugged them to her bosom, and at length, she

was able to look up with dim eyes and a smile and say: "My hair grows so fast, Jim!"

And then Della leaped up like a little singed cat and cried, "Oh, oh!"

Jim had not yet seen his beautiful present. She held it out to him eagerly upon her open palm. The dull precious metal seemed to flash with a reflection of her bright and ardent spirit.

"Isn't it a dandy, Jim? I hunted all over town to find it. You'll have to look at the time a hundred times a day now. Give me your watch. I want to see how it looks on it."

Instead of obeying, Jim tumbled down on the couch and put his hands under the back of his head and smiled.

"Dell," said he, "let's put our Christmas presents away and keep 'em a while. They're too nice to use just at present. I sold the watch to get the money to buy your combs. And now suppose you put the chops on."

The magi, as you know, were wise men—wonderfully wise men—who brought gifts to the Babe in the manger. They invented the art of giving Christmas presents. Being wise, their gifts were no doubt wise ones, possibly bearing the privilege of exchange in case of duplication. And here I have lamely related to you the uneventful chronicle of two foolish children in a flat who most unwisely sacrificed for each other the greatest treasures in their house. But in a last word to the wise of these days let it be said that of all who give gifts these two were the wisest. Of all who give and receive gifts, such as they are wisest. Everywhere they are wisest. They are the magi.

The Sin of Omission

MARGARET E. SANGSTER

Kindness is not immune to procrastination. We need
to guard against "slow compassion" as we tend to
our affairs.

It isn't the thing you do, dear,
　　It's the thing you leave undone
That gives you a bit of a heartache
　　At setting of the sun.
The tender work forgotten,
　　The letter you did not write,
The flowers you did not send, dear,
　　Are your haunting ghosts at night.
The stone you might have lifted
　　Out of a brother's way;
The bit of heartsome counsel
　　You were hurried too much to say;
The loving touch of the hand, dear,
　　The gentle, winning tone
Which you had no time nor thought for
　　With troubles enough of your own.

Those little acts of kindness
　　So easily out of mind,
Those chances to be angels
　　Which we poor mortals find—
They come in night and silence,
　　Each sad, reproachful wraith,
When hope is faint and flagging,
　　And a chill has fallen on faith.

For life is all too short, dear,
      And sorrow is all too great,
To suffer our slow compassion
      That tarries until too late;
And it isn't the thing you do, dear,
      It's the thing you leave undone
Which gives you a bit of heartache
      At the setting of the sun.

❧ Where Love Is, God Is

LEO TOLSTOY

*Here is a good man who lives the Gospel. This is a
reworking of an old Christian folk tale. Its charm
lies in its simplicity, and it remains a favorite Tolstoy
selection.*

In a little town in Russia there lived a cobbler, Martin
Avedéaitch by name. He had a tiny room in a basement, the
one window of which looked out on to the street. Through
it one could see only the feet of those who passed by, but
Martin recognized the people by their boots. He had lived
long in the place and had many acquaintances. There was
hardly a pair of boots in the neighborhood that had not
been once or twice through his hands, so he often saw his
own handiwork through the window. Some he had re-
soled, some patched, some stitched up, and to some he had
even put fresh uppers. He had plenty to do, for he worked
well, used good material, did not charge too much, and
could be relied on. If he could do a job by the day required,
he undertook it; if not, he told the truth and gave no false

promises. So he was well known and never short of work.

Martin had always been a good man, but in his old age he began to think more about his soul and to draw nearer to God.

From that time Martin's whole life changed. His life became peaceful and joyful. He sat down to his task in the morning, and when he had finished his day's work he took the lamp down from the wall, stood it on the table, fetched his Bible from the shelf, opened it, and sat down to read. The more he read the better he understood, and the clearer and happier he felt in his mind.

It happened once that Martin sat up late, absorbed in his book. He was reading Luke's Gospel, and in the sixth chapter he came upon the verses:

> *To him that smiteth thee on the one cheek offer also the other; and from him that taketh away thy cloak withhold not thy coat also. Give to every man that asketh thee; and of him that taketh away thy goods ask them not again. And as ye would that men should do to you, do ye also to them likewise.*

He thought about this, and was about to go to bed, but was loath to leave his book. So he went on reading the seventh chapter—about the centurion, the widow's son, and the answer to John's disciples—and he came to the part where a rich Pharisee invited the Lord to his house. And he read how the woman who was a sinner anointed his feet and washed them with her tears, and how he justified her. Coming to the forty-fourth verse, he read:

> *And turning to the woman, he said unto Simon,*
> *"Seest thou this woman? I entered into thine house,*

thou gavest me no water for my feet, but she hath wetted my feet with her tears, and wiped them with her hair. Thou gavest me no kiss, but she, since the time I came in, hath not ceased to kiss my feet. My head with oil thou didst not anoint, but she hath anointed my feet with ointment."

He read these verses and thought: "He gave no water for his feet, gave no kiss, his head with oil he did not anoint. . . ." And Martin took off his spectacles once more, laid them on his book, and pondered.

"He must have been like me, that Pharisee. He too thought only of himself—how to get a cup of tea, how to keep warm and comfortable, never a thought of his guest. He took care of himself, but for his guest he cared nothing at all. Yet who was the guest? The Lord himself! If he came to me, should I behave like that?"

Then Martin laid his head upon both his arms and, before he was aware of it, he fell asleep.

"Martin!" He suddenly heard a voice, as if someone had breathed the word above his ear.

He started from his sleep. "Who's there?" he asked.

He turned around and looked at the door; no one was there. He called again. Then he heard quite distinctly: "Martin, Martin! Look out into the street tomorrow, for I shall come."

Martin roused himself, rose from his chair and rubbed his eyes, but did not know whether he had heard these words in a dream or awake. He put out the lamp and lay down to sleep.

The next morning he rose before daylight, and after saying his prayers he lit the fire and prepared his cabbage soup and buckwheat porridge. Then he lit the samovar, put on his apron, and sat down by the window to his work. He looked out into the street more than he worked, and whenever anyone passed in unfamiliar boots he would stoop and look up, so as to see not only the feet but the face of the passerby as well. A house-porter passed in new felt boots, then a water-carrier. Presently an old soldier of Nicholas's reign came near the window, spade in hand. Martin knew him by his boots, which were shabby old felt once, galoshed with leather. The old man was called Stepánitch. A neighboring tradesman kept him in his house for charity, and his duty was to help the house-porter. He began to clear away the snow before Martin's window. Martin glanced at him and then went on with his work.

After he had made a dozen stitches he felt drawn to look out of the window again. He saw that Stepánitch had leaned his spade against the wall, and was either resting himself or trying to get warm. The man was old and broken down, and had evidently not enough strength even to clear away the snow.

"What if I called him in and gave him some tea?" thought Martin. "The samovar is just on the boil."

He stuck his awl in its place, and rose, and putting the samovar on the table, made tea. Then he tapped the window with his fingers. Stepánitch turned and came to the window. Martin beckoned to him to come in, and went himself to open the door.

"Come in," he said, "and warm yourself a bit. I'm sure you must be cold."

"May God bless you!" Stepánitch answered. "My bones do ache, to be sure." He came in, first shaking off the snow, and lest he should leave marks on the floor he began wiping his feet. But as did so he tottered and nearly fell.

"Don't trouble to wipe your feet," said Martin. "I'll wipe up the floor—it's all in the day's work. Come, friend, sit down and have some tea."

Filling two tumblers, he passed one to his visitor, and pouring his own tea out into the saucer, began to blow on it.

Stepánitch emptied his glass and, turning it upside down, put the remains of his piece of sugar on the top. He began to express his thanks, but it was plain that he would be glad of some more.

"Have another glass," said Martin, refilling the visitor's tumbler and his own. But while he drank his tea Martin kept looking out into the street.

"Are you expecting anyone?" asked the visitor.

"Am I expecting anyone? Well, now, I'm ashamed to tell you. It isn't that I really expect anyone, but I heard something last night which I can't get out of my mind. Whether it was a vision, or only a fancy, I can't tell. You see, friend, last night I was reading the Gospel, about Christ the Lord, how he suffered, and how he walked on earth. You have heard tell of it, I dare say."

"I have heard tell of it," answered Stepánitch. "But I'm an ignorant man and not able to read."

"Well, you see, I was reading how he walked on earth. I came to that part, you know, where he went to a Pharisee who did not receive him well. Well, friend, as I read about it, I thought how that man did not receive Christ the Lord with proper honor. Suppose such a thing could happen to such a man as myself, I thought, what would I not do to receive him! But that man gave him no reception at all. Well, friend, as I was thinking of this, I began to doze, and as I dozed I heard someone call me by name. I got up, and thought I heard someone whispering, 'Expect me. I will come tomorrow.' This happened twice over. And to tell you the truth, it sank so into my mind that, though I am ashamed of it myself, I keep on expecting him, the dear Lord!"

Stepánitch shook his head in silence, finished his tumbler, and laid it on its side, but Martin stood it up again and refilled it for him.

"Thank you, Martin Avedéaitch," he said. "You have given me food and comfort both for soul and body."

"You're very welcome. Come again another time. I am glad to have a guest," said Martin.

Stepánitch went away, and Martin poured out the last of the tea and drank it up. Then he put away the tea things and sat down to his work, stitching the back seam of a boot. And as he stitched he kept looking out of the window and thinking about what he had read in the Bible. And his head was full of Christ's sayings.

Two soldiers went by: one in Government boots, the other in boots of his own; then the master of a neighboring house, in shining galoshes; then a baker carrying a basket. All these passed on. Then a woman came up in worsted stockings and peasant-made shoes. She passed the window, but stopped by the wall. Martin glanced up at her through the window and saw that she was a stranger, poorly dressed, and with a baby in her arms. She stopped by the wall with her back to the wind, trying to wrap the baby up though she had hardly anything to wrap it in. The woman had only summer clothes on, and even they were shabby and worn. Through the window Martin heard the baby crying, and the woman trying to soothe it, but unable to do so. Martin rose, and going out of the door and up the steps he called to her. "My dear, I say, my dear!"

The woman heard, and turned around.

"Why do you stand out there with the baby in the cold? Come inside. You can wrap him up better in a warm place. Come this way!"

The woman was surprised to see an old man in an apron, with spectacles on his nose, calling to her, but she followed him in.

They went down the steps, entered the little room, and the old man led her to the bed.

"There, sit down, my dear, near the stove. Warm yourself, and feed the baby."

"Haven't any milk. I have eaten nothing myself since early morning," said the woman, but still she took the baby to her breast.

Martin shook his head. He brought out a basin and some bread. Then he opened the oven door and poured some cabbage soup into the basin. He took out the porridge pot also, but the porridge was not yet ready, so he spread a cloth on the table and served only the soup and bread.

"Sit down and eat, my dear, and I'll mind the baby. Why, bless me, I've had children of my own; I know how to manage them."

The woman crossed herself, and sitting down at the table began to eat, while Martin put the baby on the bed and sat down by it

Martin sighed. "Haven't you any warmer clothing?" he asked.

"How could I get warm clothing?" said she. "Why, I pawned my last shawl for sixpence yesterday."

Then the woman came and took the child, and Martin got up. He went and looked among some things that were hanging on the wall, and brought back an old cloak.

"Here," he said, "though it's a worn-out old thing, it will do to wrap him up in."

The woman looked at the cloak, then at the old man, and taking it, burst into tears. Martin turned away, and groping under the bed brought out a small trunk. He fumbled about in it, and again sat down opposite the woman. And the woman said, "The Lord bless you, friend."

"Take this for Christ's sake," said Martin, and gave her sixpence to get her shawl out of pawn. The woman crossed herself, and Martin did the same, and then he saw her out.

After a while Martin saw an apple-woman stop just in front of his window. On her back she had a sack full of chips, which she was taking home. No doubt she had gathered them at someplace where building was going on.

The sack evidently hurt her, and she wanted to shift it from one shoulder to the other, so she put it down on the footpath and, placing her basket on a post, began to shake down the chips in the sack. While she was doing this, a boy in a tattered cap ran up, snatched an apple out of the basket, and tried to slip away. But the old woman noticed it, and turning, caught the boy by his sleeve. He began to struggle, trying to free himself, but the old woman held on with both hands, knocked his cap off his head, and seized hold of his hair. The boy screamed and the old woman scolded. Martin dropped his awl, not waiting to stick it in its place, and rushed out of the door. Stumbling up the steps and dropping his spectacles in his hurry, he ran out into the street. The old woman was pulling the boy's hair and scolding him, and threatening to take him to the police. The lad was struggling and protesting, saying, "I did not take it. What are you beating me for? Let me go!"

Martin separated them. He took the boy by the hand and

said, "Let him go, Granny. Forgive him for Christ's sake."

"I'll pay him out, so that he won't forget it for a year! I'll take the rascal to the police!"

Martin began entreating the old woman.

"Let him go, Granny. He won't do it again."

The old woman let go, and the boy wished to run away, but Martin stopped him. "Ask the Granny's forgiveness!" said he. "And don't do it another time. I saw you take the apple."

The boy began to cry and to beg pardon.

"That's right. And now here's an apple for you," and Martin took an apple from the basket and gave it to the boy, saying, "I will pay you, Granny."

"You will spoil them that way, the young rascals," said the old woman. "He ought to be whipped so that he should remember it for a week."

"Oh, Granny, Granny," said Martin, "that's our way— but it's not God's way. If he should be whipped for stealing an apple, what should be done to us for our sins?"

The old woman was silent.

And Martin told her the parable of the lord who forgave his servant a large debt, and how the servant went out and seized his debtor by the throat. The old woman listened to it all, and the boy, too, stood by and listened.

"God bids us forgive," said Martin, "or else we shall not be forgiven. Forgive everyone, and a thoughtless youngster most of all."

The old woman wagged her head and sighed.

"It's true enough," said she, "but they are getting terribly spoiled."

"Then we old ones must show them better ways," Martin replied.

"That's just what I say," said the old woman. "I have had seven of them myself, and only one daughter is left." And the old woman began to tell how and where she was living with her daughter, and how many grandchildren she had. "There now," she said, "I have but little strength left, yet I work hard for the sake of my grandchildren; and nice children they are, too. No one comes out to meet me but the children. Little Annie, now, won't leave me for anyone. It's 'Grandmother, dear grandmother, darling grandmother.'" And the old woman completely softened at the thought.

"Of course, it was only his childishness," said she, referring to the boy.

As the old woman was about to hoist her sack on her back, the lad sprang forward to her, saying, "Let me carry it for you, Granny. I'm going that way."

The old woman nodded her head, and put the sack on the boy's back, and they went down the street together, the old woman quite forgetting to ask Martin to pay for the apple. Martin stood and watched them as they went along talking to each other.

When they were out of sight Martin went back to the house. Having found his spectacles unbroken on the steps, he picked up his awl and sat down again to work. He worked a little, but soon could not see to pass the bristle through the holes in the leather, and presently, he noticed the lamplighter passing on his way to light the street lamps.

"Seems it's time to light up," thought he. So he trimmed his lamp, hung it up, and sat down again to work. He finished off one boot and, turning it about, examined it. It was all right. Then he gathered his tools together, swept up the cuttings, put away the bristles and the thread and the awls, and, taking down the lamp, placed it on the table. Then he took the Gospels from the shelf. He meant to open them at the place he had marked the day before with a bit of morocco, but the book opened at another place. As Martin opened it, his yesterday's dream came back to his mind, and no sooner had he thought of it than he seemed to hear footsteps, as though someone were moving behind him. Martin turned round, and it seemed to him as if people were standing in the dark corner, but he could not make out who they were. And a voice whispered in his ear: "Martin, Martin, don't you know me?"

"Who is it?" muttered Martin.

"It is I," said the voice. And out of the dark corner stepped Stepánitch, who smiled and, vanishing like a cloud, was seen no more.

"It is I," said the voice again. And out of the darkness stepped the woman with the baby in her arms, and the woman smiled and the baby laughed, and they too vanished.

"It is I," said the voice once more. And the old woman and the boy with the apple stepped out and both smiled, and then they too vanished.

And Martin's soul grew glad. He crossed himself, put on his spectacles, and began reading the Gospel just where it had opened. And at the top of the page he read:

> *I was hungry, and ye gave me meat. I was thirsty, and ye gave me drink. I was a stranger, and ye took me in.*

And at the bottom of the page he read:

> *Inasmuch as ye did it unto one of these my brethren, even these least, ye did it unto me.*

And Martin understood that his dream had come true, and that the Savior had really come to him that day, and he had welcomed him.

RESPONSIBILITY

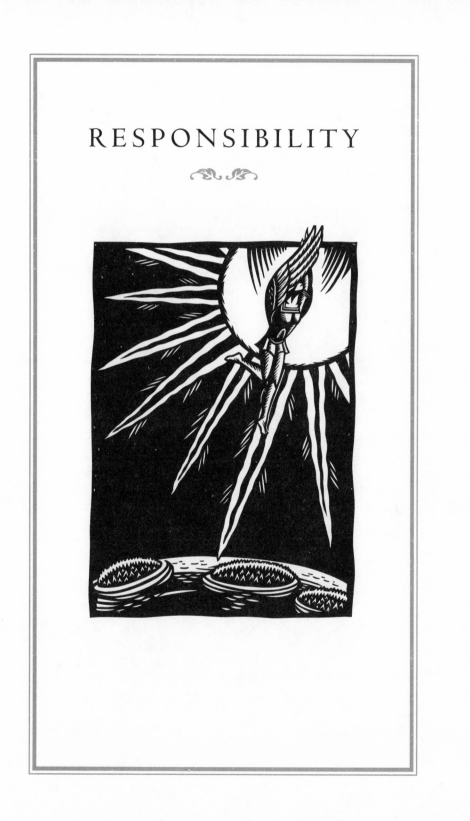

✧ Responsibility

In *King Lear,* William Shakespeare observed that when things go wrong, "we make guilty of our disasters the sun, the moon, the stars, as if we were villains on necessity, fools by heavenly compulsion." In other words, it's easy to blame our troubles on fate, the economy, bad luck, even the position of the planets—anything or anybody except ourselves.

Responsibility is the willingness to accept the consequences of your own actions and performance. It means accepting a task, doing it to the best of your ability, and then standing by what you've done. It means living up to your commitments to friends, family, community, and country. Responsible young men and women don't pass their work on to someone else or leave it forgotten. They don't make excuses. They don't point fingers of blame.

To a large degree, responsibility boils down to knowing your obligations to others (and to yourself) and seeing that you meet those obligations. We often hear about our rights. What we don't hear about as much are the responsibilities that go hand-in-hand with those rights. For every right there is a corresponding responsibility. For example, in this country you have a right to an education. The responsibility to take advantage of that right is up to you, though. You do it by paying attention in class and studying your assignments. No one else can do it for you. Likewise, you will someday have the right to vote. It will also be your responsibility to know who and what you are voting for and to get yourself to the polls on election day. Your right will not mean much if you ignore your responsibility.

We build a mature sense of responsibility the same way we develop other desirable character traits: by practice. Household chores, homework, after-school jobs, and volunteer activities are all good ways. If we can't live up to these everyday obligations, we certainly won't be ready to meet the larger ones that eventually come our way (as we see in the story of "King Alfred and the Cakes"). We also learn through experience that smaller responsibilities left unattended can lead to larger, damaging consequences (like in the story entitled "For Want Of A Horseshoe Nail").

As you grow older, you'll discover that your responsibilities are a part of who you are. So trying to avoid responsibilities will not make life any easier. It will just make you less of a successful, mature human being.

⁓ F. Scott Fitzgerald to His Daughter

Here we see a father gently and clearly telling his daughter what her duties are.

Dear Pie:

I feel very strongly about your doing duty. Would you give me a little more documentation about your reading in French? I am glad you are happy—but I never believe much in happiness. I never believe in misery either. Those are things you see on the stage or the screen or the printed page, they never really happen to you in life.

All I believe in life is the rewards for virtue (according to your talents) and the punishments for not fulfilling your duties, which are doubly costly. If there is such a volume in the camp library, will you ask Mrs. Tyson to let you look up a sonnet of Shakespeare's in which the line occurs Lilies that fester smell far worse than weeds.

Have had no thoughts today, life seems composed of getting up a Saturday Evening Post story. I think of you, and always pleasantly; but if you call me "Pappy" again I am going to take the White Cat out and beat his bottom hard, six times for every time you are impertinent. Do you react to that?

I will arrange the camp bill.

Halfwit, I will conclude. Things to worry about:

Worry about courage

Worry about cleanliness

Worry about efficiency

Worry about horsemanship . . .

Things not to worry about:

Don't worry about popular opinion

Don't worry about dolls

Don't worry about the past

Don't worry about the future

Don't worry about growing up

Don't worry about anybody getting ahead of you

Don't worry about triumph

Don't worry about failure unless it comes through
   your own fault

Don't worry about mosquitoes

Don't worry about flies

Don't worry about insects in general

Don't worry about parents

Don't worry about boys

Don't worry about disappointments

Don't worry about pleasures

Don't worry about satisfactions

Things to think about:

What am I really aiming at?

How good am I in comparison to my
   contemporaries in regard to:

(a) Scholarship

(b) Do I really understand people and am I able
   to get along with them?

(c) Am I trying to make my body a useful
   instrument or am I neglecting it?

                    With dearest love

❧ For Want of a Horseshoe Nail
ADAPTED FROM JAMES BALDWIN

This famous legend and rhyme are based on the demise of England's King Richard III, whose defeat at the Battle of Bosworth Field in 1485 has been immortalized by Shakespeare's famous line: "A horse! A horse! My kingdom for a horse!" The story is a nice foil for "King Alfred and the Cakes," which you will find later in this chapter. It reminds us that little duties neglected bring great downfalls.

King Richard the Third was preparing for the fight of his life. An army led by Henry, Earl of Richmond, was marching against him. The contest would determine who would rule England.

The morning of the battle, Richard sent a groom to make sure his favorite horse was ready.

"Shoe him quickly," the groom told the blacksmith. "The king wishes to ride at the head of his troops."

"You'll have to wait," the blacksmith answered. "I've shoed the king's whole army the last few days, and now I've got to go get more iron."

"I can't wait," the groom shouted impatiently. "The king's enemies are advancing right now, and we must meet them on the field. Make do with what you have."

So the blacksmith bent to his task. From a bar of iron he made four horseshoes. He hammered and shaped and fitted them to the horse's feet. Then he began to nail them on. But after he had fastened three shoes, he found he did not have enough nails for the fourth.

"I need one or two more nails," he said, "and it will take some time to hammer them out."

"I told you I can't wait," the groom said impatiently. "I hear the trumpets now. Can't you just use what you've got?"

"I can put the shoe on, but it won't be as secure as the others."

"Will it hold?" asked the groom.

"It should," answered the blacksmith, "but I can't be certain."

"Well, then, just nail it on," the groom cried. "And hurry, or King Richard will be angry with us both."

The armies clashed, and Richard was in the thick of the battle. He rode up and down the field, cheering his men and fighting his foes. "Press forward! Press forward!" he yelled, urging his troops toward Henry's lines.

Far away, at the other side of the field, he saw some of his men falling back. If others saw them, they too might retreat. So Richard spurred his horse and galloped toward the broken line, calling his soldiers to turn and fight.

He was barely halfway across the field when one of the horse's shoes flew off. The horse stumbled and fell, and Richard was thrown to the ground.

Before the king could grab at the reins, the frightened animal rose and galloped away. Richard looked around him. He saw that his soldiers were turning and running, and Henry's troops were closing around him.

He waved his sword in the air. "A horse!" he shouted. "A horse! My kingdom for a horse!"

But there was no horse for him. His army had fallen to pieces, and his troops were busy trying to save themselves. A moment later Henry's soldiers were upon Richard, and the battle was over.

And since that time, people have said,
For want of a battle, a kingdom was lost,
For want of a nail, a shoe was lost,
For want of a shoe, a horse was lost,
For want of a horse, a battle was lost,
For want of a battle, a kingdom was lost,
And all for the want of a horseshoe nail.

☙ Icarus and Daedalus

This famous Greek myth reminds us exactly why young people have a responsibility to obey their parents—for the same good reason parents have a responsibility to guide their children: There are many things adults know that young people do not. Successful upbringing requires a measure of obedience, as Icarus finds out the hard way.

Daedalus was the most skillful builder and inventor of his day in ancient Greece. He built magnificent palaces and gardens, and created wonderful works of art throughout the land. His statues were so beautifully crafted they were taken for living beings, and it was believed they could see and walk about. People said someone as cunning as Daedalus must have learned the secrets of his craft from the gods themselves.

Now across the sea, on the island of Crete, lived a king named Minos. King Minos had a terrible monster that was half bull and half man called the Minotaur, and he needed someplace to keep it. When he heard of Daedalus's cleverness, he invited him to come to his country and build a prison to hold the beast. So Daedalus and his young son, Icarus, sailed to Crete, and there Daedalus built the famous Labyrinth, a maze of winding passages so tangled and twisted that whoever went in could never find the way out. And there they put the Minotaur.

When the Labyrinth was finished, Daedalus wanted to sail back to Greece with his son, but Minos had made up his mind to keep them in Crete. He wanted Daedalus to stay and invent more wonderful devices for him, so he locked them both in a high tower beside the sea. The king knew Daedalus was clever enough to escape from the tower, so he also ordered that every ship be searched for stowaways before sailing from Crete.

Other men may have given up, but not Daedalus. From his high tower he watched the seagulls drifting on the ocean breezes. "Minos may control the land and the sea," he said, "but he does not rule the air. We'll go that way."

So he summoned all the secrets of his craft, and he set to work. Little by little, he gathered a great pile of feathers of all sizes. He fastened them together with thread, and molded them with wax, and at last he had two great wings like those of the seagulls. He tied them to his shoulders, and after one or two clumsy efforts, he found that by waving his arms he could rise into the air. He held himself aloft, wavering this way and that with the wind, until he taught himself how to glide and soar on the currents as gracefully as any gull.

Next he built a second pair of wings for Icarus. He taught the boy how to move the feathers and rise a few feet into the air, and then let him fly back and forth across the room. Then he taught him how to ride the air currents, climbing in circles, and hang in the winds. They practiced together until Icarus was ready.

Finally the day came when the winds were just right. Father and son strapped on their wings and prepared to fly home.

"Remember all I've told you," Daedalus said. "Above all, remember you must not fly too high or too low. If you fly too low, the ocean sprays will clog your wings and make them too heavy. If you fly too high, the heat of the sun will melt the wax, and your wings will fall apart. Stay close to me, and you'll be fine."

Up they rose, the boy after his father, and the hateful ground of Crete sank far beneath them. As they flew the plowman stopped his work to gaze, and the shepherd leaned on his staff to watch them, and people came running out of their houses to catch a glimpse of the two figures high above the treetops. Surely they were gods—Apollo, perhaps, with Cupid after him.

At first the flight seemed terrible to both Daedalus and Icarus. The wide, endless sky dazed them, and even the quickest glance down made their brains reel. But gradually they grew used to riding among the clouds, and they lost their fear. Icarus felt the wind fill his wings and lift him higher and higher, and began to sense a freedom he had never known before. He looked down with great excitement at all the islands they passed and their people, and at the broad blue sea spread out beneath him, dotted with the white sails of ships. He soared higher and higher, forgetting his father's warning. He forgot everything in the world but joy.

"Come back!" Daedalus called frantically. "You're flying too high! Remember the sun! Come down! Come down!"

But Icarus thought of nothing but his own excitement and glory. He longed to fly as close as he could to the heavens. Nearer and nearer he came to the sun, and slowly his wings began to soften. One by one the feathers began to fall and scatter in the air, and suddenly the wax melted all at once. Icarus felt himself falling. He fluttered his arms as fast as he could, but no feathers remained to hold the air. He cried out for his father, but it was too late—with a scream he fell from his lofty height and plunged into the sea, disappearing beneath the waves.

Daedalus circled over the water again and again, but he saw nothing but feathers floating on the waves, and he knew his son was gone. At last the body came to the surface, and he managed to pluck it from the sea. With a heavy burden and broken heart, Daedalus slowly flew away. When he reached land, he buried his son and built a temple to the gods. Then he hung up his wings and never flew again.

King Alfred and the Cakes
ADPATED FROM JAMES BALDWIN

Alfred the Great was king of the West Saxons in England during the ninth century. His determination to protect England from Danish conquest and his emphasis on literacy and education for his people have lifted him into the ranks of England's most popular rulers. This famous story reminds us that attention to little duties prepares us to meet larger ones. It also reminds us that leadership and responsibility walk hand in hand, and that truly great leaders do not disdain small responsibilities.

In England many years ago there ruled a king named Alfred. A wise and just man, Alfred was one of the best kings England ever had. Even today, centuries later, he is known as Alfred the Great.

The days of Alfred's rule were not easy ones in England. The country was invaded by the fierce Danes, who had come from across the sea. There were so many Danish invaders and they were so strong and bold that for a long time they won almost every battle. If they kept on winning, they would soon be masters of the whole country.

At last, after so many struggles, King Alfred's English army was broken and scattered. Every man had to save himself in the best way he could, including King Alfred. He disguised himself as a shepherd and fled alone through the woods and swamps.

After several days of wandering, he came to the hut of a woodcutter. Tired and hungry, he knocked on the door and begged the woodcutter's wife to give him something to eat and a place to sleep.

The woman looked with pity at the ragged fellow. She had no idea who he really was. "Come in," she said. "I will give you some supper if you will watch these cakes I am baking on the hearth. I want to go out and milk the cow. Watch them carefully, and make sure they don't burn while I'm gone."

Alfred thanked her politely and sat down beside the fire. He tried to pay attention to the cakes, but soon all his troubles filled his mind. How was he going to get his army together again? And even if he did, how was he going to prepare it to face the Danes? How could he possibly drive such fierce invaders out of England? The more he thought, the more hopeless the future seemed, and he began to believe there was no use in continuing to fight. Alfred saw only his problems. He forgot he was in the woodcutter's hut, he forgot about his hunger, and he forgot all about the cakes.

In a little while, the woman came back. She found her hut full of smoke and her cakes burned to a crisp. And there was Alfred sitting beside the hearth, gazing into the flames. He had never even noticed the cakes were burning.

"You lazy, good-for-nothing fellow!" the woman cried. "Look what you've done! You want something to eat, but you don't want to work for it! Now none of us will have any supper!" Alfred only hung his head in shame.

Just then the woodcutter came home. As soon as he walked through the door, he recognized the stranger sitting at his hearth. "Be quiet!" he told his wife. "Do you realize who you are scolding? This is our noble ruler, King Alfred himself."

The woman was horrified. She ran to the king's side and fell to her knees. She begged him to forgive her for speaking so harshly.

But the wise King Alfred asked her to rise. "You were right to scold me," he said. "I told you I would watch the cakes, and then I let them burn. I deserved what you said. Anyone who accepts a duty, whether it be large or small, should perform it faithfully. I have failed this time, but it will not happen again. My duties as king await me."

The story does not tell us if King Alfred had anything to eat that night. But it was not many days before he had gathered his men together again, and soon he drove the Danes out of England.

St. George and the Dragon

RETOLD BY J. BERG ESENWEIN
AND MARIETTA STOCKARD

"Somewhere perhaps there is trouble and fear," St. George says in this story before riding off to "find work which only a knight can do." Here is a morally good conscience, always aiding others. Such people who go out of their way to help are sometimes called knights, saints, and philanthropists; sometimes they are called ministers, teachers, coaches, police officers, and parents.

Long ago, when the knights lived in the land, there was one knight whose name was Sir George. He was not only braver than all the rest, but he was so noble, kind and good that the people came to call him Saint George.

No robbers ever dared to trouble the people who lived near his castle, and all the wild animals were killed or driven away, so the little children could play even in the woods without being afraid.

One day St. George rode throughout the country. Everywhere he saw the men busy at their work in the fields, the women singing at work in their homes, and the little children shouting at play.

"These people are all safe and happy. They need me no more," said St. George.

"But somewhere perhaps there is trouble and fear. There may be someplace where little children cannot play in safety, some woman may have been carried away from her home—perhaps there are even dragons left to be slain.

Tomorrow I shall ride away and never stop until I find work which only a knight can do."

Early the next morning St. George put on his helmet and all his shining armor and fastened his sword at his side. Then he mounted his great white horse and rode out from his castle gate. Down the steep, rough road he went, sitting straight and tall and looking brave and strong as a knight should look.

On through the little village at the foot of the hill and out across the country he rode. Everywhere he saw rich fields filled with waving grain, everywhere there was peace and plenty.

He rode on and on until at last he came into a part of the country he had never seen before. He noticed that there were no men working in the fields. The houses which he passed stood silent and empty. The grass along the roadside was scorched as if a fire had passed over it. A field of wheat was all trampled and burned.

St. George drew up his horse and looked carefully about him. Everywhere there was silence and desolation. "What can be the dreadful thing which has driven all the people from their homes? I must find out, and give them help if I can," he said.

But there was no one to ask, so St. George rode forward until at last far in the distance he saw the walls of a city. Here surely I shall find someone who can tell me the cause of all this," he said, so he rode more swiftly toward the city.

Just then the great gate opened and St. George saw crowds of people standing inside the wall. Some of them were weeping, all of them seemed afraid. As St. George watched, he saw a beautiful maiden dressed in white, with a girdle of scarlet about her waist, pass through the gate alone. The gate clanged shut and the maiden walked along the road, weeping bitterly. She did not see St. George, who was riding quickly toward her.

"Maiden, why do you weep?" he asked as he reached her side.

She looked up at St. George sitting there on his horse, so straight and tall and beautiful. "Oh, Sir Knight!" she cried, "ride quickly from this place. You know not the danger you are in!"

"Danger!" said St. George. "Do you think a knight would flee from danger? Besides, you, a fair girl, are here alone. Think you a knight would leave you so? Tell me your trouble that I may help you."

"No! No!" she cried. "Hasten away. You would only lose your life. There is a terrible dragon near. He may come at any moment. One breath would destroy you if he found you here. Go! Go quickly!"

"Tell me more of this," said St. George sternly. "Why are you here alone to meet this dragon? Are there no *men* left in yon city?"

"Oh," said the maiden, "my father, the King is old and feeble. He has only me to help him take care of his people. This terrible dragon has driven them from their homes, carried away their cattle, and ruined their crops. They have all come within the walls of the city for safety. For weeks now the dragon has come to the very gates of the city. We have been forced to give him two sheep each day for his breakfast."

"Yesterday there were no sheep left to give, so he said that unless a young maiden were given him today he would break down the walls and destroy the city. The people cried to my father to save them, but he could do nothing. I am going to give myself to the dragon. Perhaps if he has me, the Princess, he may spare our people."

"Lead the way, brave Princess. Show me where this monster may be found."

When the Princess saw St. George's flashing eyes and great, strong arm as he drew forth his sword, she felt afraid no more. Turning, she led the way to a shining pool.

"That's where he stays," she whispered. "See, the water moves. He is waking."

St. George saw the head of the dragon lifted from the pool. Fold on fold he rose from the water. When he saw St. George, he gave a roar of rage and plunged toward him. The smoke and flames flew from his nostrils, and he opened his great jaws as if to swallow both the knight and his horse.

St. George shouted and, waving his sword above his head, rode at the dragon. Quick and hard came the blows from St. George's sword. It was a terrible battle.

At last the dragon was wounded. He roared with pain and plunged at St. George, opening his great mouth close to the brave knight's head.

St. George looked carefully, then struck with all his strength straight down through the dragon's throat, and the dragon fell at the horse's feet—dead.

Then St. George shouted for joy at his victory. He called to the Princess. She came and stood beside him.

"Give me the girdle from about your waist, O Princess," said St. George.

The Princess gave him her girdle and St. George bound it around the dragon's neck, and they pulled the dragon after them by that little silken ribbon back to the city so that all of the people could see that the dragon could never harm them again.

When they saw St. George bringing the Princess back in safely and knew that the dragon was slain, they threw open the gates of the city and sent up great shouts of joy.

The King heard them and came out from his palace to see why the people were shouting.

When he saw his daughter safe, he was the happiest of them all.

"O brave knight," he said, "I am old and weak. Stay here and help me guard my people from harm."

"I'll stay as long as ever you have need of me," St. George answered.

So he lived in the palace and helped the old King take care of his people, and when the old King died, St. George was made King in his stead. The people felt happy and safe so long as they had such a brave and good man for their King.

ᨌ The Bell of Atri

RETOLD BY JAMES BALDWIN

This old story reminds us that justice comes from people living up to their obligations toward one another.

Atri is the name of a little town in Italy. It is a very old town and is built halfway up the side of a steep hill.

A long time ago, the King of Atri bought a fine large bell and had it hung up in a tower in the marketplace. A long rope that reached almost to the ground was fastened to the bell. The smallest child could ring the bell by pulling upon this rope.

"It is the bell of justice," said the King.

When at last everything was ready, the people of Atri had a great holiday. All the men and women and children came down to the marketplace to look at the bell of justice. It was a very pretty bell and was polished until it looked almost as bright and yellow as the sun.

"How we should like to hear it ring!" they said.

Then the king came down the street.

"Perhaps he will ring it," said the people. And everybody stood very still and waited to see what he would do.

But he did not ring the bell. He did not even take the rope in his hands. When he came to the foot of the tower, he stopped, and raised his hand.

"My people," he said, "do you see this beautiful bell? It is your bell. But it must never be rung except in case of need. If any one of you is wronged at any time, he may come and ring the bell. And then the judges shall come together at once, and hear his case, and give him justice. Rich and poor, old and young, all alike may come. But no one must touch the rope unless he knows that he has been wronged."

Many years passed by after this. Many times did the bell in the marketplace ring out to call the judges together. Many wrongs were righted, many ill-doers were punished. At last the hempen rope was almost worn out. The lower part of it was untwisted; some of the strands were broken; it became so short that only a tall man could reach it.

"This will never do," said the judges one day. "What if a child should be wronged? It could not ring the bell to let us know it."

They gave orders that a new rope should be put upon the bell at once—a rope that should hang down to the ground so that the smallest child could reach it. But there was not a rope to be found in all Atri. They would have to send across the mountains for one, and it would be many days before it could be brought. What if some wrong should be done before it came? How could the judges know about it, if the injured one could not reach the old rope?

"Let me fix it for you," said a man who stood by.

He ran into his garden, which was not far away, and soon came back with a long grapevine in his hands.

"This will do for a rope," he said. And he climbed up and fastened it to the bell. The slender vine, with its leaves and tendrils still upon it, trailed to the ground.

"Yes," said the judges, "it is a very good rope. Let it be as it is."

Now, on the hillside above the village, there lived a man who had once been a brave knight. In his youth he had ridden through many lands, and he had fought in many a battle. His best friend through all that time had been his horse—a strong, noble steed that had borne him safe through many a danger.

But the knight, when he grew older, cared no more to ride into battle; he cared no more to do brave deeds; he thought of nothing but gold; he became a miser. At last he sold all that he had, except his horse, and went to live in a little hut on the hillside. Day after day he sat among his moneybags and planned how he might get more gold. And day after day his horse stood in his bare stall, half starved and shivering with cold.

"What is the use of keeping that lazy steed?" said the miser to himself one morning. "Every week it costs me more to keep him than he is worth. I might sell him, but there is not a man that wants him. I cannot even give him away. I will turn him out to shift for himself and pick grass by the roadside. If he starves to death, so much the better."

So the brave old horse was turned out to find what he could among the rocks on the barren hillside. Lame and sick, he strolled along the dusty roads, glad to find a blade of grass or a thistle. The boys threw stones at him, the dogs barked at him, and in all the world there was no one to pity him.

One hot afternoon, when no one was upon the street, the horse chanced to wander into the marketplace. Not a man or child was there, for the heat of the sun had driven them all indoors. The gates were wide open; the poor beast could roam where he pleased. He saw the grapevine rope that hung from the bell of justice. The leaves and tendrils upon it were still fresh and green, for it had not been there long. What a fine dinner they would be for a starving horse!

He stretched his thin neck and took one of the tempting morsels in his mouth. It was hard to break it from the vine. He pulled at it, and the great bell above him began to ring. All the people in Atri heard it. It seemed to say,

Someone	has done	me wrong!
Someone	has done	me wrong!
Oh! come	and judge	my case!
Oh! come	and judge	my case!
For I've	been wronged!	

The judges heard it. They put on their robes and went out through the hot streets to the marketplace. They wondered who it could be who would ring the bell at such a time. When they passed through the gate, they saw the old horse nibbling at the vine.

"Ha!" cried one, "it is the miser's steed. He has come to call for justice. For his master, as everybody knows, has treated him most shamefully."

"He pleads his cause as well as any dumb brute can," said another.

"And he shall have justice!" said the third.

Meanwhile a crowd of men and women and children had come into the marketplace, eager to learn what cause the judges were about to try. When they saw the horse, all stood still in wonder. Then everyone was ready to tell how they had seen him wandering on the hills, unfed, uncared for, while his master sat at home counting his bags of gold.

"Go bring the miser before us," said the judges.

And when he came, they bade him stand and hear their judgment.

"This horse has served you well for many a year," they said. "He has saved you from many a peril. He has helped you gain your wealth. Therefore we order that one half of all your gold shall be set aside to buy him shelter and food, a green pasture where he may graze, and a warm stall to comfort him in his old age."

The miser hung his head and grieved to lose his gold. But the people shouted with joy, and the horse was led away to his new stall and a dinner such as he had not had in many a day.

~ The Bridge Builder

WILL ALLEN DROMGOOLE

This poem speaks of each generation's responsibilities to its successors.

An old man, going a lone highway,
Came, at the evening, cold and gray,
To a chasm, vast, and deep, and wide,
Through which was flowing a sullen tide.
The old man crossed in the twilight dim;
The sullen stream had no fears for him;
But he turned, when safe on the other side,
And built a bridge to span the tide.
"Old man," said a fellow pilgrim, near,
"You are wasting strength with building here;
Your journey will end with the ending day;
You never again must pass this way;
You have crossed the chasm, deep and wide—
Why build you the bridge at the eventide?"

The builder lifted his old gray head:
"Good friend, in the path I have come," he said,
"There followeth after me today
A youth, whose feet must pass this way.
This chasm, that has been naught to me,
To that fair-haired youth may a pitfall be.
He, too, must cross in the twilight dim;
Good friend, I am building the bridge for *him*."

The Charge of the Light Brigade

ALFRED, LORD TENNYSON

Tennyson based this famous poem on the Battle of Balaklava, fought on October 25, 1854, during the Crimean War, in which a small force of British cavalry made a daring but disastrous assault against a Russian artillery line. After the attack, only 195 of the 673 men in the Light Brigade answered muster call. There are times, such as in this tragic story, when obedient acts of self-sacrifice and courage merit both admiration and profound gratitude.

Half a league, half a league,
    Half a league onward,
All in the valley of Death
    Rode the six hundred.

"Forward, the Light Brigade!
Charge for the guns!" he said:
Into the valley of Death
    Rode the six hundred.

"Forward, the Light Brigade!"
Was there a man dismay'd?
Not tho' the soldier knew
    Someone had blunder'd:
Theirs not to make reply,
Theirs not to reason why,
Theirs but to do and die:
Into the valley of Death
    Rode the six hundred.

Cannon to right of them,
Cannon to left of them,
Cannon in front of them
    Volley'd and thunder'd;
Storm'd at with shot and shell,
Boldly they rode and well,
Into the jaws of Death,
Into the mouth of Hell
    Rode the six hundred.

Flash'd all their sabers bare,
Flash'd as they turn'd in air
Sab'ring the gunners there,
Charging an army, while
    All the world wonder'd:
Plunged in the battery smoke
Right thro' the line they broke;
Cossack and Russian
Reel'd from the saber stroke
    Shatter'd and sunder'd.
Then they rode back, but not
    Not the six hundred.

Cannon to right of them,
Cannon to left of them,
Cannon behind them
    Volley'd and thunder'd:
Storm'd at with shot and shell,
While horse and hero fell,
They that had fought so well
Came through the jaws of death
Back from the mouth of hell,

All that was left of them—
Left of six hundred.

When can their glory fade?
Oh, the wild charge they made!
All the world wonder'd.
Honor the charge they made!
Honor the Light Brigade—
Noble six hundred!

❧ The Chest of Broken Glass

Responsibilities of parents and children toward each other change with age. This tale is about that time in life when caring about someone means taking care of them. The obligation to "honor thy father and mother" does not end when father and mother grow old.

Once there was an old man who had lost his wife and lived all alone. He had worked hard as a tailor all his life, but misfortunes had left him penniless, and now he was so old he could no longer work for himself. His hands trembled too much to thread a needle, and his vision had blurred too much for him to make a straight stitch. He had three sons, but they were all grown and married now, and they were so busy with their own lives, they only had time to stop by and eat dinner with their father once a week.

Gradually the old man grew more and more feeble, and his sons came by to see him less and less. "They don't want to be around me at all now," he told himself, "because they're afraid I'll become a burden." He stayed up all night worrying what would become of him, until at last he thought of a plan.

The next morning he went to see his friend the carpenter and asked him to make a large chest. Then he went to see his friend the locksmith and asked him to give him an old lock. Finally he went to see his friend the glassblower and asked for all the old broken pieces of glass he had.

The old man took the chest home, filled it to the top with broken glass, locked it up tight, and put it beneath his kitchen table. The next time his sons came for dinner, they bumped their feet against it.

"What's in the chest?" they asked, looking under the table.

"Oh, nothing," the old man replied, "just some things I've been saving."

His sons nudged it and saw how heavy it was. They kicked it and heard a rattling inside. "It must be full of all the gold he's saved over the years," they whispered to one another.

So they talked it over and realized they needed to guard the treasure. They decided to take turns living with the old man, and that way they could look after him, too. So the first week the youngest son moved in with his father and cared and cooked for him. The next week the middle son took his place, and the week afterward the eldest son took a turn. This went on for some time.

At last the old father grew sick and died. The sons gave him a very nice funeral, for they knew there was a fortune sitting beneath the kitchen table, and they could afford to splurge a little on the old man now.

When the service was over, they hunted through the

house until they found the key, and unlocked the chest. And of course they found it full of broken glass.

"What a rotten trick!" yelled the eldest son. "What a cruel thing to do to your own sons!"

"But what else could he have done, really?" asked the middle son sadly. "We must be honest with ourselves. If it wasn't for this chest, we would have neglected him until the end of his days."

"I'm so ashamed of myself," sobbed the youngest. "We forced our own father to stoop to deceit, because we would not observe the very commandment he taught us when we were young."

But the eldest son tipped the chest over to make sure there was nothing valuable hidden among the glass after all. He poured the broken pieces onto the floor until it was empty. Then the three brothers silently stared inside, where they now read an inscription left for them on the bottom:

HONOR THY FATHER AND MOTHER.

ஐ The Devoted Son and the Thief

In this tale from China we witness one heart's remarkable sense of responsibility teaching—even reforming—another wicked heart by powerful example.

There was once a young man named Li who devoted himself to the task of taking care of his old widowed mother. He cooked for her, made sure she took her medicine every night, and brought her old friends to see her so that she wouldn't be lonely in her last years. And once a week, he took her to his father's resting place where she grieved quietly while he swept the grave.

One evening a thief broke into the house where they lived. He made Li and the old woman sit in a corner while he searched the place. He carried a cloth bag and began stuffing it with whatever he thought was worth stealing.

He took Li's silk robe, the only piece of good clothing the youth possessed. Li watched and said nothing.

He took Li's jacket, the only one he had to keep warm on bitter cold mornings.

The youth kept his mouth shut.

He took Li's jade ring, the one his father had given to him. The young man's lip trembled, but still he said nothing.

Then the thief reached for an old pot.

"Please, be kind enough to leave us that pot," Li spoke up. "If you take it, I won't be able to make my mother's dinner."

The thief dropped the pot and looked in awe at the young man and his mother.

"Heaven will surely curse me if I rob a household where such duty lives," he cried.

He emptied his bag and left with a softened heart.

The Man Who Tossed Stones

This ancient Middle Eastern tale warns us against trying to get rid of our own problems by passing them along to others.

There was once a very rich man who built for himself an immense house surrounded by a high wall. Inside the wall he kept magnificent gardens with every kind of flowering bush and tree. He loved nothing so well as his gardens, and he was always adding beds and pathways and fountains to the grounds. As his servants dug, they unearthed all sorts of useless rocks, which the rich man ordered tossed over the wall. Day after day, season after season, his servants shaped his gardens, throwing cartloads of stones into the road outside.

One day an old man passed the estate and paused at the gate.

"Tell me," he called to the rich man, who was inspecting his grounds inside, "why do you toss these stones from what is not yours to what is yours?"

"What do you mean, old man?" the rich man laughed. "This garden is mine. Everything inside these walls is mine. As to what lies outside these walls, well, I don't really care about that."

The old man gazed at him sadly.

"Everything in this world is fleeting," he said, and turned away.

"Well, he's a strange one," the rich man thought. He hurried to show his workers where to build a new pond.

The years passed, and hard times came. The man's fortune began to dwindle. His business failed and his investments soured. Soon he found himself pressed by his creditors, who forced him to sell all he possessed, including his beautiful house and gardens. He ended penniless and ragged.

One day he was wandering the streets, begging for food, when he happened to pass the grand estate he had called home. The road running beside it was full of sharp rocks;

he stumbled on one, cutting his bare feet, and sat down to tend to his wounds.

As he sat, bleeding and tired and sore, he looked up at the high wall and then down at the rocks that littered its base.

"Why did I not treat what lay outside my wall with the same respect I treated what lay within it?" he wondered. "Now I have lost my garden and inherited my own folly."

And suddenly he remembered the old man's words: "Don't toss stones from what is not yours to what is yours."

ꙮ The Sword of Damocles
ADAPTED FROM JAMES BALDWIN

This is one of our oldest "if you can't stand the heat get out of the kitchen" stories. It is a great reminder that if we aspire to any kind of high office or job, we must be willing to live with all the burdens that come with it.

There once was a king named Dionysius who ruled in Syracuse, the richest city in Sicily. He lived in a fine palace where there were many beautiful and costly things, and he was waited upon by a host of servants who were always ready to do his bidding.

Naturally, because Dionysius had so much wealth and power, there were many in Syracuse who envied his good fortune. Damocles was one of these. He was one of Dionysius's best friends, and he was always saying to him,

"How lucky you are! You have everything anyone could wish for. You must be the happiest man in the world."

One day Dionysius grew tired of hearing such talk. "Come now," he said, "do you really think I'm happier than everyone else?"

"But of course you are," Damocles replied. "Look at the great treasures you possess and the power you hold. You have not a single worry in the world. How could life be any better?"

"Perhaps you would like to change places with me," said Dionysius.

"Oh, I would never dream of that," said Damocles. "But if I could only have your riches and your pleasures for one day, I should never want any greater happiness."

"Very well. Trade places with me for just one day, and you shall have them."

And so, the next day, Damocles was led to the palace, and all the servants were instructed to treat him as their master. They dressed him in royal robes and placed on his head a crown of gold. He sat down at a table in the banquet hall, and rich foods were set before him. Nothing was wanting that could give him pleasure. There were costly wines, and beautiful flowers, and rare perfumes, and delightful music. He rested himself among soft cushions and felt he was the happiest man in all the world.

"Ah, this is the life," he sighed to Dionysius, who sat at the other end of the long table. "I've never enjoyed myself so much."

And as he raised a cup to his lips, he lifted his eyes toward the ceiling. What was that dangling above him, with its point almost touching his head?

Damocles stiffened. The smile faded from his lips, and

his face turned ashy pale. His hands trembled. He wanted no more food, no more wine, no more music. He only wanted to be out of the palace, far away, he cared not where. For directly above his head hung a sword, held to the ceiling by only a single horsehair. Its sharp blade glittered as it pointed right between his eyes. He started to jump up and run, but stopped himself, frightened that any sudden move might snap the thin thread and bring the sword down. He sat frozen to his chair.

"What is the matter, my friend?" Dionysius asked. "You seem to have lost your appetite."

"That sword! That sword!" whispered Damocles. "Don't you see it?"

"Of course I see it," said Dionysius. "I see it every day. It always hangs over my head, and there is always the chance someone or something may cut the slim thread. Perhaps one of my own advisors will grow jealous of my power and try to kill me. Or someone may spread lies about me, to turn the people against me. It may be that a neighboring kingdom will send an army to seize this throne. Or I might make an unwise decision that will bring my downfall. If you want to be a leader, you must be willing to accept these risks. They come with the power, you see."

"Yes, I do see," said Damocles. "I see now that I was mistaken, and that you have much to think about besides your riches and fame. Please take your place, and let me go back to my own house."

And as long as he lived, Damocles never again wanted to change places, even for a moment, with the king.

❧ The Ten Commandments

Western morality may be said to begin with these ten very old, very good rules for living.

1. I am the Lord thy God. Thou shalt have no other gods before me.
2. Thou shalt not make unto thee any graven image.
3. Thou shalt not take the name of the Lord thy God in vain.
4. Remember the sabbath day, to keep it holy.
5. Honor thy father and thy mother.
6. Thou shalt not kill.
7. Thou shalt not commit adultery.
8. Thou shalt not steal.
9. Thou shalt not bear false witness against thy neighbor.
10. Thou shalt not covet.

FRIENDSHIP

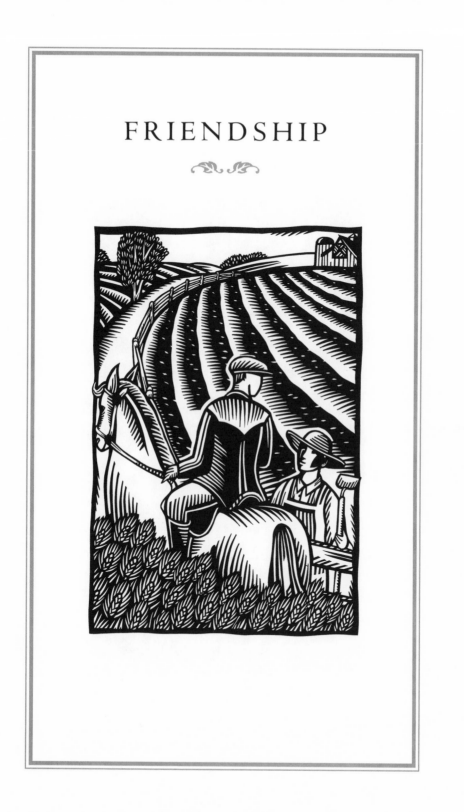

Friendship

Why do we want friends? The obvious answer is that friends make us happy. They make life more interesting and fun for us. They share our tastes, our desires, our sense of humor.

But real friendship is based on more than just hanging around with each other and joking with each other. The ancient Greek philosopher Aristotle put it this way: "We may describe friendly feeling toward any one as wishing for him what you believe to be good things, not for your own sake but for his, and being inclined, so far as you can, to bring these things about."

In other words, real friends give each other virtues, or "good things," as Aristotle put it. Friends give loyalty to one another, as in the story of Jonathan and David in this chapter. They give trust as in the story of Damon and Pythias. They give help in times of need, as in the story of Ruth and Naomi.

Friends naturally try to make each other better people. They try to lift each other. They help each other make the right decisions and aim for worthy goals. Being a friend does not always require doing what your friend wants you to do. Rather, it requires doing what you believe is best for your friend.

All of this means you must choose your friends wisely. Your friends tell you a lot about yourself. They tell you what kind of person you may turn out to be. Good friends help lift you up, but bad friends will drag you down. If they have bad habits, there's a good chance you'll end up with those bad habits, too. So if you can't persuade them to change their ways, you'll do better to find some new friends.

Of course, for many people, finding and making new friends is a tough process. But it doesn't have to be so hard if you think less about *having* friends and more about *being* a friend. You'll make many more friends by being interested in people than you will by trying to get people interested in you. And by being genuinely interested in other people, you'll discover that friendship does not just bring you happiness. It will *improve* your happiness by making you a better person.

A Time to Talk

ROBERT FROST

Work always calls us. But we make time for friends
when they call, too.

> When a friend calls to me from the road
> And slows his horse to a meaning walk,
> I don't stand still and look around
> On all the hills I haven't hoed,
> And shout from where I am, What is it?
> No, not as there is a time to talk.
> I thrust my hoe in the mellow ground,
> Blade-end up and five feet tall,
> And plod: I go up to the stone wall
> For a friendly visit.

Childhood and Poetry

PABLO NERUDA

This story by Chilean poet Pablo Neruda (1904–
1973) suggests that every time we offer friendship to
someone we do not know, we strengthen our bond
with all humanity.

One time, investigating in the backyard of our house in
Temuco the tiny objects and miniscule beings of my world,
I came upon a hole in one of the boards of the fence. I
looked through the hole and saw a landscape like that
behind our house, uncared for and wild. I moved back a
few steps, because I sensed vaguely that something was

about to happen. All of a sudden a hand appeared—a tiny hand of a boy about my own age. By the time I came close again, the hand was gone, and in its place there was a marvelous white sheep.

The sheep's wool was faded. Its wheels had escaped. All of this only made it more authentic. I had never seen such a wonderful sheep. I looked back through the hole but the boy had disappeared. I went into the house and brought out a treasure of my own: a pine cone, opened, full of odor and resin, which I adored. I set it down in the same spot and went off with the sheep.

I never saw either the hand or the boy again. And I have never again seen a sheep like that either. The toy I lost finally in a fire. But even now, in 1954, almost fifty years old, whenever I pass a toy shop, I look furtively into the window, but it's no use. They don't make sheep like that anymore.

I have been a lucky man. To feel the intimacy of brothers is a marvelous thing in life. To feel the love of people whom we love is a fire that feeds our life. But to feel the affection that comes from those whom we do not know, from those unknown to us, who are watching over our sleep and solitude, over our dangers and our weaknesses— that is something still greater and more beautiful because it widens out the boundaries of our being, and unites all living things.

That exchange brought home to me for the first time a precious idea: that all of humanity is somehow together. That experience came to me again much later; this time it stood out strikingly against a background of trouble and persecution.

It won't surprise you then that I attempted to give something resiny, earthlike and fragrant in exchange for human brotherhood. Just as I once left the pine cone by the fence, I have since left my words on the door of so many people who were unknown to me, people in prison, or hunted, or alone.

That is the great lesson I learned in my childhood, in the backyard of a lonely house. Maybe it was nothing but a game two boys played who didn't know each other and wanted to pass to the other some good things of life. Yet maybe this small and mysterious exchange of gifts remained inside me also, deep and indestructible, giving my poetry light.

Damon and Pythias

This story takes place in Syracuse in the fourth century B.C. Even today, the tale of Damon and Pythias sets the standard for the deepest friendships, which give every reason for confidence and leave no room for doubts.

Damon and Pythias had been the best of friends since childhood. Each trusted the other like a brother, and each knew in his heart there was nothing he would not do for his friend. Eventually the time came for them to prove the depth of their devotion. It happened this way.

Dionysius, the ruler of Syracuse, grew annoyed when he heard about the speeches Pythias was giving. The young scholar was telling the public that no man should have unlimited power over another, and that absolute tyrants were unjust kings. In a fit of rage, Dionysius summoned Pythias and his friend.

"Who do you think you are, spreading unrest among the people?" he demanded.

"I spread only the truth," Pythias answered. "There can be nothing wrong with that."

"And does your truth hold that kings have too much power and that their laws are not good for their subjects?"

"If a king has seized power without permission of the people, then that is what I say."

"This kind of talk is treason," Dionysius shouted. "You are conspiring to overthrow me. Retract what you've said, or face the consequences."

"I will retract nothing," Pythias answered.

"Then you will die. Do you have any last requests?"

"Yes. Let me go home just long enough to say goodbye to my wife and children and to put my household in order."

"I see you not only think I'm unjust, you think I'm stupid as well," Dionysius laughed scornfully. "If I let you leave Syracuse, I have no doubt I will never see you again."

"I will give you a pledge," Pythias said.

"What kind of pledge could you possibly give to make me think you will ever return?" Dionysius demanded.

At that instant Damon, who had stood quietly beside his friend, stepped forward.

"I will be his pledge," he said. "Keep me here in Syracuse, as your prisoner, until Pythias returns. Our friendship is well known to you. You can be sure Pythias will return so long as you hold me."

Dionysius studied the two friends silently. "Very well," he said at last. "But if you are willing to take the place of your friend, you must be willing to accept his sentence if he breaks his promise. If Pythias does not return to Syracuse, you will die in his place."

"He will keep his word," Damon replied. "I have no doubt of that."

Pythias was allowed to go free for a time, and Damon was thrown into prison. After several days, when Pythias failed to reappear, Dionysius's curiosity got the better of him, and he went to the prison to see if Damon was yet sorry he had made such a bargain.

"Your time is almost up," the ruler of Syracuse sneered. "It will be useless to beg for mercy. You were a fool to rely on your friend's promise. Did you really think he would sacrifice his life for you or anyone else?"

"He has merely been delayed," Damon answered steadily. "The winds have kept him from sailing, or perhaps he has met with some accident on the road. But if it is humanly possible, he will be here on time. I am as confident of his virtue as I am of my own existence."

Dionysius was startled at the prisoner's confidence. "We shall soon see," he said, and left Damon in his cell.

The fatal day arrived. Damon was brought from prison and led before the executioner. Dionysius greeted him with a smug smile.

"It seems your friend has not turned up," he laughed. "What do you think of him now?"

"He is my friend," Damon answered. "I trust him."

Even as he spoke, the doors flew open and Pythias staggered into the room. He was pale and bruised and half speechless from exhaustion. He rushed to the arms of his friend.

"You are safe, praise the gods," he gasped. "It seemed

as though the fates were conspiring against us. My ship was wrecked in a storm, and then bandits attacked me on the road. But I refused to give up hope, and at last I've made it back in time. I am ready to receive my sentence of death."

Dionysius heard his words with astonishment. His eyes and his heart were opened. It was impossible for him to resist the power of such constancy.

"The sentence is revoked," he declared. "I never believed that such faith and loyalty could exist in friendship. You have shown me how wrong I was, and it is only right that you be rewarded with your freedom. But I ask that in return you do me one great service."

"What service do you mean?" the friends asked.

"Teach me how to be part of so worthy a friendship."

🐦 Helen Keller and Anne Sullivan

There is no friendship more sacred than that between student and teacher, and one of the greatest of these was the friendship of Helen Keller (1880–1968) and Anne Mansfield Sullivan (1866–1936).

Illness destroyed Helen Keller's sight and hearing when she was not two years old, leaving her cut off from the world. For nearly five years she grew up, as she later described it, "wild and unruly, giggling and chuckling to express pleasure; kicking, scratching, uttering the choked screams of the deaf-mute to indicate the opposite."

Anne Sullivan's arrival at the Kellers' Alabama home from the Perkins Institution for the Blind in

Boston changed Helen's life. Sullivan herself had been half-blind from an eye infection from which she never fully recovered, and she came to Helen with experience, unbending dedication, and love. Through the sense of touch she was able to make contact with the young girl's mind, and within three years she had taught Helen to read and write in Braille. By sixteen, Helen could speak well enough to go to preparatory school and college. She graduated cum laude *from Radcliffe in 1904, and devoted the rest of her life to helping the blind and deaf-blind, as her teacher had done. The two women continued their remarkable friendship until Anne's death.*

Helen wrote about Anne Sullivan's arrival in her autobiography, The Story of My Life.

The most important day I remember in all my life is the one on which my teacher, Anne Mansfield Sullivan, came to me. I am filled with wonder when I consider the immeasurable contrasts between the two lives which it connects. It was the third of March, 1887, three months before I was seven years old.

On that afternoon of the eventful day, I stood on the porch, dumb, expectant. I guessed vaguely from my mother's signs and from the hurrying to and fro in the house that something unusual was about to happen, so I went to the door and waited on the steps. The afternoon sun penetrated the mass of honeysuckle that covered the porch, and fell on my upturned face. My fingers lingered almost unconsciously on the familiar leaves and blossoms which had just come forth to greet the sweet Southern spring. I did not know what the future held of marvel or surprise for me.

Anger and bitterness had preyed upon me continually for weeks and a deep languor had succeeded this passionate struggle.

Have you ever been at sea in a dense fog, when it seemed as if a tangible white darkness shut you in, and the great ship, tense and anxious, groped her way toward the shore with plummet and sounding-line, and you waited with beating heart for something to happen? I was like that ship before my education began, only I was without compass or sounding-line, and had no way of knowing how near the harbor was. "Light! give me light!" was the wordless cry of my soul, and the light of love shone on me in that very hour.

I felt approaching footsteps. I stretched out my hand as I supposed to my mother. Someone took it, and I was caught up and held close in the arms of her who had come to reveal all things to me and, more than all things else, to love me.

The morning after my teacher came she led me into her room and gave me a doll. The little blind children at the Perkins Institution had sent it and Laura Bridgman had dressed it; but I did not know this until afterward. When I had played with it a little while, Miss Sullivan slowly spelled into my hand the word "d-o-l-l." I was at once interested in this finger play and tried to imitate it. When I finally succeeded in making the letters correctly I was flushed with childish pleasure and pride. Running downstairs to my mother I held up my hand and made the letters for *doll*. I did not know that I was spelling a word or even that words existed; I was simply making my fingers go in monkey-like imitation. In the days that followed I learned to spell in this uncomprehending way a great many words, among them, *pin, hat, cup* and a few verbs like *sit, stand,* and *walk.* But my teacher had been with me several weeks before I understood that everything has a name.

One day, while I was playing with my new doll, Miss Sullivan put my big rag doll into my lap also, spelled "d-o-l-l" and tried to make me understand that "d-o-l-l" applied to both. Earlier in the day we had had a tussle over the words "m-u-g" and "w-a-t-e-r." Miss Sullivan had tried to impress upon me that "m-u-g" is *mug* and that "w-a-t-e-r" is *water,* but I persisted in confounding the two. In despair she had dropped the subject for the time, only to renew it at the first opportunity. I became impatient at her repeated attempts and, seizing the new doll, I dashed it upon the floor. I was keenly delighted when I felt the fragments of the broken doll at my feet. Neither sorrow nor regret followed my passionate outburst. I had not loved the doll. In the still, dark world in which I lived, there was no strong sentiment or tenderness. I felt my teacher sweep the fragments to one side of the hearth, and I had a sense of satisfaction that the cause of my discomfort was removed. She brought me my hat, and I knew I was going out into the warm sunshine. This thought, if a wordless sensation may be called a thought, made me hop and skip with pleasure.

We walked down the path to the well-house, attracted by the fragrance of the honeysuckle with which it was covered. Someone was drawing water and my teacher placed my hand under the spout. As the cool stream gushed over one hand she spelled into the other the word *water,* first slowly, then rapidly. I stood still, my whole attention fixed upon the motions of her fingers. Suddenly I felt a misty consciousness as of something forgotten—a thrill of returning thought; and somehow the mystery of language was revealed to me. I knew then that "w-a-t-e-r" meant the wonderful cool something that was flowing over my hand. That living word awakened my soul, gave it light, hope, joy, set it free! There were barriers still, it is true, but barriers that could in time be swept away.

I left the well-house eager to learn. Everything had a name, and each name gave birth to a new thought. As we returned to the house every object which I touched seemed to quiver with life. That was because I saw everything with the strange, new sight that had come to me. On entering the door I remembered the doll I had broken. I felt my way to the hearth and picked up the pieces. I tried vainly to put them together. Then my eyes filled with tears; for I realized what I had done, and for the first time I felt repentance and sorrow.

I learned a great many new words that day. I do not remember what they all were; but I do know that *mother, father, sister, teacher* were among them—words that were to make the world blossom for me, "like Aaron's rod, with flowers." It would have been difficult to find a happier child than I was as I lay in my crib at the close of that eventful day and lived over the joys it had brought me, and for the first time longed for a new day to come.

Anne Sullivan, in her letters, described the "miracle" she saw taking place in Helen.

March 20, 1887
My heart is singing for joy this morning. A miracle has happened! The light of understanding has shone upon my little pupil's mind, and behold, all things are changed!

The wild little creature of two weeks ago has been transformed into a gentle child. She is sitting by me as I write, her face serene and happy, crocheting a long red chain of Scotch wool. She learned the stitch this week, and is very proud of the achievement. When she succeeded in making a chain that would reach across the room, she patted herself on the arm and put the first work of her hands lovingly against her cheek. She lets me kiss her now, and when she is in a particularly gentle mood, she will sit in my lap for a minute or two; but she does not return my caresses. The great step—the step that counts—has been taken. The little savage has learned her first lesson in obedience, and finds the yoke easy. It now remains my pleasant task to direct and mold the beautiful intelligence that is beginning to stir in the child-soul. Already people remark the change in Helen. Her father looks in at us morning and evening as he goes to and from his office, and sees her contentedly stringing her beads or making horizontal lines on her sewing card, and exclaims, "How quiet she is!" When I came, her movements were so insistent that one always felt there was something unnatural and almost weird about her. I have noticed also that she eats much less, a fact which troubles her father so much that he is anxious to get her home. He says she is homesick. I don't agree with him; but I suppose we shall have to leave our little bower very soon.

Helen has learned several nouns this week. "M-u-g" and "m-i-l-k," have given her more trouble than other words. When she spells *milk,* she points to the mug, and when she spells *mug,* she makes the sign for pouring or drinking, which shows that she has confused the words. She has no idea yet that everything has a name.

April 5, 1887

I must write you a line this morning because something very important has happened. Helen has taken the second great step in her education. She has learned that *everything has a name, and that the manual alphabet is the key to everything she wants to know.*

In a previous letter I think I wrote you that "mug" and "milk" had given Helen more trouble than all the rest. She confused the nouns with the verb "drink." She didn't know the word for "drink," but went through the pantomime of drinking whenever she spelled "mug" or "milk." This morning, while she was washing, she wanted to know the name for "water." When she wants to know the name of anything, she points to it and pats my hand. I spelled "w-a-t-e-r" and thought no more about it until after breakfast. Then it occurred to me that with the help of this new word I might succeed in straightening out the "mug-milk" difficulty. We went out to the pump-house, and I made Helen hold her mug under the spout while I pumped. As the cold water gushed forth, filling the mug, I spelled "w-a-t-e-r" in Helen's free hand. The word coming so close upon the sensation of cold water rushing over her hand seemed to startle her. She dropped the mug and stood as one transfixed. A new light came into her face. She spelled "water" several times. Then she dropped on the ground and asked for its name and pointed to the pump and the trellis, and suddenly turning round she asked for my name. I spelled "Teacher." Just then the nurse brought Helen's little sister into the pump-house, and Helen spelled "baby" and pointed to the nurse. All the way back to the house she was highly excited, and learned the name of every object she touched, so that in a few hours she had thirty new words to her vocabulary. Here are some of them: *Door, open, shut, give, go, come,* and a great many more.

P.S.—I didn't finish my letter in time to get it posted last night; so I shall add a line. Helen got up this morning like a radiant fairy. She has flitted from object to object, asking the name of everything and kissing me for very gladness. Last night when I got in bed, she stole into my arms of her own accord and kissed me for the first time, and I thought my heart would burst, so full was it of joy.

❧ Jonathan and David

RETOLD BY JESSE LYMAN HURLBUT

Sometimes the duties of friendship compete with other obligations and affections. The story of Jonathan, told in the first book of Samuel in the Bible, is one such instance. Jonathan was the eldest son and heir of King Saul of Israel. He was also David's sworn friend. After David killed Goliath, Saul grew jealous of his popularity, and fearing that he would eventually become king, sought to murder him. Jonathan's defense of David, made doubly painful because of his duties to his father and his own claim to the throne, is one of our greatest examples of loyalty and friendship.

After David had slain the giant he was brought before King Saul, still holding the giant's head. Saul did not remember in this bold fighting man the boy who a few years before had played in his presence. He took him into his own house and made him an officer among his soldiers. David was as wise and as brave in the army as he had been when facing the giant, and very soon he was in command of a thousand men. All the men loved him, both in Saul's court and in his camp, for David had the spirit that drew all hearts toward him.

When David was returning from his battle with the Philistines, the women of Israel came to meet him out of the cities, with instruments of music, singing and dancing, and they sang:

> "Saul has slain his thousands,
> And David his ten thousands."

This made Saul very angry, for he was jealous and suspicious in his spirit. He thought constantly of Samuel's words, that God would take the kingdom from him and would give it to one who was more worthy of it. He began to think that perhaps this young man, who had come in a single day to greatness before the people, might try to make himself king.

His former feeling of unhappiness again came over Saul. He raved in his house, talking as a man talks who is crazed. By this time they all knew that David was a musician, and they called him again to play on his harp and to sing before the troubled king. But now, in his madness, Saul would not listen to David's voice. Twice he threw his spear at him; but each time David leaped aside, and the spear went into the wall of the house.

Saul was afraid of David, for he saw that the Lord was with David, as the Lord was no longer with himself. He would have killed David, but did not dare kill him, because everybody loved David. Saul said to himself, "Though I cannot kill him myself, I will have him killed by the Philistines."

And he sent David out on dangerous errands of war; but David came home in safety, all the greater and the more beloved after each victory. Saul said, "I will give you my daughter Merab for your wife if you will fight the Philistines for me."

David fought the Philistines; but when he came home from the war he found that Merab, who had been promised to him, had been given as wife to another man. Saul had another daughter, named Michal. She loved David, and showed her love for him. Then Saul sent word to David, saying, "You shall have Michal, my daughter, for your wife when you have killed a hundred Philistines."

Then David went out and fought the Philistines, and killed two hundred of them; and they brought the word to Saul. Then Saul gave him his daughter Michal as his wife; but he was all the more afraid of David as he saw him growing in power and drawing nearer the throne of the kingdom.

But if Saul hated David, Saul's son Jonathan saw David's courage, and the soul of Jonathan was knit to the soul of David, and Jonathan loved him as his own soul. He took off his own royal robe and his sword and his bow, and gave them all to David. It grieved Jonathan greatly that his father, Saul, was so jealous of David. He spoke to his father and said: "Let not the king do harm to David; for David has been faithful to the king, and he has done great things for the kingdom. He took his life in his hand, and killed the Philistine, and won a great victory for the Lord and for the people. Why should you seek to kill an innocent man?"

For the time Saul listened to Jonathan, and said, "As the Lord lives, David shall not be put to death."

And again David sat at the king's table, among the princes; and when Saul was troubled again David played on his harp and sang before him. But once more Saul's jealous anger arose, and he threw his spear at David. David was watchful and quick. He leaped aside and, as before, the spear fastened into the wall.

Saul sent men to David's house to seize him; but Michal, Saul's daughter, who was David's wife, let David down out of the window, so that he escaped. She placed an image on David's bed and covered it with the bedclothes. When the men came, she said, "David is ill in the bed and cannot go."

They brought the word to Saul, and he said, "Bring him to me in the bed, just as he is."

When the image was found in David's bed, David was in a safe place, far away. David went to Samuel at Ramah, and stayed with him among the men who were prophets worshipping God and singing and speaking God's word. Saul heard that David was there and sent men to take him. But when these men came and saw Samuel and the prophets praising God and praying, the same spirit came on them, and they began to praise and to pray. Saul sent other men, but these also, when they came among the prophets, felt the same power and joined in the worship.

Finally, Saul said, "If no other man will bring David to me, I will go myself and take him."

And Saul went to Ramah; but when he came near to the company of the worshippers, praising God, and praying, and preaching, the same spirit came on Saul. He, too, began to join in the songs and the prayers, and stayed there all that day and that night, worshipping God very earnestly. When the next day he went again to his home in Gibeah, his feeling was changed for the time, and he was again friendly to David.

But David knew that Saul was at heart his bitter enemy and would kill him if he could as soon as his madness came upon him. He met Jonathan out in the field away from the palace. Jonathan said to David:

"Stay away from the king's table for a few days, and I will find out how he feels toward you, and will tell you. Perhaps even now my father may become your friend. But if he is to be your enemy, I know that the Lord is with you and that Saul will not succeed against you. Promise me that as long as you live you will be kind to me, and not only to me while I live, but to my children after me."

Jonathan believed, as many others believed, that David would yet become the king of Israel, and he was willing to give up to David his right to be king, such was his great love for him. That day a promise was made between Jonathan and David, that they and their children and those who should come after them, should be friends forever.

Jonathan said to David, "I will find how my father feels toward you and will bring you word. After three days I will be here with my bow and arrows, and I will send a little boy out near your place of hiding, and I will shoot three arrows. If I say to the boy, 'Run, find the arrows, they are on this side of you,' then you can come safely, for the king will not harm you. But if I call out to the boy, 'The arrows are away beyond you,' that will mean that there is danger, and you must hide from the king."

So David stayed away from Saul's table for two days. At first Saul said nothing of his absence, but at last he said:

"Why has not the son of Jesse come to meals yesterday and today?"

And Jonathan said, "David asked leave of me to go to his home at Bethlehem and visit his oldest brother."

Then Saul was very angry. He cried out, "You are a disobedient son! Why have you chosen this enemy of mine as your best friend? Do you not know that as long as he is alive you can never be king? Send after him, and let him be brought to me, for he shall surely die!"

Saul was so fierce in his anger that he threw his spear at his own son Jonathan. Jonathan rose up from the table, so anxious for his friend David that he could eat nothing. The next day, at the hour agreed upon, Jonathan went out into the field with a little boy. He said to the boy, "Run out yonder, and be ready to find the arrows that I shoot."

And as the boy was running Jonathan shot arrows beyond him, and he called out, "The arrows are away beyond you; run quickly and find them."

The boy ran and found the arrows, and brought them to Jonathan. He gave the bow and arrows to the boy, saying to him, "Take them back to the city. I will stay here awhile."

And as soon as the boy was out of sight David came from his hiding place and ran to Jonathan. They fell into each other's arms and kissed each other again and again, and wept together. For David knew now that he must no longer hope to be safe in Saul's hands. He must leave home, wife, friends, and his father's house, and hide wherever he could from the hate of King Saul.

Jonathan said to him, "Go in peace; for we have sworn

together saying, 'The Lord shall be between you and me and between your children and my children forever.'"

Then Jonathan went again to his father's palace, and David went out to find a hiding place.

✑ Ruth and Naomi
RETOLD BY JESSE LYMAN HURLBUT

The book of Ruth in the Bible is the story of a widow's courageous decision to leave Moab, her homeland, and travel to Judah with her Hebrew mother-in-law, who has lost her own husband and sons. Ruth's words to Naomi are one of the greatest statements of friendship and loyalty in all of literature:"Whither thou goest, I will go; and where thou lodgest, I will lodge: thy people shall be my people, and thy God my God. Where thou diest, will I die, and there will I be buried." In Judah, Ruth's fidelity and kindness were rewarded with the love of Boaz, and through marriage to him she became the great-grandmother of King David.

In the time of the judges in Israel, a man named Elimelech was living in the town of Bethlehem, in the tribe of Judah, about six miles south of Jerusalem. His wife's name was Naomi, and his two sons were Mahlon and Chilion. For some years the crops were poor, and food was scarce in Judah; and Elimelech, with his family, went to live in the land of Moab, which was on the east of the Dead Sea, as Judah was on the west.

There they stayed ten years, and in that time Elimelech

died. His two sons married women of the country of Moab, one woman name Orpah, the other named Ruth. But the two young men also died in the land of Moab, so that Naomi and her two daughters-in-law were all left widows.

Naomi heard that God had given again good harvests and bread to the land of Judah, and she rose up to go from Moab back to her own land and her own town of Bethlehem. Her two daughters-in-law loved her and both would have gone with her, though the land of Judah was a strange land to them, for they were of the Moabite people.

Naomi said to them, "Go back, my daughters, to your own mothers' homes. May the Lord deal kindly with you, as you have been kind to your husbands and to me. May the Lord grant that each of you may yet find another husband and a happy home." Then Naomi kissed them in farewell, and the three women all wept together. The two young widows said to her, "You have been a good mother to us, and we will go with you, and live among your people."

"No, no," said Naomi. "You are young and I am old. Go back and be happy among your own people."

Then Orpah kissed Naomi and went back to her people, but Ruth would not leave her. She said, "Do not ask me to leave you, for I never will. Where you go, I will go; where you live, I will live; your people shall be my people; and your God shall be my God. Where you die, I will die, and be buried. Nothing but death itself shall part you and me."

When Naomi saw that Ruth was firm in her purpose, she ceased trying to persuade her; so the two women went together. They walked around the Dead Sea, and crossed the river Jordan, and climbed the mountains of Judah, and came to Bethlehem.

Naomi had been absent from Bethlehem for ten years,

but her friends were all glad to see her again. They said, "Is this Naomi, whom we knew years ago?" Now the name *Naomi* means "pleasant." And Naomi said:

"Call me not Naomi; call me Mara, for the Lord has made my life bitter. I went out full, with my husband and two sons; now I come home empty, without them. Do not call me 'Pleasant'; call me 'Bitter.'" The name "*Mara,*" by which Naomi wished to be called, means "bitter." But Naomi learned later that "Pleasant" was the right name for her after all.

There was living in Bethlehem at that time a very rich man named Boaz. He owned large fields that were abundant in their harvests; and he was related to the family of Elimelech, Naomi's husband, who had died.

It was the custom in Israel when they reaped the grain not to gather all the stalks, but to leave some for the poor people, who followed after the reapers with their sickles, and gathered what was left. When Naomi and Ruth came to Bethlehem it was the time of the barley harvest; and Ruth went out into the fields to glean the grain which the reapers had left. It so happened that she was gleaning in the field that belonged to Boaz, this rich man.

Boaz came out from the town to see his men reaping, and he said to them, "The Lord be with you"; and they answered him, "The Lord bless you." And Boaz said to his master of the reapers, "Who is this young woman that I see gleaning in the field?"

The man answered, "It is the young woman from the land of Moab, who came with Naomi. She asked leave to glean after the reapers and has been here gathering grain since yesterday."

Then Boaz said to Ruth, "Listen to me, my daughter.

Do not go to any other field, but stay here with my young women. No one shall harm you; and when you are thirsty, go and drink at our vessels of water."

Then Ruth bowed to Boaz, and thanked him for his kindness, all the more because she was a stranger in Israel. Boaz said:

"I have heard how true you have been to your mother-in-law, Naomi, in leaving your own land and coming with her to this land. May the Lord, under whose wings you have come, give you a reward!" And at noon, when they sat down to rest and to eat, Boaz gave her some of the food. And he said to the reapers:

"When you are reaping, leave some of the sheaves for her; and drop out some sheaves from the bundles, where she may gather them."

That evening Ruth showed Naomi how much she had gleaned and told her of the rich man Boaz, who had been so kind to her. And Naomi said, "This man is a near relation of ours. Stay in his fields as long as the harvest lasts." And so Ruth gleaned in the fields of Boaz until the harvest had been gathered.

At the end of the harvest, Boaz held a feast on the threshing floor. And after the feast, by the advice of Naomi, Ruth went to him, and said to him, "You are a near relation of my husband and of his father, Elimelech. Now will you not do good to us for his sake?"

And when Boaz saw Ruth he loved her; and soon after this he took her as his wife. And Naomi and Ruth went to live in his home, so that Naomi's life was no more bitter, but pleasant. And Boaz and Ruth had a son, whom they named Obed; and later Obed had a son named Jesse; and Jesse was the father of David, the shepherd boy who became king. So Ruth, the young woman of Moab, who chose the people and the God of Israel, became the mother of kings.

The Lover Pleads With His Friend for Old Friends
WILLIAM BUTLER YEATS

We cannot afford to make new friends at the expense of our old ones.

> Though you are in your shining days,
> Voices among the crowd
> And new friends busy with your praise,
> Be not unkind or proud,
> But think about old friends the most:
> Time's bitter flood will rise,
> Your beauty perish and be lost
> For all eyes but these eyes.

Friendship

This poem reminds us of some of the "rules" of friendship, as well as some of the rewards.

> Friendship needs no studied phrases.
> Polished face, or winning wiles;
> Friendship deals no lavish praises,
> Friendship dons no surface smiles.

Friendship follows Nature's diction,
    Shuns the blandishments of art.
Boldly severs truth from fiction,
    Speaks the language of the heart.

Friendship favors no condition,
    Scorns a narrow-minded creed,
Lovingly fulfills its mission,
    Be it word or be it deed.

Friendship cheers the faint and weary,
    Makes the timid spirit brave,
Warns the erring, lights the dreary,
    Smooths the passage to the grave.

Friendship—pure, unselfish friendship,
    All through life's allotted span,
Nurtures, strengthens, widens, lengthens,
    Man's relationship with man.

❧ The Bear and the Travelers

AESOP

*Fair-weather friends were around in the days of
Aesop, in the sixth century B.C., and they still
abound today. Everyone should learn how to recognize and how not to be one.*

Two travelers were on the road together, when a Bear
suddenly appeared on the scene. Before he observed them,
one made for a tree at the side of the road and climbed up

into the branches and hid there. The other was not so nimble as his companion; and as he could not escape, he threw himself on the ground and pretended to be dead. The Bear came up and sniffed all round him, but he kept perfectly still and held his breath; for they say that a bear will not touch a dead body. The Bear took him for a corpse and went away. When the coast was clear, the Traveler in the tree came down and asked the other what it was the Bear had whispered to him when he put his mouth to his ear. The other replied, "He told me never again to travel with a friend who deserts you at the first sign of danger."

Misfortune tests the sincerity of friendship.

WORK

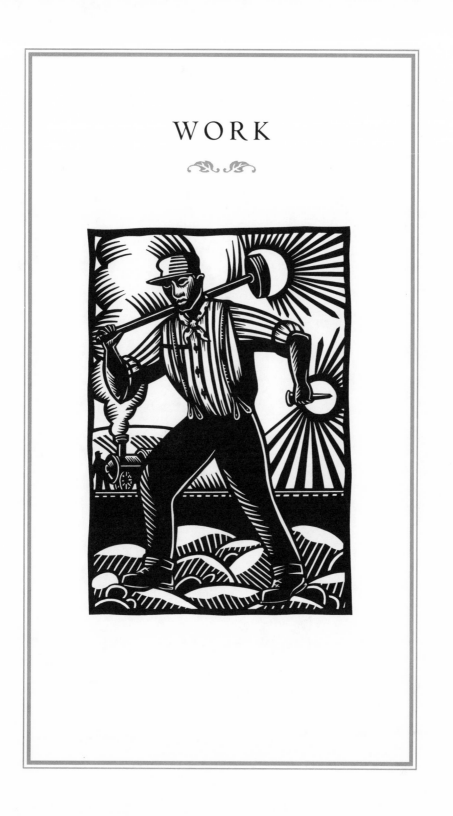

⚚ Work

As you grow older, you find that work of one kind or another takes up a greater and greater part of your life. The school day gets longer. Homework assignments get harder and more time-consuming. Your parents ask you to begin to take on a few more household chores. Eventually you begin to take summer jobs. Meanwhile, hopefully, you make time to do some volunteer work for those less fortunate than you.

You are discovering that work is a necessary, unavoidable fact of life. And you are learning that, generally speaking, no one else is going to do your work for you, as we see in Aesop's fable of "Hercules and the Wagoner." The first English settlers in this country learned that lesson, too. Many of them were "gentlemen" who weren't used to working very hard in England, and they brought their habits with them to Jamestown, Virginia. Their motivation wasn't very high until their leader, Captain John Smith, announced a new rule. Those who did not pitch in and help would not get a share of the colony's food. In other words, if you don't work, you don't eat. Suddenly, many more people became a lot more motivated.

As you spend more time working, you will naturally spend less time playing. Don't be alarmed. It does not mean life gets less enjoyable. In fact, if you approach your work in the right way, just the opposite is true. Life will be richer, fuller, and, yes, more fun. That's because work brings all sorts of rewards. Obviously, it can bring monetary reward, as we see in another Aesop story, "The Farmer and His Sons." But Aesop has more in mind that just the money. He is also pointing to the satisfaction of a job well done. There are few experiences more enjoyable than such satisfaction, and those who miss it are missing one of the best parts of life.

The attitude you take in approaching your work is all-important, both in terms of doing the job well and in terms of whether or not you are going to enjoy it. It can be done thoroughly or carelessly, cheerfully or with bad temper. It's up to you. The mistake many people make is not realizing that it's usually not the work itself but the attitude you bring to the work that makes it a good or bad experience.

Another mistake people make is trying to avoid work because they think that somehow life will be better without it. The truth is, most people find life without work boring, as we see in the tale "A Week of Sundays." And life without work makes most people feel worthless. Work brings dignity to life, as we see in the story of John Henry.

Of course, some work is simply unpleasant. We'd rather not have to do it, but we have no choice, so the best course is to buckle down and get it over with. Even here, though, there is an important lesson to be heeded. Since life is full of work, it makes sense, when possible, to choose the kind of work we like, even love.

For most people, that idea is an important key to satisfaction in life. Remember that the word *vocation* comes from the Latin root "to call." Hopefully your vocation—your life's work—will be a calling, something you love to spend your time doing. For the Wright Brothers, a fascination with tinkering in their Ohio bicycle shop led them to Kitty Hawk, North Carolina. As they showed us, a love of labor leads to some of life's greatest joys and accomplishments.

Hercules and the Wagoner

AESOP

Sometimes we should complain less and work more.

A wagoner was driving his team along a muddy lane with a full load behind them, when the wheels of his wagon sank so deep in the mire that no efforts of his horses could move them. As he stood there, looking helplessly on and calling loudly at intervals upon Hercules for assistance, the god himself appeared and said to him, "Put your shoulder to the wheel, man, and goad on your horses, and then you may call on Hercules to assist you. If you won't lift a finger to help yourself, you can't expect Hercules or anyone else to come to your aid."

Heaven helps those who help themselves.

Hercules Cleans the Augean Stables

The cleaning of the Augean stables was the fifth of the famous Twelve Labors of Hercules, which the great Greek hero performed by order of his cousin, King Eurystheus of Mycenae. We usually think of Hercules for his strength, but here we admire his intelligence as much as his brute force in tackling a nearly impossible job.

The fifth labor of Hercules was the famous cleaning of the Augean stables. Augeas, the king of Elis, had a herd of three thousand cattle, and he had built a stable miles long for them. Year after year his herd kept growing, and he could not get enough men to take care of the barns. The cows could hardly get into them because of the filth, or if they did get in, they were never quite sure of getting out again because the dirt was piled so high. It was said the stables had not been cleaned in thirty years.

Hercules told Augeas he would clean the barns in one day if the king would give him one tenth of all his cows. Augeas thought the great hero could never do it in so short a time, so he made the agreement in the presence of his young son.

The king's stables were near the two rivers Alpheus and Peneus. Hercules cut a great channel to bring the two streams together and then run into the stables. They rushed along and carried the dirt out so quickly the king could not believe it. He did not intend to pay the reward, so he pretended he had never made a promise.

The dispute was taken before a court for the judges to decide. Hercules called the little prince as a witness, and the boy told the truth about it, which caused the king to fall into such a rage he sent both his son and Hercules out of the country. So Hercules left the land of Elis and continued his twelve labors, but his heart was filled with contempt for the faithless king.

Kill Devil Hill

HARRY COMBS

Here is one of the all-time great American success stories. A childhood fascination with a toy helicopter powered by rubber bands ultimately led

*Wilbur (1867–1912) and Orville (1871–1948)
Wright to what can only be described as one of
mankind's most spectacular achievements. In 1900
the Wright brothers began taking their gliders to
Kitty Hawk, on North Carolina's Outer Banks,
because the ocean breezes and lofty dunes were an
ideal environment for testing their odd-looking flying contraptions. On December 17, 1903, numerous
experiments and several "failures" later, Orville
made the first powered flight of 120 feet. Wilbur, in
the fourth and longest flight of the day, described
below, made 852 feet in 59 seconds. If ever we need
inspiration as we toil toward some distant, elusive
goal, surely we find it here. Here is great work begun
by genius, but finished by labor.*

The people of Kitty Hawk had always been generous
and kind to Wilbur and Orville—friendly and warm, sharing their food and worldly goods, sparing no effort to assist
in any way they could to provide physical comfort, and
open in their respect for the brothers. Most of them, however, felt less convinced about the Wrights' ability to fly;
Kitty Hawk was an area where the reaction to flight was
often expressed in such familiar bits of folk wisdom as "If
God had wanted man to fly, He would have given him
wings."

Bill Tate, who from the beginning had been a close
friend to the Wrights, was not present at the camp on
December 17, 1903. This was not a sign of lack of faith; he
had assumed that "no one but a crazy man would attempt
to fly in such a wind."

The brothers had different ideas. Shortly before twelve

o'clock, for the fourth attempt of the day, Wilbur took his position on the flying machine, the engine sputtering and clattering in its strange thunder. His peaked cap was pulled snug across his head, and the wind blowing across the flats reached him with a sandpapery touch. As he had felt it do before, the machine trembled in the gusts, rocking from side to side on the sixty-foot launching track. He settled himself in the hip cradle, feet snug behind him, hands on the controls, studying the three instrument gauges. He looked to each side to be certain no one was near the wings. There were no assistants to hold the wings as they had done with the gliders, for Wilbur believed that unless a man was skilled in what he was doing he ought not touch anything, and he had insisted on a free launch, for he knew the craft would require only forty feet in the stiff wind to lift itself into the air.

Wilbur shifted his head to study the beach area. Today was different. The wintry gale had greatly reduced the bird population, as far as he could see. It had been that way since they awoke. Very few of the familiar seagulls were about beneath the leaden skies.

Wilbur turned to each side again, looked at his brother, and nodded. Everything was set, and Wilbur reached to the restraining control and pulled the wire free. Instantly, the machine rushed forward and, as he expected, was forty feet down the track when he eased into the air. He had prepared himself for almost every act of the wind, but the gusts were too strong, and he was constantly correcting and overcorrecting. The hundred-foot mark fell behind as the aircraft lunged up and down like a winged bull. Then he was two hundred feet from the start of his run, and the pitch motions were even more violent. The aircraft seemed to stagger as it struck a sudden down draft and darted toward the sands. Only a foot above the ground Wilbur regained control, and eased it back up.

Three hundred feet—and the bucking motions were easing off.

And then the five witnesses and Orville were shouting and gesturing wildly, for it was clear that Wilbur had passed some invisible wall in the sky and had regained control. Four hundred feet out, he was still holding the safety altitude of about fifteen feet above the ground, and the airplane was flying smoother now, no longer darting and lunging about, just easing with the gusts between an estimated eight and fifteen feet.

The seconds ticked away and it was a quarter of a minute since Wilbur had started, and there was no question, now: the machine was under control and was sustaining itself by its own power.

It was flying.

The moment had come. It was here, now.

Five hundred feet.

Six hundred.

Seven hundred!

My God, he's trying to reach Kitty Hawk itself, nearly four miles away! And indeed, this is just what Wilbur was trying to do, for he kept heading toward the houses and trees still well before him.

Eight hundred feet . . .

Still going; still flying. Ahead of him, a rise in the ground, a sprawling hump, a hummock of sand. Wilbur brought the elevator into position to raise the nose, to gain altitude to clear the hummock; for beyond this point lay clear sailing, good flying, and he was lifting, the machine rising slowly. But hummocks do strange things to winds blowing at such high speeds. The wind soared up from the sands, rolling and tumbling, and reached out invisibly to push the flying machine downward. The nose dropped too sharply; Wilbur brought it up; and instantly the oscillations began again, a rapid jerking up and down of the nose. The winds were simply too much, the ground-induced roll too severe, and the *Flyer* "suddenly darted into the ground," as Orville later described it.

They knew as they ran that the impact was greater than that of an intentional landing. The skids dug in, and all the weight of the aircraft struck hard, and above the wind they heard the wood splinter and crack. The aircraft bounced once, borne as much by the wind as by its own momentum, and settled back to the sands, the forward elevator braces askew, broken so that the surfaces hung at an angle. Unhurt, aware that he had been flying a marvelously long time, mildly disappointed at not having continued his flight, stuck in the sand with the wind blowing into his face and the engine grinding out its now familiar clattering, banging roar, Wilbur reached out to shut off power. The propellers whistled and whirred as they slowed, the sounds of the chains came to him more clearly, and then only the wind could be heard. The wind, the sand hissing against fabric and his own clothes and across the ground, and perhaps a gull or two, and certainly the beating of his own heart.

It had happened.

He had flown for fifty-nine seconds.

The distance across the surface from his start to his finish was 852 feet.

The air distance, computing airspeed and wind and all the other factors—more than half a mile.

He—they—had done it.

The air age was *now.*

Just fifty-six days before, Simon Newcomb, the only American scientist since Benjamin Franklin to be an associate of the Institute of France, in an article in *The Independent* had shown by "unassailable logic" that human flight was impossible.

They ran up to the machine, where Wilbur stood waiting for them. No one ever recorded what Wilbur's words were at that moment, and no amount of research has been able to unearth them. It is unfortunate, but they are lost forever. . . .

Orville and Wilbur, stiff with cold, went to their living quarters, where they prepared and ate lunch. They rested for several minutes, washed their dishes, and, ready at last to send word of their achievement, at about two o'clock in the afternoon began the walk to the weather station four miles distant in Kitty Hawk. From the station, still run by Joseph J. Dosher, they could dispatch a wire via government facilities to Norfolk, where the message would be continued by telephone to a commercial telegraph office near Dayton. The message, as it was received in Dayton, read:

176 C KA CS 33 PAID.   VIA NORFOLK VA
KITTY LAWK N C DEC 17
BISHOP M WRIGHT
        7 HAWTHORNE ST
SUCCESS FOUR FLIGHTS THURSDAY MORNING ALL
AGAINST TWENTY ONE MILE WIND STARTED FROM
LEVEL WITH ENGINE POWER ALONE AVERAGE SPEED
THROUGH AIR THIRTY ONE MILES LONGEST 57 SEC-
ONDS INFORM PRESS HOME ##### CHRISTMAS.
                    OREVELLE WRIGHT 525P

While this slightly garbled message was being transmitted, including the error of flight time of fifty-seven seconds rather than fifty-nine, the brothers went to the life-saving station nearby to talk with the crew on duty. Captain S.J. Payne, who skippered the facility, told the Wrights he had watched through binoculars as they soared over the ground.

Orville and Wilbur went on to the post office, where they visited Captain and Mrs. Hobbs, who had hauled materials and done other work for them, spent some time with a Dr. Cogswell, and then started their trek back to their camp. It would take them several days to dismantle and pack their *Flyer* into a barrel and two boxes, along with personal gear, and they went to work with their usual thoroughness. It was a strange and quiet aftermath, and several times they went back outside to stand and look at the ground over which they had flown.

❧ Mr. Meant-To

Hear the famous words of Benjamin Franklin: "One today is worth two tomorrows; never leave that till tomorrow which you can do today."

> Mr. Meant-To has a comrade,
>   And his name is Didn't-Do;
> Have you ever chanced to meet them?
>   Did they ever call on you?

These two fellows live together
   In the house of Never-Win,
And I'm told that it is haunted
   By the ghost of Might-Have-Been.

◆ Results and Roses

EDGAR GUEST

Efforts bring roses, laziness nothing.

The man who wants a garden fair,
   Or small or very big,
With flowers growing here and there,
   Must bend his back and dig.

The things are mighty few on earth
   That wishes can attain,
Whate'er we want of any worth
   We've got to work to gain.

It matters not what goal you seek
   Its secret here reposes:
You've got to dig from week to week
   To get Results or Roses.

The Ballad of John Henry

The John Henry of American folklore was an African-American railroad worker celebrated for his feats of great strength and skill. His most famous exploit was his classic man-versus-machine battle against the new steam drill, which threatened to take the place of the "steel–drivin'" men who hammered long steel bits into solid rock to make holes for dynamite. The story is said to be based on the digging of the Big Bend Tunnel for the Chesapeake and Ohio Railroad in West Virginia's Allegheny Mountains in the 1870's. It is a great American tale of pride and dignity in work.

John Henry was a little baby boy
You could hold him in the palm of your hand.
He gave a long and lonesome cry,
"Gonna be a steel-drivin' man, Lawd, Lawd,
Gonna be a steel-drivin' man."
They took John Henry to the tunnel,
Put him in the lead to drive,
The rock was so tall, John Henry so small,
That he laid down his hammer and he cried,
     "Lawd, Lawd,"
Laid down his hammer and he cried.

John Henry started on the right hand,
The steam drill started on the left,
"Fo' I'd let that steam drill beat me down,
I'd hammer my fool self to death, Lawd, Lawd,
Hammer my fool self to death."

John Henry told his captain,
"A man ain't nothin' but a man,
Fo' I let your steam drill beat me down
I'll die with this hammer in my hand, Lawd, Lawd,
Die with this hammer in my hand."
Now the captain told John Henry,
"I believe my tunnel's sinkin' in."
"Stand back, Captain, and doncha be afraid,
That's nothin' but my hammer catchin' wind,
        Lawd, Lawd,
That's nothin' but my hammer catchin' wind."

John Henry told his cap'n,
"Look yonder, boy, what do I see?
Your drill's done broke and your hole's done choke,
And you can't drive steel like me, Lawd, Lawd,
You can't drive steel like me."

John Henry hammerin' in the mountain,
Til the handle of his hammer caught on fire,
He drove so hard till he broke his po' heart,
Then he laid down his hammer and he died,
        Lawd, Lawd,
He laid down his hammer and he died.

They took John Henry to the tunnel,
And they buried him in the sand,
An' every locomotive come rollin' by
Say, "There lies a steel-drivin' man, Lawd, Lawd,
There lies a steel-drivin' man."

↪ The Farmer and His Sons
AESOP

A farmer, being at death's door and desiring to impart to his sons a secret of much moment, called them round him and said, "My sons, I am shortly about to die. I would have you know, therefore, that in my vineyard there lies a hidden treasure. Dig, and you will find it." As soon as their father was dead, the sons took spade and fork and turned up the soil of the vineyard over and over again, in their search for the treasure which they supposed to lie buried there. They found none, however: but the vines, after so thorough a digging, produced a crop such as had never before been seen.

There is no treasure without toil.

↪ The Poor Man and His Seeds

This tale from East Africa reminds us that unexpected reward often has more to do with hard work than with luck.

There was once a poor man who possessed only a very small plot of land and one small bag of seeds. When his field was ready for planting, he rose at sunrise and carefully began to sow his meager crop. At mid-day, when the sun was beating fiercely on his shoulders, he stopped by a tree stump to rest. As he sat, a handful of seeds spilled out of his bag and fell down a hole under the stump.

"Well, they can do no growing down there, the man sighed. "I cannot afford to lose even these few."

So he took a shovel and began digging at the roots of the stump. The day grew hotter, and the sweat ran from his back and brow, but he kept digging. When he finally reached his seeds, he found them lying on top of a buried box. And inside the box he found gold—enough gold coins to make him rich for the rest of his life!

Afterward, people would say to him, "You must be the luckiest man alive."

"Yes, I was lucky," he would say. "I was in my field by sunrise, I dug throughout the hot day, and I did not waste a single seed."

❧ The Rebellion Against the Stomach

We find variations of this story all over the world. Aesop told it as one of his fables. Paul used it in his first letter to the Corinthians. Shakespeare employed it in his play Coriolanus. *It teaches two lessons. First, most of us are better off worrying about our own jobs than criticizing others. Second, many big jobs require the cooperation of many workers.*

Once a man had a dream in which his hands and feet and mouth and brain all began to rebel against his stomach.

"You good-for-nothing sluggard!" the hands said. "We work all day long, sawing and hammering and lifting and carrying. By evening we're covered with blisters and scratches, and our joints ache, and we're covered with dirt. And meanwhile you just sit there, hogging all the food."

"We agree!" cried the feet. "Think how sore we get, walking back and forth all day long. And you just stuff yourself full, you greedy pig, so that you're that much heavier to carry about."

"That's right!" whined the mouth. "Where do you think all that food you love comes from? I'm the one who has to chew it all up, and as soon as I'm finished you suck it all down for yourself. Do you call that fair?"

"And what about me?" called the brain. "Do you think it's easy being up here, having to think about where your next meal is going to come from? And yet I get nothing at all for my pains."

And one by one the parts of the body joined the complaint against the stomach, which didn't say anything at all.

"I have an idea," the brain finally announced. Let's all rebel against this lazy belly, and stop working for it."

"Superb idea!" all the other members and organs agreed. "We'll teach you how important we are, you pig. Then maybe you'll do a little work of your own."

So they all stopped working. The hands refused to do any lifting or carrying. The feet refused to walk. The mouth promised not to chew or swallow a single bite. And the brain swore it wouldn't come up with any more bright ideas. At first the stomach growled a bit, as it always did when it was hungry. But after a while it was quiet.

Then, to the dreaming man's surprise, he found he could not walk. He could not grasp anything in his hands. He could not even open his mouth. And he suddenly began to feel rather ill.

The dream seemed to go on for several days. As each day passed, the man felt worse and worse. "This rebellion had better not last much longer," he thought to himself, "or I'll starve."

Meanwhile, the hands and feet and mouth and brain

just lay there, getting weaker and weaker. At first they roused themselves just enough to taunt the stomach every once in a while, but before long they didn't even have the energy for that.

Finally the man heard a faint voice coming from the direction of his feet.

"It could be that we were wrong," they were saying. "We suppose the stomach might have been working in his own way all along."

"I was just thinking the same thing," murmured the brain. "It's true he's been getting all the food. But it seems he's been sending most of it right back to us."

"We might as well admit our error," the mouth said. "The stomach has just as much work to do as the hands and feet and brain and teeth."

"Then let's all get back to work," they cried together. And at that the man woke up.

To his relief, he discovered his feet could walk again. His hands could grasp, his mouth could chew, and his brain could now think clearly. He began to feel much better.

"Well, there's a lesson for me," he thought as he filled his stomach at breakfast. "Either we all work together, or nothing works at all."

ᴄᴇᴠ The Village Blacksmith

HENRY WADSWORTH LONGFELLOW

Longfellow said that he wrote this poem in praise of an ancestor, and that it was suggested to him by a blacksmith shop beneath a horse chestnut tree near his house in Cambridge, Massachusetts. Here is the character of true, honest, willing labor. It is surely one of the most appealing images in American verse.

Under a spreading chestnut tree
    The village smithy stands;
The smith, a mighty man is he,
    With large and sinewy hands;
And the muscles of his brawny arms
    Are strong as iron bands.
His hair is crisp, and black, and long,
    His face is like the tan;
His brow is wet with honest sweat,
    He earns whate'er he can,
And looks the whole world in the face,
    For he owns not any man.

Week in, week out, from morn till night,
    You can hear his bellows blow;
You can hear him swing his heavy sledge,
    With measured beat and slow,
Like a sexton ringing the village bell,
    When the evening sun is low.

And children coming home from school
    Look in at the open door;

They love to see the flaming forge,
    And hear the bellows roar;
And catch the burning sparks that fly
    Like chaff from a threshing floor.
He goes on Sunday to the church,
    And sits among his boys;
He hears the parson pray and preach,
    He hears his daughter's voice,
Singing in the village choir,
    And it makes his hear rejoice.

It sounds to him like her mother's voice,
    Singing in Paradise!
He needs must think of her once more,
    How in the grave she lies;
And with his hard, rough hand he wipes
    A tear out of his eyes.

Toiling—rejoicing—sorrowing
    Onward through life he goes;
Each morning sees some task begin,
    Each evening sees it close;
Something attempted, something done,
    Has earned a night's repose.

Thanks, thanks to thee, my worthy friend,
    For the lesson thou hast taught!
Thus at the flaming forge of life
    Our fortunes must be wrought;
Thus on its sounding anvil shaped
    Each burning deed and thought!

The Week of Sundays

In this old tale we see the difference between idle time, which we steal, and leisure time, which we earn. The truth is that people who never have anything to do are usually the most dissatisfied because they are the most bored. Our leisure time, on the other hand, we enjoy largely because we've put plenty of work behind us to get it.

Once upon a time there was a man named Bobby O'Brien who never did a stitch of work in his life unless he absolutely had to.

"Come now, Bobby," his friends used to say, "what's so wrong with a little hard work? You'd think it was the black plague itself, the way you guard yourself against it."

"My friends, I have no more against work than the next man," Bobby would reply. "In fact, nothing fascinates me more than work. I can sit here and watch it all day, if you'll only give me the chance."

And of course, he was perfectly useless around the house.

"Aren't you ashamed of yourself, now?" his wife, Katie, moaned one afternoon. "A fine example you're setting for the children! Do you want them to grow up to be lazy slobs too?"

"It's Sunday, my dear, the day of rest," Bobby pointed out. "Now why would you want to be disturbing it? If you want my opinion, it's the only day out of the whole week worth getting out of bed for. The only problem with Sunday is that as soon as it's over, the rest of the week starts up again." Bobby was a great philosopher, having so much time on his hands.

That very night the whole family was sitting around the fire, waiting for their soup to boil, when what should they hear but a tap-tap-tap at the window. Bobby strolled over and raised the sash, and into the room hopped a little man no bigger than a strutting rooster.

"I was just passing by," the wee man said, "and smelled something good and strong, and thought I might have a bite to eat."

"You're welcome to as much as you want," Bobby said, thinking that such a little man couldn't possibly hold more than a spoonful or two. So the tiny fellow sat down at the fireside, but no sooner had Katie given him a steaming bowl than he slurped it down and asked for another. Katie gave him seconds, and he swallowed that one faster than the first. She gave him thirds, and he drained the bowl almost before she had filled it up.

"What a little pig," Bobby thought to himself. "He'll have all of our suppers, before he's through. Still, I asked him in, and he is our guest, so we must hold our tongues."

After five or six bowls the little man smacked his lips and jumped off his stool.

"It's most kind you've been," he laughed. "A more hospitable family I've never met. Now I must be on my way, but as a way of thanks I'll be more than happy to grant the next wish uttered aloud beneath this roof." And with that he hopped through the window and vanished into the night.

Well, everyone wanted to wish for something different. One child wanted a bag of sweets, and the other child wanted a box of toys. Katie thought a new bed would be nice, as the old one was showing signs of collapse. Bobby could name a dozen or so things he'd like to have, right off the top of his head, perhaps a new fishing pole, or maybe a chocolate cake.

"We need more time to think it over," he declared. "The trouble is, tomorrow's Monday morning, and there'll be work and chores to get in the way of our thinking. I wish we had a week of Sundays, and then we could take our time and figure it out."

"Now you've done it!" Katie cried. "You've gone and wasted our only wish on a week of Sundays! You might have wished for a few more brains in that thick head of yours before you opened your mouth for a wish like that!"

"Well, well, it's not such a bad wish, you know," said Bobby, who was just now realizing what he had done. "A week of Sundays will be a fine thing, after all. I've been needing a little rest, and this will give me the chance."

"Rest is the last thing you need, you lazy bag of bones," Katie moaned, hustling the children off to bed.

But the next morning when Bobby woke up to hear the churchbells pealing, and he remembered he had seven whole days before him of not having a thing in the world to do, he decided he'd made the wisest of all possible wishes. He lolled around bed all morning, while Katie took the children to church, and didn't bother to rouse himself until he finally smelled a nice plump chicken coming out of the oven for Sunday dinner.

"What a remarkable event!" he yawned and stretched as he sat down at the table. "King Solomon himself could never have wished for such a wonderful thing as a week of Sundays." And after he stuffed himself, he wandered outside and took a nap beneath his favorite tree.

The next day he lay in bed all morning again, and got

up only when church was safely over. But the only thing Katie put on the table was a few chicken bones left from the day before, when Bobby had eaten the whole Sunday dinner. The next day was even worse. Bobby sat down with a roaring appetite, only to find porridge and potatoes gracing the table.

"Now what kind of dinner is this?" he asked. "Have you forgotten what day of the week it is? Porridge and potatoes aren't fit for Sunday, my dear."

"And what else did you expect?" Katie cried. "How am I supposed to buy a new chicken with every shop in the village closed for seven straight days? It's all we have in the cupboard, so you'd better get used to it, my good man."

Well, the next morning Bobby's stomach was growling so fiercely he couldn't help but getting out of bed a little earlier than his usual Sunday custom. He wandered around the kitchen a bit, checking here and there for a bite to eat, but he found only a loaf of stale bread in the pantry.

"You know, my dear," he said, "I've been thinking I need a bit of exercise. I believe I'll go out to the garden and dig a few potatoes for dinner."

"You'll do nothing of the sort," Katie snapped. "I won't have you digging potatoes on Sunday morning, with the neighbors passing by on their way to church. That won't do at all."

"But there's nothing in the house but bits of stale bread," Bobby cried.

"And who do you have to blame but yourself and your week of Sundays for that?" Katie asked.

The next day Bobby was up at the crack of dawn, pacing back and forth across the house and drumming his fingers on every windowsill. The children followed him everywhere he went until the churchbells began to peal, and then they bawled and whimpered to no end.

"What's wrong with these young ones?" Bobby whined. "Have all their manners gone and left them?"

"And what do you expect, after all?" Katie cried. "The poor little things have sat through more sermons in a week now than you've snored through all year. Their backs are sore from living in pews, and they've tossed every last penny they've been saving into that collection plate."

"They should be in school, that's where," Bobby declared.

"And who, may I ask, is to blame for that?" Katie inquired.

On the sixth Sunday, Bobby was so fidgety and bored, he decided to go to church with the rest of the family. Every head in the congregation swung around when he came through the door and crept up the aisle.

"There's the man!" the preacher cried from the pulpit. "Here's the rascal who's kept me up every night this week, wracking my poor brain for another new sermon! Here's the troublemaker who's ruined every last throat in the choir, and almost worn the fingers off the poor organist! I guess you've come to survey your dirty work now, have you?"

And when the service was over, Bobby found his neighbors lined up to greet him.

"Well, now," asked one, "did you stop to think of how we're to bring in the harvest with so many Sundays getting in the way?"

"And how are the rest of us to make a living, having to keep our doors closed all week?" asked the butcher and the baker.

"And what about the washing and ironing and mending?"

someone called. "Do you know how much is piled up for next Monday, should it ever come again?"

"And by the way," said the schoolmaster, "have you been taking care of your children's lessons, or have they forgotten how to read and write by now?"

Bobby made his way home as fast as he could.

"Thank goodness there's only one Sunday left!" he sighed as soon as he was safe behind his own door. "Any more would be dangerous to a man's health."

That last Sunday was the longest day of Bobby O'Brien's life. The minutes passed like hours, and the hours stretched into eternities. Bobby twiddled his thumbs, and stood on one foot, and walked in circles, and watched the clock.

"Is this thing broken?" he cried, grabbing it from the mantel and shaking it till its insides rattled. "You can't tell me the time has ever dragged by so slow!"

"When have you ever wanted a Sunday to end?" Katie asked. "Aren't you forgetting that tomorrow is Monday?"

"Forgetting it? It's all I can think about," Bobby exclaimed. "I've never in my life looked forward to any day as much as this Monday morning."

The shadows slowly crept across the lawn, the sun finally went down, and just as the first star popped into the sky, who should come rapping at the window but the same little man who visited one week ago.

"And how did you enjoy your wish?" he asked Bobby.

"Not very much, I'm afraid," said Bobby.

"Really?" exclaimed the little man. "Then you wouldn't want to trade another bite to eat for another week of Sundays?"

"For goodness' sake, no!" cried Bobby. "The only days

of rest I want are the ones I've worked six days to earn. It took me all week to learn that lesson, and I won't be forgetting it anytime soon. So I'll thank you to be gone with your wishes, my friend."

And at that the little man disappeared and was never seen again.

COURAGE

❧ Courage

T he most common misunderstanding about courage
is the belief that courage means not feeling afraid.
In truth, courage is not at all about emotions. It is
not about how you feel. It's about how you *act*.

Everybody is afraid of something—it's perfectly normal.
You might be scared of being alone in a strange place, or
asking someone out on a date, or saying the wrong thing
and having people laugh at you. Feeling fear is an unavoidable part of life.

The question is, what do you *do* when you have those
fears? Do you run and hide? Or do you stand and face the
situation?

This is the essence of courage—mustering the strength
and will to do what you know you should do, even though
you are afraid. The great philosopher Aristotle put it this
way: "We become brave by doing brave acts." He meant
that we may not *feel* very brave when we do something
courageous. Nevertheless, by *acting* brave, by doing what is
right and required, we turn ourselves into courageous people. It's the only way to overcome fear.

So courage requires practice. One step at a time, little by little, you have to try facing your fears and acting the way you know you should act. And as you practice, some of your fears will go away. Here is a part of life where it makes sense to reach higher and higher. When you do, you'll find you have more courage than you thought.

Courage also requires wisdom. That is, you have to know the things you fear as well as the way you need to act to face those fears. You'll need the virtue of honesty for that—honesty with yourself.

As you'll see in this chapter, there are many different kinds of true courage. There is the kind that stays cool and calm in troubled times, as in the story of Dolley Madison. There is the courage that stands up for what is right, as Rosa Parks and Susan B. Anthony did. There is the courage of acting according to your faith in God, as David did when he fought Goliath. And there is the courage of trusting yourself and refusing to follow the crowd when the crowd is wrong, as Rudyard Kipling tells us in his poem "If—." But there are also varieties of false courage, too, and you should always guard against them. Simply being loud and talking as if you are brave is one kind. We see it in the story of "Chanticleer and Partlet," and we see how it often rises from our own vanity. The strong beating up the weak is another kind of false courage. It's really cowardice, as we see in the story "The Leopard's Revenge." And there is nothing courageous about taking stupid, unnecessary risks just for thrills or to show off. Again, true courage requires wisdom—the wisdom of being able to distinguish between those circumstances you fear but need to face and those circumstances you fear and rightly need to avoid.

An Appeal from the Alamo

WILLIAM BARRET TRAVIS

The Alamo in San Antonio, Texas, has become an American symbol of unyielding courage and self-sacrifice. A force of Texans captured the mission fort in late 1835 after the outbreak of revolution against the dictatorship of Mexican General Antonio López de Santa Anna. By early 1836, Lieutenant Colonel William Barret Travis and the fort's garrison found themselves hemmed in by a Mexican army swelling to 6,000 troops. On February 24, Travis dispatched couriers to nearby Texas towns, carrying frantic appeals for aid. Fewer than three dozen men picked their way through enemy lines to join the Alamo's defenders. The siege continued until March 6, when Santa Anna's forces overwhelmed the fort. The entire garrison was killed, some 180 men, including Colonel Travis, James Bowie, and Davy Crockett.

COMMANDANCY OF THE ALAMO, TEXAS
February 24, 1836

To the People of Texas and
All Americans in the World.
FELLOW CITIZENS AND COMPATRIOTS

I am besieged by a thousand or more of the Mexicans under Santa Anna. I have sustained a continual bombardment and cannonade for twenty-four hours and have not lost a man. The enemy has demanded a surrender at discretion; otherwise the garrison are to be put to the sword if the fort is taken. I have answered the demand with a cannon shot, and our flag still waves proudly from the walls. *I shall never surrender nor retreat.* Then, I call on you in the name of Liberty, of patriotism, and of everything dear to the American character, to come to our aid with all dispatch. The enemy is receiving reinforcements daily and will no doubt increase to three or four thousand in four or five days. If this call is neglected, I am determined to sustain myself as long as possible and die like a soldier who never forgets what is due to his own honor and that of his country.

VICTORY OR DEATH

WILLIAM BARRET TRAVIS

Lieutenant Colonel, Commandant

Chanticleer and Partlet

RETOLD BY J. BERG ESENWEIN
AND MARIETTA STOCKARD

This story comes from "Nun's Priest's Tale," one of Geoffrey Chaucer's Canterbury Tales. It reminds us that there is such a thing as false courage, which may rise from our own vanity.

Once there was a barnyard close to a wood, in a little valley. Here dwelt a cock, Chanticleer by name. His comb was redder than coral, his feathers were like burnished gold, and his voice was wonderful to hear. Long before dawn each morning his crowing sounded over the valley, and his seven wives listened in admiration.

One night as he sat on the perch by the side of Dame Partlet, his most loved mate, he began to make a curious noise in his throat.

"What is it, my dear?" said Dame Partlet. "You sound frightened."

"Oh!" said Chanticleer. "I had the most horrible dream. I thought that as I roamed down by the wood a beast like a dog sprang out and seized me. His color was red, his nose was small, and his eyes were like coals of fire. Ugh! It was fearful!"

"Tut, tut! Are you a coward to be frightened by a dream? You've been eating more than was good for you. I wish my husband to be wise and brave if he would keep my love!" Dame Partlet clucked, as she smoothed her feathers and slowly closed her scarlet eyes. She felt disgusted at having her sleep disturbed.

"Of course you are right, my love, yet I have heard of many dreams which came true. I am sure I shall meet with some misfortune, but we will not talk of it now. I am quite happy to be here by your side. You are very beautiful, my dear!"

Dame Partlet unclosed one eye slowly and made a pleased sound, deep in her throat.

The next morning, Chanticleer flew down from the perch and called his hens about him for their breakfast. He walked about boldly, calling, "Chuck! chuck!" at each grain of corn which he found. He felt very proud as they all looked at him so admiringly. He strutted about in the sunlight, flapping his wings to show off his feathers, and now and then throwing back his head and crowing exultantly. His dream was forgotten; there was no fear in his heart.

Now all this time, Reynard, the fox, was lying hidden in the bushes on the edge of the wood bordering the barnyard. Chanticleer walked nearer and nearer his hiding place. Suddenly he saw a butterfly in the grass, and as he stooped toward it, he spied the fox.

"Cok! cok!" he cried in terror, and turned to flee.

"Dear friend, why do you go?" said Reynard in his gentlest voice. "I only crept down here to hear you sing. Your voice is like an angel's. Your father and mother once visited my house. I should so love to see you there too. I wonder if you remember your father's singing? I can see him now as he stood on tiptoe, stretching out his long slender neck, sending out his glorious voice. He always flapped his wings and closed his eyes before he sang. Do you do it in the same way? Won't you sing just once and let me hear you? I am so anxious to know if you really sing better than your father."

Chanticleer was so pleased with this flattery that he flapped his wings, stood up on tiptoe, shut his eyes, and crowed as loudly as he could.

No sooner had he begun than Reynard sprang forward, caught him by the throat, threw him over his shoulder, and made off toward his den in the woods.

The hens made a loud outcry when they saw Chanticleer being carried off, so that the people in the cottage nearby heard and ran out after the fox. The dog heard and ran yelping after him. The cow ran, the calf ran, and the pigs began to squeal and run too. The ducks and geese quacked in terror and flew up into the treetops. Never was there heard such an uproar. Reynard began to feel a bit frightened himself.

"How swiftly you do run!" said Chanticleer from his back. "If I were you I should have some sport out of those slow fellows, who are trying to catch you. Call out to them and say, 'Why do you creep along like snails? Look! I am far ahead of you and shall soon be feasting on this cock in spite of all of you!'"

Reynard was pleased at this and opened his mouth to call to his pursuers; but as soon as he did so, the cock flew away from him and perched up in a tree safely out of reach.

The fox saw he had lost his prey and began his old tricks again. "I was only proving to you how important you are in the barnyard. See what a commotion we caused! I did not mean to frighten you. Come down now and we will go along together to my home. I have something very interesting to show you there."

"No, no," said Chanticleer. "You will not catch me again. A man who shuts his eyes when he ought to be looking deserves to lose his sight entirely."

By this time, Chanticleer's friends were drawing near, so Reynard turned to flee. "The man who talks when he should be silent deserves to lose what he has gained," he said as he sped away through the wood.

◈ David and Goliath

RETOLD BY J. BERG ESENWEIN
AND MARIETTA STOCKARD

Here is the famous story of a brave youth who forges his courage through his faith.

Long ago, in the land of Bethlehem, there lived a man named Jesse, who had eight stalwart sons. The youngest of these sons was David.

Even as a little lad, David was ruddy, beautiful of countenance, and strong of body. When his older brothers drove the flocks to the fields, he ran with them. Each day as he leaped over the hillsides and listened to the gurgling water in the brooks and the songs of birds in the trees, he grew stronger of limb and more filled with joy and courage. Sometimes he made songs of the beautiful things he saw and heard. His eye was keen, his hands strong, and his aim sure. When he fitted a stone into his sling, he never missed the mark at which he threw it.

As he grew older, he was given the care of a part of the flocks. One day as he lay on the hillside keeping watch over his sheep, a lion rushed out of the woods and seized a lamb. David leaped to his feet and ran forward. He had no fear in his heart, no thought but to save the lamb. He sprang upon the lion, seized him by his hairy head and, with no weapon but the staff in his strong young hands, he slew him. Another day, a bear came down upon them. Him also, David slew.

Now, soon after this, the Philistines marshaled their armies and came across the hills to drive the children of Israel away from their homes. King Saul gathered his armies and went out to meet them. David's three oldest brothers went with the king, but David was left at home to tend the sheep. "Thou art too young; stay in the fields and keep the flocks safe," they said to David.

Forty days went by, and no news of the battle came; so Jesse [David's father] called David to him and said: "Take this food for thy brethren, and go up to the camp to see how they fare."

David set out early in the morning and journeyed up to the hill on which the army was encamped. There was great shouting and the armies were drawn up in battle array when David arrived. He made his way through the ranks and found his brethren. As he stood talking with them, silence fell upon King Saul's army; and there on the hillside opposite stood a great giant. He strode up and down, his armor glittering in the sun. His shield was so heavy that the strongest man in King Saul's army could not have lifted it, and the sword at his side was so great that the strongest arm could not have wielded it.

"It is the great giant, Goliath," David's brethren told him. "Each day he strides over the hill and calls out his challenge to the men of Israel, but no man amongst us dares to stand before him."

"What! Are the men of Israel afraid?" asked David. "Will they let this Philistine defy the armies of the living God? Will no one go forth to meet him?" He turned from one to another, questioning them.

Eliab, David's oldest brother, heard him and was angry. "Thou art naughty and proud of heart," he said. "Thou has stolen away from home thinking to see a great battle. With whom has thou left the sheep?"

"The keeper hath charge of them; and our father, Jesse, sent me hither; and my heart is glad that I am come," answered David. "I myself will go forth to meet this giant. The God of Israel will go with me, for I have no fear of Goliath nor all of his hosts!"

The men standing near hastened to the tent of King Saul and told him of David's words.

"Let him stand before me," commanded the king.

When David was brought into his presence and Saul saw that he was but a youth, he attempted to dissuade him. But David told him how he had slain the lion and the bear with his naked hands. "The Lord who delivered me from them will deliver me out of the hand of this Philistine," he said.

Then King Saul said: "Go, and the Lord go with thee!"

He had his own armor fetched for David, his helmet of

brass, his coat of mail, and his own sword. But David said: "I cannot fight with these. I am not skilled in their use." He put them down, for he knew that each man must win his battles with his own weapons.

Then he took his staff in his hand, his shepherd's bag and sling he hung at his side, and he set out from the camp of Israel. He ran lightly down the hillside, and when he came to the brook which ran at the foot of the hill, he stooped, and choosing five smooth stones from the brook, dropped them into his bag.

The army of King Saul upon one hill, and the host of the Philistines upon the other, looked on in silent wonder. The great giant strode toward David, and when Goliath saw that he was but a youth, ruddy and fair of countenance, his anger knew no bounds.

"Am I a dog, that thou comest to me with sticks?" he shouted. "Do the men of Israel make mock of me to send a child against me? Turn back, or I will give thy flesh to the birds of the air and to the beasts of the field!" Then Goliath cursed David in the name of all his gods.

But no fear came to David's heart. He called out bravely: "Thou comest to me with a sword, and with a spear, and with a shield: But I come to thee in the name of the Lord of hosts, the God of the armies of Israel, whom thou has defied. This day will the Lord deliver thee into mine hands; and I will smite thee, that all the earth may know that there is a God in Israel!"

Then Goliath rushed forward to meet David, and David ran still more swiftly to meet the giant. He put his hand into his bag and took one of the stones from it. He fitted it into his sling, and his keen eye found the place in the giant's forehead where the helmet joined. He drew his sling and, with all the force of his strong right arm, he hurled the stone.

It whizzed through the air and struck deep into Goliath's forehead. His huge body tottered—then fell crashing to the ground. As he lay with his face upon the earth, David ran swiftly to his side, drew forth the giant's own sword, and severed his huge head from his body.

When the army of Israel saw this, they rose up with a great shout and rushed down the hillside to throw themselves upon the frightened Philistines who were fleeing in terror. When they saw their greatest warrior slain by this lad, they fled toward their own land, leaving their tents and all their riches to be spoiled by the men of Israel.

When the battle was ended, King Saul caused David to be brought before him, and he said: "Thou shalt go no more to the house of thy father but thou shalt be as mine own son."

So David stayed in the tents of the king, and at length he was given command over the king's armies. All Israel honored him, and long years after, he was made the king in King Saul's stead.

ᔐ Dolley Madison Saves the National Pride

DOROTHEA PAYNE MADISON

In August 1814, a British army marched on Washington, D.C., thinking that by burning the American capital it could bring an end to the War of 1812. Panic reigned in the city as the red-coated columns approached. Many public records, including the Declaration of Independence, had already been stuffed into linen bags and carted off to Virginia, where they were piled up in a vacant house. Now the roads leading out of town began to fill with flee- ing American soldiers and statesmen as well as wag- ons loaded with families and their valuables.

Dolley Madison, wife of the fourth president, calmly directed evacuation details at the White House. A large portrait of George Washington by Gilbert Stuart hung in the dining room. It would be an unbearable disgrace if it fell into British hands. Mrs. Madison ordered the doorkeeper and gardener to bring it along, but the huge frame was screwed so tightly to the wall that no one could get it down. Minutes ticked by as they tugged and pulled. At last someone found an ax. They chopped the frame apart, removed the canvas, and sent it off for safe- keeping. Soon afterward the British entered the District of Columbia, setting fire to the Capitol and the White House.

The rescue of Washington's portrait quickly took its place as one of America's most cherished acts of heroism. This letter, written by Dolley to her sister, Anna, even as the city fell, speaks to us of unflinch- ing courage and levelheadedness amid chaos and retreat.

Tuesday, August 23, 1814

Dear Sister:

My husband left me yesterday morning to join General Winder. He inquired anxiously whether I had courage or firmness to remain in the President's house until his return on the morrow, or succeeding day, and on my assurance that I had no fear but for him, and the success of our army, he left, beseeching me to take care of myself, and of the Cabinet papers, public and private. I have since received two dispatches from him, written with a pencil. The last is alarming, because he desires I should be ready at a moment's warning to enter my carriage, and leave the city; that the enemy seemed stronger than had at first been reported, and it might happen that they would reach the city with the intention of destroying it. I am accordingly ready; I have pressed as many Cabinet papers into trunks as to fill one carriage; our private property must be sacrificed, as it is impossible to procure wagons for its transportation.

I am determined not to go myself until I see Mr. Madison safe, so that he can accompany me, as I hear of much hostility toward him. Disaffection stalks around us. My friends and acquaintances are all gone, even Colonel C. with his hundred, who were stationed as a guard in this enclosure. French John [a faithful servant], with his usual activity and resolution, offers to spike the cannon at the gate, and lay a train of powder, which would blow up the British, should they enter the house. To this last proposition I positively object, without being able to make him understand why all advantages in war may not be taken.

Wednesday morning, twelve o'clock. Since sunrise I have been turning my spyglass in every direction, and watching with unwearied anxiety, hoping to discover the approach of my dear husband and his friends; but, alas! I can descry only groups of military, wandering in all directions, as if there was a lack of arms, or of spirit to fight for their own fireside.

Three o'clock. Will you believe it, my sister? we have had a battle, or skirmish, near Bladensburg, and here I am still, within sound of the cannon! Mr. Madison comes not. May God protect us! Two messengers, covered with dust, come to bid me fly; but here I mean to wait for him. . . At this late hour a wagon has been procured, and I have had it filled with plate and the most valuable portable articles belonging to the house. Whether it will reach its destination, the "Bank of Maryland," or fall into the hands of British soldiery, events must determine. Our kind friend, Mr. Carroll, has come to hasten my departure, and in a very bad humor with me, because I insist on waiting until the large picture of General Washington is secured, and it requires to be unscrewed from the wall. This process was found too tedious for these perilous moments; I have ordered the frame to be broken, and the canvas taken out. It is done! and the precious portrait placed in the hands of two gentlemen of New York, for safekeeping. And now, dear sister, I must leave this house, or the retreating army will make me a prisoner of it by filling up the road I am directed to take. When I shall again write to you, or where I shall be tomorrow, I cannot tell!

Dolley

❧ Excerpt from the Diary of Anne Frank

Anne Frank was born in Germany in 1929, but in 1933, after Nazis began to persecute Jews, she moved with her family to Amsterdam. In 1942, after the Nazis occupied the Netherlands, the Franks went into hiding in a secret annex behind Anne's father's business. Two years later, they were discovered and arrested. Anne died in a Nazi concentration camp.

Anne's diary, which she addressed as "Kitty," remains one of our most moving testaments to the courage of the human spirit. "Peter," mentioned in this excerpt, was Peter Van Daan, who with his parents had joined the Franks in hiding.

Tuesday, 7 March, 1944

Dear Kitty,

If I think now of my life in 1942, it all seems so unreal. It was quite a different Anne who enjoyed that heavenly existence from the Anne who has grown wise within these walls. Yes, it was a heavenly life. Boy friends at every turn, about twenty friends and acquaintances of my own age, the darling of nearly all the teachers, spoiled from top to toe by Mummy and Daddy, lots of sweets, enough pocket money, what more could one want?

You will certainly wonder by what means I got around all these people. Peter's word "attractiveness" is not altogether true. All the teachers were entertained by my cute answers, my amusing remarks, my smiling face, and my questioning looks. That is all I was—a terrible flirt, coquettish and amusing. I had one or two advantages, which kept me rather in favor. I was industrious, honest, and frank. I would never have dreamed of cribbing from anyone else. I shared my sweets generously, and I wasn't conceited.

Wouldn't I have become rather forward with so much admiration? It was a good thing that in the midst of, at the height of, all this gaiety, I suddenly had to face reality, and it took me at least a year to get used to the fact that there was no more admiration forthcoming.

How did I appear at school? The one who thought of

new jokes and pranks, always "king of the castle," never in a bad mood, never a crybaby. No wonder everyone liked to cycle with me, and I got their attentions.

Now I look back at that Anne as an amusing, but very superficial girl, who has nothing to do with the Anne of today. Peter said quite rightly about me: "If ever I saw you, you were always surrounded by two or more boys and a whole troupe of girls. You were always laughing and always the center of everything!

"What is left of this girl? Oh, don't worry, I haven't forgotten how to laugh or to answer back readily. I'm just as good, if not better, at criticizing people, and I can still flirt if . . . I wish. That's not it though, I'd like that sort of life again for an evening, a few days, or even a week; the life which seems so carefree and gay. But at the end of that week, I should be dead beat and would be only too thankful to listen to anyone who began to talk about something sensible. I don't want followers, but friends, admirers who fall not for a flattering smile but for what one does and for one's character.

I know quite well that the circle around me would be much smaller. But what does that matter, as long as one still keeps a few sincere friends?

Yet I wasn't entirely happy in 1942 in spite of everything; I often felt deserted, but because I was on the go the whole day long, I didn't think about it and enjoyed myself as much as I could. Consciously or unconsciously, I tried to drive away the emptiness I felt with jokes and pranks. Now I think seriously about life and what I have to do. One period of my life is over forever. The carefree schooldays are gone, never to return.

I don't even long for them any more; I have outgrown

them, I can't just only enjoy myself as my serious side is always there.

I look upon my life up till the New Year, as it were, through a powerful magnifying glass. The sunny life at home, then coming here in 1942, the sudden change, the quarrels, the bickerings. I couldn't understand it, I was taken by surprise, and the only way I could keep up some bearing was by being impertinent.

The first half of 1943: my fits of crying, the loneliness, how I slowly began to see all my faults and shortcomings, which are so great and which seemed much greater then. During the day I deliberately talked about anything and everything that was farthest from my thoughts, tried to draw Pim to me; but couldn't. Alone I had to face the difficult task of changing myself, to stop the everlasting reproaches, which were so oppressive and which reduced me to such terrible despondency.

Things improved slightly in the second half of the year, I became a young woman and was treated more like a grownup. I started to think, and write stories, and came to the conclusion that the others no longer had the right to throw me about like an india-rubber ball. I wanted to change in accordance with my own desires. But *one* thing that struck me even more was when I realized that even Daddy would never become my confidant over everything. I didn't want to trust anyone but myself any more.

At the beginning of the New Year: the second great change, my dream. . . . And with it I discovered my longing, not for a girl friend, but for a boy friend. I also discovered my inward happiness and my defensive armor of superficiality and gaiety. In due time I quieted down and discovered my boundless desire for all that is beautiful and good.

And in the evening, when I lie in bed and end my prayers with the words, "I thank you, God, for all that is good and dear and beautiful," I am filled with joy. Then I think about "the good" of going into hiding, of my health and with my whole being of "dearness" of Peter, of that which is still embryonic and impressionable and which we neither of us dare to name or touch, of that which will come sometime; love, the future, happiness and of "the beauty" which exists in the world; the world, nature, beauty and all, all that is exquisite and fine.

I don't think then of all the misery, but of the beauty that still remains. This is one of the things that Mummy and I are so entirely different about. Her counsel when one feels melancholy is: "Think of all the misery in the world and be thankful that you are not sharing in it!" My advice is: "Go outside, to the fields, enjoy nature and the sunshine, go out and try to recapture happiness in yourself and in God. Think of all the beauty that's still left in and around you and be happy!"

I don't see how Mummy's idea can be right, because then how are you supposed to behave if you go through the misery yourself? Then you are lost. On the contrary, I've found that there is always some beauty left—in nature, sunshine, freedom, in yourself; these can all help you. Look at these things, then you find yourself again, and God, and then you regain your balance.

And whoever is happy will make others happy too. He who has courage and faith will never perish in misery!

Yours, Anne

If—

RUDYARD KIPLING

Brave men and women (as well as cowardly men and women) are not born that way; they become that way through their acts. Here are the acts that make us not just grow up, but grow up well.

If you can keep you head when all about you
    Are losing theirs and blaming it on you;
If you can trust yourself when all men doubt you,
    But make allowance for their doubting too;
If you can wait and not be tired by waiting,
    Or, being lied about, don't deal in lies,
Or, being hated, don't give way to hating,
    And yet don't look too good, nor talk too wise;

If you can dream—and not make dreams your master;
If you can think—and not make thoughts your aim;
If you can meet with triumph and disaster
    And treat those two impostors just the same;
If you can bear to hear the truth you've spoken
    Twisted by knaves to make a trap for fools,
Or watch the things you gave your life to broken,
    And stoop and build 'em up with worn-out tools;

If you can make one heap of all your winnings
    And risk it on one turn of pitch-and-toss,
And lose, and start again at your beginnings
    And never breathe a word about your loss;
If you can force you heart and nerve and sinew
    To serve your turn long after they are gone,

And so hold on when there is nothing in you
  Except the Will which says to them: "Hold on!"

If you can talk with crowds and keep your virtue,
  Or walk with kings—nor lose the common touch;
If neither foes nor loving friends can hurt you;
  If all men count with you, but none too much;
If you can fill the unforgiving minute
  With sixty seconds' worth of distance run—
Yours is the Earth and everything that's in it,
  And—which is more—you'll be a Man, my son!

It Can Be Done

Courageous people think things through and ask:
"Is this the best way to do this?" Cowards, on the
other hand, always say, "It can't be done."

The man who misses all the fun
Is he who says, "It can't be done."
In solemn pride he stands aloof
And greets each venture with reproof.
Had he the power he'd efface
The history of the human race;
We'd have no radio or motor cars,
No streets lit by electric stars;
No telegraph nor telephone,
We'd linger in the age of stone.
The world would sleep if things were run
By men who say, "It can't be done."

Our Heroes

PHOEBE CARY

*Seeing what is right and doing it with confidence is
the mark of moral courage. Going against the crowd
when the crowd is wrong is something most courageous people must do more than once in their lives.*

Here's a hand to the boy who has courage
    To do what he knows to be right;
When he falls in the way of temptation,
    He has a hard battle to fight.
Who strives against self and his comrades
    Will find a most powerful foe.
All honor to him if he conquers.
    A cheer for the boy who says "NO!"

There's many a battle fought daily
    The world knows nothing about;
There's many a brave little soldier
    Whose strength puts a legion to rout.
And he who fights sin singlehanded
    Is more of a hero, I say,
Than he who leads soldiers to battle
    And conquers by arms in the fray.

Be steadfast, my boy, when you're tempted,
    To do what you know to be right.
Stand firm by the colors of manhood,
    And you will o'ercome in the fight.

"The right," be your battle cry ever
In waging the warfare of life,
And God, who knows who are the heroes,
Will give you the strength for the strife.

❧ Rosa Parks

KAI FRIESE

When Rosa Parks refused to give up her seat on a bus, it led to one of the most important chapters in the story of civil rights in America. Parks's courage led to profound change for African Americans.

It was Thursday, December 1, 1955. The workday was over, and crowds of people boarded the green-and-white buses that trundled through the streets of Montgomery. Rosa Parks was tired after a full day of stitching and ironing shirts at the Montgomery Fair department store. She thought she was lucky to have gotten one of the last seats in the rear section of the Cleveland Avenue bus that would take her home.

Soon the back of the bus was full, and several people were standing in the rear. The bus rolled on through Court Square, where African Americans had been auctioned off during the days of the Confederacy, and came to a stop in front of the Empire Theater. The next passenger aboard stood in the front of an aisle. He was a white man.

When he noticed that a white person had to stand, the bus driver, James F. Blake, called out to the four black people who were sitting just behind the white section. He said they would have to give up their seats for the new passenger.

No one stood up. "You'd better make it light on yourself and let me have those seats," the driver said threateningly. Three men got up and went to stand at the back of the bus. But Rosa Parks wasn't about to move. She had been in this situation before, and she had always given up her seat. She had always felt insulted by the experience. "It meant that I didn't have a right to do anything but get on the bus, give them my fare, and then be pushed around wherever they wanted me," she said.

By a quirk of fate, the driver of the bus on this December evening was the same James F. Blake who had once before removed the troublesome Rosa Parks from his bus for refusing to enter by the back door. That was a long time ago, in 1943. Rosa Parks didn't feel like being pushed around again. She told the driver that she wasn't in the white section and she wasn't going to move.

Blake knew the rules, though. He knew that the white section was wherever the driver said it was. If more white passengers got on the bus, he could stretch the white section to the back of the bus and make all the blacks stand. He shouted to Rosa Parks to move to the back of the bus. She wasn't impressed. She told him again that she wasn't moving. Everyone in the bus was silent, wondering what would happen next. Finally Blake told Rosa Parks that he would have her arrested for violating the racial segregation codes. In a firm but quiet voice, she told him that he could do what he wanted to do because she wasn't moving.

Blake got off the bus and came back with an officer of the Montgomery Police Department. As the officer placed Rosa Parks under arrest, she asked him plainly, "Why do you people push us around?"

With the eyes of all the passengers on him, the officer

could only answer in confusion. "I don't know. I'm just obeying the law," he said.

Rosa Parks was taken to the police station, where she was booked and fingerprinted. While the policemen were filling out forms, she asked if she could have a drink of water. She was told that the drinking fountain in the station was for whites only. Then a policewoman marched her into a long corridor facing a wall of iron bars. A barred door slid open. She went inside. The door clanged shut, and she was locked in. She was in jail.

Rosa Parks's decision to challenge her arrest in court led Montgomery's black community to organize a bus boycott as a show of support.

Rosa Parks woke up on the morning of Monday, December 5, thinking about her trial. As she and her husband got out of bed, they heard the familiar sound of a City Lines bus pulling up to a stop across the road. There was usually a crowd of people waiting for the bus at this time. The Parkses rushed to the window and looked out. Except for the driver, the bus was empty and there was no one getting on either. The bus stood at the stop for more than a minute, puffing exhaust smoke into the cold December air as the puzzled driver waited for passengers. But no one appeared, and the empty bus chugged away.

Rosa Parks was filled with happiness. Her neighbors were actually boycotting the buses. She couldn't wait to drive to the courthouse so that she could see how the boycott was going in the rest of Montgomery. When Fred Gray arrived to drive her to the trial, she wasn't disappointed. Rosa Parks had expected some people to stay off the buses.

She thought that with luck, maybe even half the usual passengers would stay off. But these buses were just plain empty.

All over the city, empty buses bounced around for everyone to see. There was never more than the usual small group of white passengers in front and sometimes a lonely black passenger in back, wondering what was going on. The streets were filled with black people walking to work.

As Rosa Parks and her lawyer drove up to the courthouse, there was another surprise waiting for them. A crowd of about five hundred blacks had gathered to show their support for her. Mrs. Parks and the lawyer made their way slowly through the cheering crowd into the courtroom. Once they were inside, the trial didn't take long. Rosa Parks was quickly convicted of breaking the bus segregation laws and fined ten dollars, as well as four dollars for the cost of her trial. This was the stage at which Claudette Colvin's trial had ended seven months earlier. Colvin had had little choice but to accept the guilty verdict and pay the fine.

This time, however, Fred Gray rose to file an appeal on Rosa Parks's case. This meant that her case would be taken to a higher court at a later date. Meanwhile, Mrs. Parks was free to go.

Outside the courthouse, the crowd was getting restless. Some of them were carrying sawed-off shotguns, and the policemen were beginning to look worried. E. D. Nixon went out to calm them, but nobody could hear him in the din. Voices from the crowd shouted out that they would storm the courthouse if Rosa Parks didn't come out safely within a few minutes. When she did appear, a great cheer went up again.

After seeing the empty buses that morning, and this

large and fearless crowd around her now, Rosa Parks knew that she had made the right decision. Black people were uniting to show the city administration that they were tired of the insults of segregation. Together, they could change Montgomery. They could do some good.

❧ Susan B. Anthony

JOANNA STRONG AND TOM B. LEONARD

The Nineteenth Amendment to the Constitution, which provides for full woman suffrage, was not ratified until fourteen years after Susan B. Anthony's death in 1906. Nevertheless, her name more than any other is associated with American women's long struggle to vote. Her firm resolve made her one of our greatest examples of political courage.

"What the blazes are you doing here?" shouted the man at the big desk. "You women go home about your business. Go home and wash the dishes. And if you don't clear out of here fast, I'll get the cops to put you out!"

Everybody in the store stopped and listened. Some of the men just turned around and sneered. Others looked at the fifteen women mockingly and guffawed. One man piped, "Beat it, youse dames. Your kids are dirty." And at that, every man in the place bellowed with laughter.

But this banter didn't faze the tall, dignified woman who stood with a piece of paper in her hand at the head of the fourteen other ladies. She didn't budge an inch.

"I've come here to vote for the President of the United States," she said. "He will be my President as well as yours.

We are the women who bear the children who will defend this country. We are the women who make your homes, who bake your bread, who rear your sons and give you daughters. We women are citizens of this country just as much as you are, and we insist on voting for the man who is to be the leader of this government."

Her words rang out with the clearness of a bell, and they struck to the heart. No man in the place dared move now. The big man at the desk who had threatened her was turned to stone. And then, in silence and dignity, Susan B. Anthony strode up to the ballot box and dropped into it the paper bearing her vote. Each of the other fourteen women did the same, while every man in the room stood silent and watched.

It was the year 1872. Too long now had women been denied the rights that should naturally be theirs. Too long now had they endured the injustice of an unfair law—a law that made them mere possessions of men.

Women could earn money, but they might not own it. If a woman was married and went to work, every penny she earned became the property of her husband. In 1872, a man was considered complete master of the household. His wife was taken to be incapable of managing her own affairs. She was supposed to be a nitwit unable to think clearly, and therefore the law mercifully protected her by appointing a guardian—a male guardian, of course—over any property that she was lucky enough to possess.

Women like Susan Anthony writhed at this injustice. Susan saw no reason why her sex should be discriminated against. "Why should only men make the laws?" she cried. "Why should men forge the chains that bind us down? No!" she exclaimed. "It is up to us women to fight for our rights." And then she vowed that she would carry on an everlasting battle, as long as the Lord gave her strength to see that women were made equal in the sight of the law.

And fight she did. Susan B. Anthony was America's greatest champion of women's rights. She traveled unceasingly, from one end of the country to the other. She made thousands of speeches, pleading with men, and trying to arouse women to fight for their rights. She wrote hundreds of pamphlets and letters of protest. It was a bitter and difficult struggle that she entered upon, for the people who opposed her did not hesitate to say all kinds of ugly and untrue things about her and her followers. "No decent woman would talk like that. No refined lady would force her way before judges and men's associations and insist on talking. She is vulgar!"

Many women who knew that Susan Anthony was a refined, intelligent, and courageous woman were afraid to say so. They were afraid that *they* would be looked down on. But in time, they grew to love her for trying to help them.

After a while, many housewives gained courage from her example. Then, in great meetings, they joined her by the thousands. Many a man began to change his notions when his wife, inspired by Susan B. Anthony, made him feel ashamed at the unfair treatment accorded women. Slowly the great Susan B. Anthony was undermining the fierce stubbornness of men.

On that important day in 1872, she and her faithful followers cast their first ballots for President. But though the men in the polling place were momentarily moved, their minds were not yet opened. In a few days, Susan was arrested and brought before a judge, accused of having illegally entered a voting booth.

"How do you plead?" asked the judge.

"Guilty!" cried Susan. "Guilty of trying to uproot the slavery in which you men have placed us women. Guilty of trying to make you see that we mothers are as important to this country as are the men. Guilty of trying to lift the standard of womanhood, so that men may look with pride upon their wives' awareness of public affairs."

And then, before the judge could recover from this onslaught, she added, "But, Your Honor, *not* guilty of acting against the Constitution of the United States, which says that no person is to be deprived of equal rights under the law. Equal rights!" she thundered. "How can it be said that we women have equal rights, when it is you and you alone who take upon yourselves the right to make the laws, the right to choose your representatives, the right to send only sons to higher education. You, you blind men, have become slaveholders of your own mothers and wives."

The judge was taken aback. Never before had he heard these ideas expressed to him in such a forceful manner. However, the law was the law! The judge spoke quietly, and without much conviction. "I am forced to fine you one hundred dollars," he said.

"I will not pay it!" said Susan Anthony. "Mark my words, the law will be changed!" And with that, she strode from the court.

"Shall I follow her and bring her back?" said the court clerk to the judge. "No, let her go," answered the elderly judge. "I fear that she is right, and that the law will soon be changed."

And Susan did go on, on to further crusades, on across the vast stretches of the United States, proclaiming in every hamlet where her feet trod, her plea for womanhood.

Today, voting by women is an established fact. Women may keep what they earn; and whether married or single, own their own property. It is taken for granted that a woman may go to college and work in any business or profession she may choose. But these rights, enjoyed by the women of today, were secured through the valiant effort of many fighters for women's freedom, such as the great Susan B. Anthony.

❧ The Leopard's Revenge

Courage involves knowing what to fear, but that in itself is not enough, as this African folktale reminds us. The father leopard of this story may be smart to know his limits, but his taking revenge on a weaker, innocent party is hardly courageous.

Once a leopard cub strayed from his home and ventured into the midst of a great herd of elephants. His mother and father had warned him to stay out of the way of the giant beasts, but he did not listen. Suddenly, the elephants began to stampede, and one of them stepped on the cub without even knowing it. Soon afterward, a hyena found his body and went to tell his parents.

"I have terrible news," he said. "I've found your son lying dead in the field."

The mother and father leopard gave great cries of grief and rage.

"How did it happen?" the father demanded. "Tell me who did this to our son! I will never rest until I have my revenge!"

"The elephants did it," answered the hyena.

"The elephants?" asked the father leopard, quite startled. "You say it was the elephants?"

"Yes," said the hyena, "I saw their tracks."

The leopard paced back and forth for a few minutes, growling and shaking his head.

"No, you are wrong," he said at last. "It was not the elephants. It was the goats. The goats have murdered my boy!"

And at once he bounded down the hill and sprang upon a herd of goats grazing in the valley below, and in a violent rage killed as many as he could in revenge.

ᨠ The Minotaur

ADAPTED FROM ANDREW LANG

This Greek myth is a story of compassion and courage. There are two heroes here: The first is Theseus, who goes into the maze to save his countrymen. The second is Ariadne, who searches her heart and realizes she must defy her own father to save Theseus and the others. We can be sure that both Theseus and Ariadne were afraid of the danger they faced, but they did the right thing anyway. It is not the absence of fear that defines courage, but doing the right thing despite one's fears.

This story begins in Athens, one of the greatest and most noble cities of ancient Greece. At the time it takes place, however, Athens was only a little town, perched on the top of a cliff rising out of the plain, two or three miles from the sea. King Aegeus, who ruled Athens in those days, had just welcomed home a son he had not seen since the child's birth, a youth named Theseus, who was destined to become one of Greece's greatest heroes.

Aegeus was overjoyed at having his son home at last, but Theseus could not help but notice moments when the king seemed distracted and sad. Gradually, Theseus began to sense the same melancholy among the people of Athens. Mothers were silent, fathers shook their heads, and young people watched the sea all day, as if they expected something fearful to come from it. Many of the Athenian youth seemed to be missing, and were said to have gone to visit friends in faraway parts of Greece. At last Theseus decided to ask his father what troubled the land.

"I'm afraid you've come home at an unhappy time," Aegeus sighed. "There is a curse upon Athens, a curse so terrible and strange that not even you, Prince Theseus, can deal with it."

"Tell me all," said Theseus, "for though I am but one man, yet the ever-living gods protect me and help me."

"The trouble is an old one," Aegeus said. "It dates to a time when young men came to Athens from all over Greece and other lands to take part in contests in running, boxing, wrestling, and foot races. The son of the great Minos, king of Crete, was among the contestants, and he died while he was here. His death is still a puzzle to me. Some say it was an accident; others say he was murdered by jealous rivals. At any rate, his comrades fled in the night, bearing the news to Crete.

"The sea was black with King Minos's ships when he arrived seeking vengeance. His army was far too powerful for us. We went humbly out of the city to meet him and ask for mercy. 'This is the mercy I will show you,' he said. 'I will not burn your city, I will not take your treasures, and I will not make your people my captives. But every seven years, you must pay a tribute. You must swear to choose by lot seven youths and seven maidens, and send them to me.' We had no choice but to agree. Every seven years, a ship with black sails arrives from Crete and bears away the captives. This is the seventh year, and the coming of the ship is at hand."

"And what happens to them once they reach Crete?" Theseus asked.

"We do not know, because they never return. But the sailors of Minos say he places them in a strange prison, a kind of maze, called the Labyrinth. It is full of dark winding ways, cut in the solid rock, and therein lives a horrible monster called the Minotaur. This monster has the body of a man, but his head is the head of a bull, and his teeth are the teeth of a lion, and he devours everyone he meets. That, I fear, is the fate of our Athenian youth."

"We could burn the black-sailed ship when it arrives, and slay its sailors," Theseus said.

"Yes, we could," answered Aegeus, "but then Minos would return with his fleet and his army, and destroy all of Athens."

"Then let me go as one of the captives," said Theseus, rising to his feet, "and I will slay the Minotaur. I am your son and heir, and it is only right that I try to free Athens of this awful curse."

Aegeus tried to persuade his son that such a plan was useless, but Theseus was determined, and when the ship with black sails touched the shore, he joined the doomed group. His father came to tell him goodbye for the last time, weeping bitterly.

"If you do manage to come back alive," he said to Theseus, "lower the black sails as you approach, and hoist white sails in their place, so that I may know you did not die in the Labyrinth."

"Do not worry," Theseus told him. "Look for white sails. I will return in triumph." As he spoke, the dark ship put to sea and soon sailed past the horizon.

After many days' sailing, the ship reached Crete. The Athenian prisoners were marched to the palace, where King Minos sat on his gilded throne, surrounded by his chiefs and princes, all gloriously clothed in silken robes and jewels of gold. Minos, a dark-faced man with touches of white in his hair and long beard, sat with his elbow on his knee and his chin in his hand, and he fixed his eyes on the eyes of Theseus. Theseus bowed and then stood erect, with his eyes on the eyes of Minos.

"You are fifteen in number," Minos said at last, "and my law claims only fourteen."

"I came of my own will," answered Theseus.

"Why?" asked Minos.

"The people of Athens have a mind to be free, O King."

"There is a way," said Minos. "Slay the Minotaur, and you are free of my tribute."

"I am minded to slay him," said Theseus, and as he spoke, there was a stir in the throng of chiefs and princes, and a beautiful young woman glided through them and stood a little behind the throne. This was Ariadne, the daughter of Minos, a wise and tender-hearted maiden. Theseus bowed low, and again stood erect, with his eyes on the face of Ariadne.

"You speak like a king's son," Minos said with a smile. "Perhaps one who has never known hardship."

"I have known hardship, and my name is Theseus, Aegeus's son. I have come to ask you to let me face the Minotaur alone. If I cannot slay it, my companions will follow me into the Labyrinth."

"I see," Minos said. "Very well. The king's son wishes to die alone. Let him do so."

The Athenians were led upstairs and along galleries, each to a chamber more rich and beautiful than they had seen before in their dreams. Each was taken to a bath, and washed and clothed in new garments, and then treated to a lavish feast. None had the appetite to eat, though, except Theseus, who knew he would need his strength.

That night as he was preparing for bed, Theseus heard a soft knock at his door, and suddenly Ariadne, the king's daughter, was standing in his room. Once again Theseus gazed into her eyes and saw there was a kind of strength and compassion he had never known before.

"Too many of your countrymen have disappeared into my father's Labyrinth," she said quietly. "I have brought you a dagger, and I can show you and your friends the way to flee."

"I thank you for the dagger," Theseus answered, "but I cannot flee. If you wish to show me a way, show me the way to the Minotaur."

"Even if you are strong enough to kill the monster," Ariadne whispered, "you will need to find your way out of the Labyrinth. It is made of so many dark twists and turns, so many dead ends and false passages, not even my father knows the secrets of its windings. If you are determined to go forward with your plan, you must take this with you." She took from her gown a spool of gold thread, and pressed it into Theseus's hand.

"As soon as you get inside the Labyrinth," she said, "tie the end of the thread to a stone, and hold tight to the spool as you wander through the maze. When you are ready to come back, the thread will be your guide."

Theseus gazed at her, hardly knowing what to say. "Why are you doing this?" he finally asked. "If your father finds out, you'll be in great danger."

"Yes," Ariadne answered slowly, "but if I had not acted, you and your friends would be in far greater danger."

And Theseus knew then that he loved her.

The next morning Theseus was led to the Labyrinth. As soon as the guards shut him inside, he fastened one end of the thread to a pointed rock, and began to walk slowly, keeping firm hold of the precious string. He made his way down the broadest corridor, from which others turned off to the right and left, until he came to a wall. He retraced his steps, and tried another hallway, and then another, always stopping every few feet to listen for the monster. He passed through many dark, winding passages, sometimes coming to places he had already been before, but gradually descending further and further into the Labyrinth. Finally he reached a room heaped high with bones, and he knew now he was very near the beast.

He sat still, and from far away he heard a faint sound, like the end of the echo of a roar. He stood up and listened keenly. The sound came nearer and louder, not deep like the roar of a bull, but more shrill and thin. Theseus stooped quickly and scooped up a handful of dirt from the floor of the Labyrinth, and with his other hand drew his dagger.

The roars of the Minotaur came nearer and nearer. Now his feet could be heard thudding along the echoing floor. There was a heavy rustling, then sniffing, then silence. Theseus moved to the shadowy corner of the narrow path and crouched there. His heart was beating quickly. On came the Minotaur—it caught sight of the crouching figure, gave a great roar, and rushed straight for it. Theseus leaped up and, dodging to one side, dashed his handful of dirt into the beast's eyes.

The Minotaur bellowed in pain. It rubbed its eyes with its monstrous hands, shrieking and confused. It tossed its great head up and down, and it turned around and around, feeling with its hands for the wall. It was quite blind. Theseus drew his dagger, crept up behind the monster, and quickly slashed at its legs. Down fell the Minotaur, with a crash and a roar, biting at the rocky floor with its lion's teeth, waving its hands, and clawing at the empty air. Theseus waited for his chance, when the clutching hands rested, and then three times he drove the sharp blade through the heart of the Minotaur. The body leaped and lay still.

Theseus kneeled and thanked all the gods, and when he had finished his prayer, he took his dagger and hacked off the head of the Minotaur. With the head in his hand, he began following the string out of the Labyrinth. It seemed he would never come out of those dark, gloomy passages. Had the thread snapped somewhere, and had he, after all, lost his way? But still he followed it anxiously, until at last he came to the entrance, and he sank to the ground, worn out with his struggle and his wanderings.

"I don't know what miracle caused you to come out of the Labyrinth alive," Minos said when he saw the monster's head, "but I will keep my word. I promised you freedom if you slew the Minotaur. You and your comrades may go. Now let there be peace between your people and mine. Farewell."

Theseus knew he owed his life and his country's freedom to Ariadne's courage, and he knew he could not leave without her. Some say he asked Minos for her hand in marriage, and that the king gladly consented. Others says she stole onto the departing ship at the last minute without her father's knowledge. Either way, the two lovers were together when the anchor lifted and the dark ship sailed away from Crete.

But this happy ending is mixed with tragedy, as stories sometimes are. For the Cretan captain of the vessel did not know he was to hoist white sails if Theseus came home in triumph, and King Aegeus, as he anxiously watched the waters from a high cliff, spied the black sails coming over the horizon. His heart broke at once, and he fell from the towering cliff into the sea, which is now called the Aegean.

PERSEVERANCE

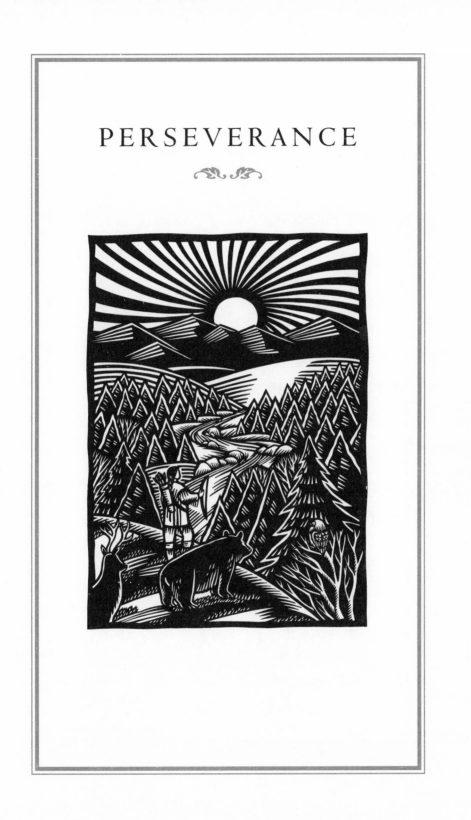

∾ Perseverance

Once a beaten man went to see a rabbi for advice. "Help me," he cried. "I'm so tired of failing. At least half the time, whatever I try doesn't seem to work. What should I do?"

"I'll tell you what to do," the rabbi answered. "Go look on page 720 of the *World Almanac*."

The man went to the library, turned to the right page, and found a listing of the lifetime batting averages of the greatest baseball players. At the top was Ty Cobb, the greatest slugger of all time. His average was .367.

The man went back to the rabbi.

"I don't understand," he said. "What does Ty Cobb's batting average have to do with my failures?"

"His average was .367," the rabbi said. "One out of every three times he stood at the plate, he got a hit. But two out of every three times, he did not. And he was the greatest."

Life isn't just about winning. Much of life is about losing. It's something we all do, over and over again. That's where the virtue of perseverance comes in. We fail and we fail and we fail until, finally, we succeed. There are always going to be discouraging times when we want to walk away from a task. But perseverance is that voice inside your head that says, "If at first you don't succeed, try, try again." Listening to that voice is an important part of growing up.

Perseverance may be one of the most underrated virtues. That's because when we see people who have "made it," whether they are famous sports figures or actresses or businessmen, we tend to credit their success to how much talent they have, or how smart they are, or even how lucky they are. We don't think about all the false starts, all the humiliating rejections, all the lonely hours they suffered before finally succeeding. We remember Thomas Edison as the brilliant inventor of the electric lightbulb and phonograph and many other modern-day wonders. We never really think about all of his ideas that didn't work out. But, then, neither did Edison. Once, when a friend was consoling him after many unsuccessful attempts to make a storage battery work, Edison said, "I have not failed. I've just found a thousand ways that don't work."

Edison knew what most successful people know. Talent and skills and even luck can take you a long way. But perseverance can take you further. Those who learn to stick to their tasks usually end up doing very well in life.

Of course, persevering is no guarantee you'll get the prize you're after. You may do all the drills and still not win the championship game. You may do all the homework assignments and still not get an A on the test. But you'll be a better, stronger person. And you'll be all the more ready to go after the next prize, the next goal.

Even when you *do* reach that goal, the time for trying

isn't over. Living well isn't a destination but a journey. It's a journey of striving, of seeking, of learning from mistakes and failures, and trying to better ourselves from each one. So you set a new, higher goal, and the perseverance begins again.

🐎 Bruce and the Spider
BERNARD BARTON

*Robert Bruce (1274–1329) was the king of Scotland
who freed his land from English rule. But the fight
was long and hard, as this famous story tells in
verse.*

For Scotland's and for freedom's right
　　The Bruce his part had played,
In five successive fields of fight
　　Been conquered and dismayed;
Once more against the English host
His band he led, and once more lost
　　The meed for which he fought;
And now from battle, faint and worn,
The homeless fugitive forlorn
　　A hut's lone shelter sought.

And cheerless was that resting place
　　For him who claimed a throne:
His canopy, devoid of grace,
　　The rude, rough beams alone;
The heather couch his only bed—
Yet well I ween had slumber fled
　　From couch of eiderdown!
Through darksome night till dawn of day,
Absorbed in wakeful thoughts he lay
　　Of Scotland and her crown.

The sun rose brightly, and its gleam
　　Fell on that hapless bed,
And tinged with light each shapeless beam
　　Which roofed the lowly shed;
When, looking up with wistful eye,
The Bruce beheld a spider try
　　His filmy thread to fling
From beam to beam of that rude cot;
And well the insect's toilsome lot
　　Taught Scotland's future king.

Six times his gossamery thread
　　The wary spider threw;
In vain the filmy line was sped,
　　For powerless or untrue
Each aim appeared, and back recoiled
The patient insect, six time foiled,
　　And yet unconquered still;
And soon the Bruce, with eager eye,
Saw him prepare once more to try
　　His courage, strength, and skill.

One effort more, his seventh and last—
　　The hero hailed the sign!—
And on the wished-for beam hung fast
　　That slender, silken line!
Slight as it was, his spirit caught
The more than omen, for his thought
　　The lesson well could trace,
Which even "he who runs may read,"
That Perseverance gains its meed,
　　And Patience wins the race.

Can't

EDGAR GUEST

The word can't *is a favorite of some young people.*
This poem makes a strong case against it.

Can't is the worst word that's written or spoken;
    Doing more harm here than slander and lies;
On it is many a strong spirit broken,
    And with it many a good purpose dies.
It springs from the lips of the thoughtless each morning
    And robs us of courage we need through the day:
It rings in our ears like a timely sent warning
    And laughs when we falter and fall by the way.

Can't is the father of feeble endeavor,
    The parent of terror and halfhearted work;
It weakens the efforts of artisans clever,
    And makes of the toiler an indolent shirk.
It poisons the soul of the man with a vision,
    It stifles in infancy many a plan;
It greets honest toiling with open derision
    And mocks at the hopes and the dreams of a man.

Can't is a word none should speak without blushing;
    To utter it should be a symbol of shame;
Ambition and courage it daily is crushing;
    It blights a man's purpose and shortens his aim.
Despise it with all of your hatred of error;
    Refuse it the lodgment it seeks in your brain;
Arm against it as a creature of terror,
    And all that you dream of you someday shall gain.

Can't is the word that is foe to ambition,
    An enemy ambushed to shatter your will;
Its prey is forever the man with a mission
    And bows but to courage and patience and skill.
Hate it, with hatred that's deep and undying,
    For once it is welcomed 'twill break any man;
Whatever the goal you are seeking, keep trying
    And answer this demon by saying: "I *can*."

ꙮ Carry On!

ROBERT SERVICE

*Here's another good poem to read out loud—and a
good one to keep inside the head and heart.*

It's easy to fight when everything's right,
And you're mad with the thrill and the glory;
It's easy to cheer when victory's near,
And wallow in fields that are gory.
It's a different song when everything's wrong,
When you're feeling infernally mortal;
When it's ten against one, and hope there is none,
Buck up, little soldier, and chortle:

Carry on! Carry on!
There isn't much punch in your blow.
You're glaring and staring and hitting out blind;
You're muddy and bloody, but never you mind.
Carry on! Carry on!
You haven't the ghost of a show.
It's looking like death, but while you've a breath,
Carry on, my son! Carry on!

And so in the strife of the battle of life
It's easy to fight when you're winning;
It's easy to slave, and starve and be brave,
When the dawn of success is beginning.
But the man who can meet despair and defeat
With a cheer, there's the man of God's choosing;
The man who can fight to Heaven's own height
Is the man who can fight when he's losing.

Carry on! Carry on!
Things never were looming so black.
But show that you haven't a cowardly streak,
And though you're unlucky you never are weak.
Carry on! Carry on!
Brace up for another attack.
It's looking like hell, but—you never can tell:
Carry on, old man! Carry on!

There are some who drift out in the deserts of doubt,
And some who in brutishness wallow;
There are others, I know, who in piety go
Because of a Heaven to follow.
But to labor with zest, and to give of your best,
For the sweetness and joy of the giving;
To help folks along with a hand and a song;
Why, there's the real sunshine of living.

Carry on! Carry on!
Fight the good fight and true;
Believe in your mission, greet life with a cheer;
There's big work to do, and that's why you are here.

Carry on! Carry on!
Let the world be the better for you;
And at last when you die, let this be your cry:
Carry on, my soul! Carry on!

❧ Keep Your Eyes on the Prize

One of the most famous freedom songs of the civil rights movement, "Keep Your Eyes on the Prize" evolved from a traditional gospel song, "Keep Your Hand on the Plow." All great causes require people to hold on, hold on.

Paul and Silas bound in jail,
Had no money for to go their bail.
Keep your eyes on the prize,
Hold on, hold on.
    Hold on, hold on.
Keep your eyes on the prize,
    Hold on, hold on.
Paul and Silas begin to shout,
The jail door open and they walked out.
Keep your eyes on the prize,
Hold on, hold on.

Freedom's name is mighty sweet,
Soon one day we're gonna meet.
Keep your eyes on the prize,
Hold on, hold on.

Got my hand on the Gospel plow,
I wouldn't take nothing for my journey now.
Keep your eyes on the prize,
Hold on, hold on.

The only chain that a man can stand,
Is that chain of hand in hand.
Keep your eyes on the prize,
Hold on, hold on.

The only thing that we did wrong,
Stayed in the wilderness a day too long.
Keep your eyes on the prize,
Hold on, hold on.

But the one thing we did right,
Was the day we started to fight.
Keep your eyes on the prize,
Hold on, hold on.

We're gonna board that big Greyhound,
Carryin' love from town to town.
Keep your eyes on the prize,
Hold on, hold on.

We're gonna ride for civil rights,
We're gonna ride both black and white.
Keep your eyes on the prize,
Hold on, hold on.

We've met jail and violence too,
But God's love has seen us through.

Keep your eyes on the prize,
Hold on, hold on.

Haven't been to Heaven but I've been told,
Streets up there are paved with gold.
Keep your eyes on the prize,
Hold on, hold on.

ᕤ Sail on! Sail on!

JOAQUIN MILLER

This poem is about Christopher Columbus. We admire his imagination, we celebrate his daring, and we should imitate his determination.

Behind him lay the gray Azores,
    Behind the gates of Hercules;
Before him not the ghost of shores,
    Before him only shoreless seas.
The good mate said: "Now must we pray,
    For lo! the very stars are gone;
Speak, Admiral, what shall I say?"
    "Why say, sail on! and on!"

"My men grow mut'nous day by day;
    My men grow ghastly wan and weak."
The stout mate thought of home; a spray
    Of salt wave wash'd his swarthy cheek.
"What shall I say, brave Admiral,
    If we sight naught but seas at dawn?"

"Why, you shall say, at break of day:
  'Sail on! sail on! and on!'"

They sailed and sailed, as winds might blow,
  Until at last the blanch'd mate said:
"Why, now, not even God would know
  Should I and all my men fall dead.
These very winds forget their way,
  For God from these dread seas is gone.
Now speak, brave Admiral, and say—"
  He said: "Sail on! and on!"

They sailed, they sailed, then spoke his mate:
  "This mad sea shows his teeth tonight,
He curls his lip, he lies in wait,
  With lifted teeth as if to bite!
Brave Admiral, say but one word;
  What shall we do when hope is gone?"
The words leaped as a leaping sword:
  "Sail on! sail on! and on!"

Then, pale and worn, he kept his deck,
  And thro' the darkness peered that night.
Ah, darkest night! and then a speck—
  A light! a light! a light! a light!
It grew—a star-lit flag unfurled!
  It grew to be Time's burst of dawn;
He gained a world! he gave that world
  Its watchword: "On! and on!"

The Story of Scarface

RETOLD BY AMY CRUSE

The dictionary defines fortitude *as "strength that enables a person to encounter danger with coolness and courage." The English philosopher John Locke called fortitude the "guard to every other virtue." In this Blackfoot Indian tale, we find honesty, loyalty, friendship, courage, self-discipline, and more in a young brave's fortitude.*

There lived once among a tribe of Indians a poor boy whose father and mother were dead, and who had no friends to take care of him. The kindly Indian women helped him as well as they could, giving him what they could spare of food and clothing, and shelter in the hard days of winter; and the men let him go with them on hunting expeditions, and taught him the Indian woodcraft, just as they taught their own sons. The boy grew up strong and brave, and the men of the tribe said that he would one day make a mighty hunter. While he was quite young he met on one of the hunting parties a great grizzly bear, and fought a desperate fight with him, and at last killed him. But during the struggle the bear set its claws in the boy's face and tore it cruelly; and when the wound healed there was left a red, unsightly mark, so that he thereafter was called Scarface.

The boy thought little of the disfigurement until he fell in love with the beautiful daughter of the chief of his tribe. Then when he saw all the handsome young braves dressing themselves in the splendid dress of the Indian warrior and going to pay court to this maiden at her father's wigwam, his heart ached very sorely because he was poor and friendless, and above all because he bore upon his face the terrible disfiguring scar.

But the maiden did not care for the finery and boastful talk of the young Indians who crowded round her, and each in turn, when he ventured to ask her hand in marriage, found himself refused. Scarface scarcely dared to approach her, but the girl often saw him as he went about the forest, and she felt that he was braver and truer than the other lovers who boldly sought her favor.

One day, as she sat outside her father's lodge, Scarface passed by, and as he passed he looked at her, and his eyes showed the love and admiration that possessed him. A young Indian whose suit the girl had refused noticed the look, and said with a sneer, "Scarface has become a suitor for our chief's daughter. She will have nothing to do with men unblemished; perhaps she desires a man marked and marred. Try then, Scarface, and see if she will take you."

Scarface felt anger rise hot within him against the man who thus mocked him. He stood proudly, as though he were a chief's son instead of a poor, common, disfigured warrior, and, looking very steadily at the young brave, he said, "My brother speaks true words, though he speaks them with an ill tongue. I go indeed to ask the daughter of our great chief to be my wife."

The young brave laughed loudly in mockery. Some other young men of the tribe came up, and he told them what Scarface had said, and they also laughed, calling him the great chief, speaking of his vast wealth and of his marvelous beauty, and pretending to bow down before him. Scarface took no notice, but walked away quietly and with an unmoved face, though in his heart he yearned to spring at them, as the great grizzly had sprung at him in the forest. But when he came down to the river, following the chief's daughter, who had gone there to gather rushes for the baskets she was weaving, his anger died away. He drew near to her, knowing that if he did not speak at once his courage would leave him, for though she was so gentle and so kind, he trembled in her presence as the fiercest warrior or the most terrible bear could not make him tremble.

"Maiden," he said, "I am poor and little thought of, because I have no store of furs or pemmican, as the great warriors of the tribe have. I must gain day by day with my bow and my spear and with hard toil the means by which I live. And my face is marred and unsightly to look upon. But my heart is full of love for you, and I greatly desire you for my wife. Will you marry Scarface and live with him in his poor lodge?"

The maiden looked at him, and in her face he saw the love for which he asked.

"That you are poor," she said, "matters little. My father would give me great store of all needful things for a wedding portion. But I may not be your bride, nor the bride of any man of the tribe. The great Lord of the Sun has laid his commands on me, forbidding me to marry."

The heart of poor Scarface sank at these terrible words, yet he would not give up hope. "Will he not release you?" he asked. "He is kind and gives us many good gifts. He would not wish to make us both miserable."

"Go to him, then," said the girl, "and make your prayer to him that he will set me free from my promise. And ask him, that I may know that he has done so, to take the scar from off your face as a sign."

"I will go," said Scarface, "I will seek out the bright god in his own land, and beseech him to pity us." So he turned and left the maiden by the riverside.

Scarface started at once on his journey, and traveled for many, many miles. Sometimes he went cheerfully, saying to himself, "The sun god is kind; he will give me my bride." Sometimes his heart was sad, and he went heavily, for he thought, "Maybe the sun god desires to marry her himself, and who could expect him to give up a maiden so beautiful?" Through forests and over mountains he went, searching ever for the golden gates which marked the entrance to the country of the great god. The wild animals he met knew that this time he had not come out as a hunter to take them, so they drew near to him and willingly answered his questions. But not one of them could tell him where lay the sun god's land. "We have not traveled beyond the forest," they said. "Perhaps the birds, who fly swiftly and very far, can tell you what you want to know."

Scarface called to the birds who were flying overhead, and they came down and listened. But they answered. "We fly far and see many things, but we have never seen two gleaming gates of gold, nor looked on the face of the bright god of the sun."

Scarface was disappointed, but he went bravely on. One day, when he was very weary, he met a wolverine and asked him the question he had asked so many times before. To his great joy the wolverine answered, "I have seen the gleaming gates, and have entered the bright country of the Lord of the Sun. But the way to it is long and hard, and you will be tired indeed when you reach the end of your journey. I will put you on your way, and if your heart does not fail you, someday you will see what I have seen."

With fresh courage Scarface went on. Day after day he journeyed, walking until he was weary, and taking but short rest. Each morning when he started he had hope that evening would bring him to the golden gates, and then one day came to a great water, very broad and deep so that he could not cross it.

Now it seemed that his labor and weariness had been all for nothing, and he sat down on the shore of the great water and felt hope dying out of his heart. But very soon he saw drawing near to him from the other side two beautiful swans. "We will take you across," they said. "Step on our backs and we will swim with you to the farther shore." Up started Scarface, joyful once again, and poised himself carefully on the backs of the two swans; and they glided across and landed him safely on the opposite shore.

"You seek the kingdom of the sun god?" they said. "Go then along the road that lies before you, and you will soon come to it." Scarface thanked them with all his heart. He felt happier than he had done since he had started on his journey, and he walked along with quick, light steps. He had not gone far when he saw lying on the ground a very beautiful bow and arrows. He stopped for a moment to look at them. "These belong to some mighty hunter," he thought, "they are finer than those of a common warrior." But he left them lying where he found them, for though his hunter's heart coveted them, Scarface was honest, and would not take what was not his own. He went on, even lighter of heart than before, and soon he saw a beautiful youth coming gaily along the road toward him. It seemed to Scarface that a soft, bright light shone around as the youth stopped and said, "I have lost a bow and arrows somewhere along the road. Have you seen them?"

"They lie but a little distance behind me," said Scarface, "I have but just passed them."

"Thank you many times," said the youth. "It is well for me that it was an honest man who passed, or I should never have seen my bow and arrows again." He smiled at Scarface, and the Indian felt great joy in his heart, and all the air seemed flecked with golden points of light. "Where are you going?" inquired the stranger.

And Scarface answered, "I seek the land of the great Lord of the Sun, and I believe it is very near."

"It is near indeed," replied the youth. "I am Apisirahts, the Morning Star, and the Sun is my father. Come and I will take you to him."

So the two went down the broad, bright road and passed through the golden gates. Inside they saw a great lodge, shining and glorious, gaily bedecked with such beautiful pictures and carvings as Scarface had never in his life seen before. At the door stood a woman with a fair face and bright clear eyes that looked kindly at the wayworn stranger. "Come in," she said. "I am Kokomikis, the moon goddess, and this youth is my son. Come, for you are tired and footsore and need food and rest."

Scarface, almost bewildered by the beauty of everything around him, went in, and Kokomikis cared for him tenderly, so that he soon felt refreshed and strong. After a time the great Lord of the Sun came home to the lodge, and he, too, was very kind to Scarface. "Stay with us," he said, "you have traveled a weary way to find me, now be my guest for a season. You are a great hunter, and here you will find good game. My son who loves the chase will go with you, and you will live with us and be happy."

Very gladly Scarface replied, "I will stay, great lord." So

for many days he lived with the sun god and Kokomikis and Apisirahts, and every morning he and Morning Star went hunting and returned at night to the shining lodge. "Do not go near the Great Water," the Lord of the Sun warned them, "for savage birds dwell there, who will seek to slay the Morning Star."

But Apisirahts secretly longed to meet these savage birds and kill them, so one day he stole away from Scarface and hastened toward the Great Water. For a little while Scarface did not miss him, but believed him to be nearby; but after a time he looked round and could not find his companion. He searched anxiously, and then a terrible fear came into his heart, and he set off as fast as he could toward the haunt of the dread birds. Horrid cries came to his ears as he hastened on, and soon he saw a crowd of the monstrous creatures surrounding Morning Star, and pressing on him so closely that he could use his weapons to little purpose to defend himself. Scarface feared to loose an arrow, but he dashed in among the hideous creatures, taking them by surprise, so that they flew off in alarm. Then he seized Morning Star, and hurried him back through the forest to safety.

When they returned to the lodge that night Apisirahts told his father of his own disobedience and the courage of Scarface. The great Lord of the Sun turned to the poor stranger. "You have saved my son from a dreadful death," he said. "Ask of me some boon, that I may repay you. Why was it that you sought me here? Surely you had some desire in your heart or you would not have traveled so far and fared so hardly."

Now all the while he had been at the Shining Lodge the thing he had come to ask had been ever in Scarface's mind.

Many times he had thought, "The hour is come when I may speak." But because it was so great a boon he craved his heart failed him, and he thought again, "I will have patience just a little longer. It is too soon to beg so great a favor of the god who has already been so kind to me." But when he heard the words of the sun god, so graciously spoken, he took courage and replied, "In my own land, O mighty Lord, I love a maiden who is the daughter of the chief of my tribe. I am only a poor warrior and, as you see, I am disfigured and hideous to look upon. Yet she of her goodness loves me, and would marry me, but for the reverence in which she holds your commands laid upon her. For she has promised you, O great Lord, that she will marry no man. So I came to seek you in hope that you would free her from her promise, that she might come to my lodge, and we might live in happiness together."

Then the sun god smiled, and looked kindly upon the Indian, who spoke bravely, though in his heart he trembled. "Go back," he said, "and take this maiden for your wife. Tell her that it is my will she marry you, and for a token"— he passed his hand before the Indian's face, and immediately the disfiguring scar had vanished—"tell her to look upon you and see how the Lord of the Sun has wrought upon your face."

They loaded the Indian—Scarface no longer—with gifts and changed his poor clothes for the rich dress of an Indian chief. Then they led him out from the country of the Sun, through the golden gates, and showed him a short and easy path by which he could return to his own land.

He traveled quickly, and soon was at home once more. All his tribe came out to look at the richly clad young brave, who walked with such a quick, light step, and looked so eager and happy; but none knew him for Scarface, at whom they had mocked and jeered. Even the chief's daughter did not recognize him when she first looked upon him, but a second look told her who he was, and she called his name; then, realizing that the scar was gone, and remembering what its disappearance meant, she sprang toward him with a cry of joy. The story of his wonderful journey was told, and the chief gladly gave his daughter to this warrior on whom the great sun god had looked with favor. That same day they were married, and the chief gave his daughter a splendid wigwam for her marriage portion. There the two lived happily for many years; and Scarface lost his old name and was known to all the tribe as Smoothface.

Will

ELLA WHEELER WILCOX

There is no chance, no destiny, no fate,
    Can circumvent or hinder or control
    The firm resolve of a determined soul.
Gifts count for nothing; will alone is great;
All things give way before it, soon or late.
    What obstacle can stay the mighty force
    Of the sea-seeking river in its course,
Or cause the ascending orb of day to wait?

Each well-born soul must win what it deserves.
    Let the fool prate of luck. The fortunate

Is he whose earnest purpose never swerves,
Whose slightest action or inaction serves
The one great aim. Why, even Death stands still,
And waits an hour sometimes for such a will.

◈ You Mustn't Quit

When things go wrong, as they sometimes will,
When the road you're trudging seems all uphill,
When the funds are low and the debts are high
And you want to smile, but you have to sigh,
When care is pressing you down a bit,
Rest! if you must—but never quit.

Life is queer, with its twists and turns,
As every one of us sometimes learns,
And many a failure turns about
When he might have won if he'd stuck it out;
Stick to your task, though the pace seems slow—
You may succeed with one more blow.

Success is failure turned inside out—
The silver tint of the clouds of doubt—
And you never can tell how close you are,
It may be near when it seems afar;
So stick to the fight when you're hardest hit—
It's when things seem worst that YOU MUSTN'T QUIT.

Solitude

ELLA WHEELER WILCOX

Sometimes we persevere with the help and compassion of friends and loved ones. Sometimes we have to do it alone. This poem speaks a hard truth but one we have to accept: Pain is harder to share than joy. But if we can bring ourselves to endure pain without too much complaint, we'll find more company along the way.

Laugh, and the world laughs with you;
        Weep, and you weep alone;
For the sad old earth must borrow its mirth,
        But has trouble enough of its own.
Sing, and the hills will answer;
        Sigh, it is lost on the air;
The echoes bound to a joyful sound,
        But shrink from voicing care.

Rejoice, and men will seek you;
        Grieve, and they turn and go;
They want full measure of all your pleasure,
        But they do not need your woe.
Be glad, and your friends are many;
        Be sad, and you lose them all—
There are none to decline your nectared wine,
        But alone you must drink life's gall.

Feast, and your halls are crowded;
        Fast, and the world goes by.

Succeed and give, and it helps you live,
But no man can help you die.
There is room in the halls of pleasure
For a large and lordly train,
But one by one we must all file on
Through the narrow aisles of pain.

◌᠍᠍᠍ The Long, Hard Way
Through the Wilderness

RETOLD BY WALTER RUSSELL BOWIE

*The story of the Hebrews' flight from Egypt and
their 40 years of wandering in the wilderness is told
primarily in the biblical book of Exodus. It is one of
our greatest accounts of endurance, not only by a
people but also by a people's leader. As God's agent,
Moses led the Hebrews through trial after trial, helping them find their way past starvation, sickness,
impatience, and despair.*

Moses had brought the people out of Egypt. They had
come safely across the water, in spite of the chariots of
Pharaoh. Now they thought there would be no danger or
trouble anymore. But soon they found that they had a long,
hard way ahead of them. The country to which they had
come was a strip of land, not very wide, between the sea on
the one side and great mountains of rock on the other side.
The ground between the sea and the mountains was flat
sand and gravel. In the daytime the sun beat down with
blistering heat, and there were no trees to give shade.

Mile after mile the people traveled without finding water. When at last they came to a pool in the sands, the water tasted so bad that they could not drink it. They named the place Marah, which means bitterness, and they demanded of Moses, "What shall we drink?"

Moses prayed to God to show him what to do. He found some shrubs growing in the sand, and he put these into the pool. Their leaves changed the taste of the water so that it became fit to drink.

After that Moses led the people to a place called Elim. There they found twelve springs of water with seventy palm trees growing nearby. To the people who had been dragging their feet through the hot desert, Elim seemed like heaven, and they made camp there at the oasis.

But they could not stay long at Elim, for they had used up all the food they had brought with them out of Egypt. They had to go on farther in the hope of finding something they could eat. But when they had left the oasis, all that they saw around them was the desert again, and they seemed to be worse off than ever. Most of the Israelites were not as brave as Moses, and some of them began to complain aloud. They said to Moses, "Would to God that we had been let alone to die in the land of Egypt. There we had meat to cook, and plenty of bread. And here you have brought us out into this wilderness to kill us all with hunger."

But Moses kept his temper, and he kept his courage. He said that God would send them help.

That evening as the people looked at the sky they saw what seemed like a cloud. As it came near, they saw that it was not a cloud but hundreds and hundreds of quail, blown to land by a strong wind from islands out in the sea. When the tired birds came to earth, the people caught and ate them.

That night there was a heavy dew. In the morning when the people woke up, there on the ground were small white patches like frost. Moses said, "This is the bread that the Lord has given you to eat." The people of Israel called it manna. It was a kind of gum that fell from the desert bushes, and it had to be picked up before the sun rose, for after that it melted and disappeared.

From the place where they were fed with the quail and the manna, the people of Israel went on farther along the sea. Then Moses told them to turn and head for the mountains. Terrible looking mountains they were, high and bare and grim. Again the people grew so thirsty that their tongues were dry. "Give us water!" they cried to Moses. "Is this what you brought us out of Egypt for—to kill us all with thirst?"

But Moses had been in these mountains before, and there was much that God had helped him learn. He led the people to a great rock cliff in a mountain called Horeb. There he struck the cliff with his staff and showed them water flowing. For a while the Hebrews were satisfied. They liked it still better when Moses brought them after that to another oasis. This was the greenest spot in all that bleak and barren land. Row after row of palm trees were there and springs bubbled up and overflowed, so that the waters made a murmuring stream. Centuries later this oasis was still known as the Pearl of Sinai because of its beauty.

The people of Israel might have liked to pitch their tents here and stay always, but it was a dangerous place in which to linger. An oasis was the one place most wanted, and so most fought for, by all the wild desert tribes. Moses chose a young man named Joshua to be the commander of the fighting men if there was danger.

The people had not been at the oasis long when a band of Amalekites appeared. They were mounted on camels and carried spears. They rode in fiercely to attack the Israelites. But Moses stood on a hill and held up his staff. He prayed to God. As he went on praying, Aaron and a man named Hur held up Moses' hands. While he prayed, Joshua and his fighting men drove the Amalekites away.

All the same, they could not stay at the oasis. Moses knew that other tribes, stronger than the Amalekites, might come there any day. Besides, the country to which Moses hoped to bring them, so that they might settle there, was a long way off on the other side of the mountain.

So on over rocky paths and up deep ravines Moses led the people of Israel. Great mountain peaks frowned over them. Some of these mountains had been volcanoes, and now and then there were rumblings among them, and sometimes even an earthquake. But it was in country like this that Moses, when he had first fled from Pharaoh, had seen the burning bush and heard the voice of God telling him to bring his people out of Egypt. In these same mountains Moses was to hear something else from God—something even more important.

While the people were camped in a valley, Moses climbed high on the greatest of the mountains—Mount Sinai. The people watched him until he disappeared in the distance. Hours and hours went by and he did not come back.

Up there, all alone, with only the rocks around him and the sky above, Moses thought and prayed. What did God want him to teach the people? How did God want them to behave?

Then it was as though Moses saw what he wanted to know. He saw the glory of God passing by, and heard God's voice telling him what he needed to understand. God would give him the Commandments which from this time on all people must obey.

After Moses had taught the people the Ten Commandments, he taught them a great deal more about how they were to live together. He taught them how to arrange the camps on the march, how to keep clean, how to be healthy, and what to do when anyone was sick. He told them what to do to remember God and worship him. They were to make a beautiful little chest, called the ark, and in it they were to carry the stone tablets on which were written the Ten Commandments. They were also to make a tabernacle, which was a tent made of the skins of animals. They were to put this tent up wherever they camped and have it for the place where they would pray to God.

Before long the Israelites left the valley at the foot of Mount Sinai and started on their way again. The ark was carried before them. Moses was still their leader. Often he had a hard time, just as he had had when they first came out of Egypt, because some of the people were forever grumbling. They said they were tired of eating manna all the time. They were tired of going thirsty on long journeys when there was not even so much as a water hole in the barren ground. They kept thinking of Egypt and telling one another that they wished they were back there. When they were there, they had wanted more than anything to be out of the country; but they forgot that now. What they remembered was the good things they had had to eat.

"We remember the fish," they said, "the cucumbers, and the melons." In Egypt there was the Nile with fish for anybody's taking, and there were fresh vegetables and fruits. But here there was nothing but sand and blistering sun and emptiness. Once or twice the people nearly rebelled.

Whenever Moses went by the tents and heard the people in them complaining, he was sad. But he would not let them think he was discouraged. He went off by himself and told everything to God in prayer. It seemed to him that God had given him more to do than any one man could manage. "I am not able to take care of all these people alone," he said. "It is too much for me." But when he prayed, God gave him new strength, and he went on.

All this time, by slow marches, the people were traveling farther north, beyond the mountains, toward the country where Moses believed God meant them to be. It was the same country to which Abraham had come long before, and it was called the Promised Land. They were near enough to its borders now for Moses to plan how they should enter it. But first he had to learn exactly what the land was like, and what sort of people were living there. He chose twelve scouts, one of whom was Joshua and one a young man named Caleb, and he sent them out secretly in advance.

"Go see the land," he told them, "and the people who live there. Notice whether they are strong or weak, few or many. Is the land good or bad, and is it wooded or not? What sort of homes do the people have? Do they live in tents, or in towns with walls around them? Be of good courage, and bring back with you some of the fruits of the land."

So on ahead the scouts went. From the region around Mount Sinai it was a hundred miles or more to the shores of the Dead Sea. Beyond that they went, up over the high rock country of Moab, and along the valley of the Jordan River. Across the Jordan lay the Promised Land.

After forty days the scouts came back and made their report to Moses. They all said that the country they had looked at was a good land. Compared with the mountains and deserts they had been through, it seemed like a paradise. There were fields of grain in it and olive trees and vineyards, and springs of water in the hills. They brought back a great bunch of grapes which they had taken from a valley they called Eshcol, and they also brought figs and other fruit.

But after that, the scouts began to disagree. Ten of them said that the people in the land were so strong and so warlike they would never let the Israelites in. They said that the people living there looked like giants. Measured against them, the ten scouts said they felt like grasshoppers. But Caleb and Joshua, the other two, said all that was nonsense. The people living in the country were no different from any other people. The thing for the Israelites to do was to march straight ahead and go in.

Most of the Israelites who crowded around and listened believed the ten men instead of the two. They were afraid to trust the ones who were courageous. Then, because it made them uncomfortable to feel cowardly, they pretended that Caleb and Joshua were trying to lead them into trouble. If they had dared, they would have stoned the two brave men to death. They started again to say that they wished they were back in Egypt. They even talked of choosing a captain of their own who would take them there. But they could not find any real leader, so their angry muttering came to nothing.

Yet all this was enough to make Moses know that such fainthearted people could not win the Promised Land. There was no use trying to lead them into it now. He would have to wait a long time, until some of the older ones who had been slaves in Egypt died, and younger and braver men grew up.

Many years went by, and now at last Moses did have a different sort of people under him—people who had been born and had grown up in the wilderness. They moved to the borders of the land of Edom, which lies at the south of the Dead Sea. They asked the Edomites to let them pass through their country peacefully. When the Edomites would not do this, the Israelites circled around that country and came to the land of the Amorites, to the west of the Jordan River.

Moses sent a message to Sihon, the chief of the Amorites, saying: "Let us pass through your land. We will not turn into the fields, nor into the vineyards. We will not drink from your wells. But we will go along the high roads until we have passed your borders."

The Amorites were fierce fighters. Instead of letting the Israelites through, they rode into the camp to attack them. But the younger men who followed Moses and Joshua now were no cowards. They beat off Sihon and his Amorites. And afterward, when Og, the chief of another one of the desert tribes, tried to stop them, they defeated him, too.

They were coming close to the Promised Land. But Moses was not to go in with them. He was an old man now. He went up one day to the top of Mount Nebo, four thousand feet above the waters of the Dead Sea. Across the Jordan River he could see the walled city of Jericho. The springs there were fed by the streams that flowed from the hills above. Moses could see mile after mile of the Promised Land which his people would surely enter. There on the mountaintop he died, and it is written that he was buried "in a valley in the land of Moab; but no man knoweth of his grave unto this day."

HONESTY

❦ Honesty

When you think of someone's reputation, you usually think first of his or her honesty. If you say, "He's a man of honor," you mean that person is someone who tells the truth, keeps his word, and does what he says he's going to do. When you are deciding whether or not you want to associate with someone, his honesty is probably one of the first yardsticks you'll use to measure him.

George Washington wrote, "I hope I shall always possess firmness and virtue enough to maintain what I consider the most enviable of all titles, the character of an honest man." He knew that honesty is usually a good reputation's greatest possession, as well as its greatest armor for staying good. Whatever other good traits someone possesses, they do a reputation no good without honesty. Someone may be smart, friendly, hard-working, and determined, but all those qualities are poisoned by deceit.

Very early on, you will be identified by classmates and friends as an honest or dishonest person. When people know you are honest they will like you, rely on you, and want to be around you. Here, however, is the sober truth about dishonest reputations: No one wants to be around a liar. So it is very important that you guard your honest reputation. Just one or two lies can destroy it very quickly. A reputation for not telling the truth, on the other hand, may take a very long time to erase.

You guard your honest reputation by constantly practicing honesty. Like any other habit, honesty must be cultivated. The more you do it, the more it becomes a part of your nature.

Lying, like any other bad habit, usually starts in small, seemingly harmless measures. "He who permits himself to tell a lie once," Thomas Jefferson wrote, "finds it much easier to do it a second time, til at length it becomes habitual. He tells lies without attending to it, and truths without the world's believing him. This falsehood of the tongue leads to that of the heart, and in time depraves all its good dispositions." So we have to guard against "little white lies" that eventually may destroy our love of the truth.

Sometimes honesty has its costs. A friend may want you to do something wrong, and you may make him angry— even lose the friendship—by saying no. Or you may have to watch others get ahead by cheating or playing loose with the rules. At times like that, you may be tempted to think that perhaps crime does pay. And occasionally it does—but only for a short while. Eventually, dishonesty catches up with those who practice it. In the meantime, it's best to remember the words of Sir Thomas More in Robert Bolt's play, *A Man For All Seasons*: "Since in fact we see that avarice, anger, envy, pride, sloth, lust, and stupidity commonly profit far beyond humility, chastity, fortitude, justice, and thought, and have to choose, to be human at all . . . then perhaps we *must* stand fast a little—even at the risk of being heroes."

In the end, honesty is more than telling the truth to other people. It also means being honest with ourselves. It means doing the right thing even when we know no one else is looking. Why? One reason is that deceit takes a terrible toll on our own sense of self-respect. It can make us nothing but unhappy. Another reason was stated by the ancient Greek philosopher Demosthenes, who pointed out that "what we have in us of the image of God is the love of truth."

❧ Honest Abe

RETOLD BY HORATIO ALGER

*Our two most beloved American presidents,
Washington and Lincoln, are remembered for their
honesty. The following tales remind us that honesty
in private life makes honesty in public office. More
important, they show us that habits of a truthful
heart begin early in life.*

The Young Storekeeper

As a clerk, Abe proved honest and efficient, and my
readers will be interested in some illustrations of the former
trait which I find in Dr. Holland's interesting volume.

One day a woman came into the store and purchased
sundry articles. They footed up two dollars and six and a
quarter cents, or the young clerk thought they did. We do
not hear nowadays of six and a quarter cents, but this was
a coin borrowed from the Spanish currency, and was well
known in my own boyhood.

The bill was paid, and the woman was entirely satisfied.
But the young storekeeper, not feeling quite sure as to the
accuracy of his calculation, added up the items once more.
To his dismay he found that the sum total should have been
but two dollars.

"I've made her pay six and a quarter cents too much,"
said Abe, disturbed.

It was a trifle, and many clerks would have dismissed it
as such. But Abe was too conscientious for that.

"The money must be paid back," he decided.

This would have been easy enough had the woman lived "just round the corner," but, as the young man knew, she lived between two and three miles away. This, however, did not alter the matter. It was night, but he closed and locked the store, and walked to the residence of his customer. Arrived there, he explained the matter, paid over the six and a quarter cents, and returned satisfied. If I were a capitalist, I would be will to lend money to such a young man without security.

Here is another illustration of young Lincoln's strict honesty:

A woman entered the store and asked for half a pound of tea.

The young clerk weighed it out and handed it to her in a parcel. This was the last sale of the day.

The next morning, when commencing his duties, Abe discovered a four-ounce weight on the scales. It flashed upon him at once that he had used this in the sale of the night previous, and so, of course, given his customer short weight. I am afraid that there are many country merchants who would not have been much worried by this discovery. Not so the young clerk in whom we are interested. He weighed out the balance of the half pound, shut up the store, and carried it to the defrauded customer. I think my young readers will begin to see that the name so often given, in later times to President Lincoln, of "Honest Old Abe," was well deserved. A man who begins by strict honesty in his youth is not likely to change as he grows older, and mercantile honesty is some guarantee of political honesty.

Working Out a Book

All the information we can obtain about this early time is interesting for it was then that Abe was laying the foundation of his future eminence. His mind and character were slowly developing, and shaping themselves for the future.

From Mr. Lamon's *Life* I quote a paragraph which will throw light upon his habits and tastes at the age of seventeen:

"Abe loved to lie under a shade tree, or up in the loft of the cabin, and read, cipher, and scribble. At night he sat by the chimney jamb, and ciphered by the light of the fire, on the wooden fire shovel. When the shovel was fairly covered, he would shave it off with Tom Lincoln's drawing knife, and begin again. In the daytime he used boards for the same purpose, out of doors, and went through the shaving process everlastingly. His stepmother repeats often that 'he read every book he could lay his hands on.' She says, 'Abe read diligently. He read every book he could lay his hands on, and when he came across a passage that struck him, he would write it down on boards if he had no paper, and keep it there until he did get paper. Then he would rewrite it, look at it, repeat it. He had a copybook, a kind of scrapbook, in which he put down all things, and thus preserved them.'"

I am tempted also to quote a reminiscence of John Hanks, who lived with the Lincolns from the time Abe was fourteen to the time he became eighteen years of age: "When Lincoln—Abe—and I returned to the house from work, he would go to the cupboard, snatch a piece of cornbread, take down a book, sit down on a chair, cock his legs up as high as his head, and read. He and I worked barefooted, grubbed it, plowed, mowed, and cradled together; plowed corn, gathered it, and shucked corn. Abraham read constantly when he had opportunity."

It may well be supposed, however, that the books upon which Abe could lay hands were few in number. There were no libraries, either public or private, in the neighborhood, and he was obliged to read what he could get rather than those which he would have chosen, had he been able to select from a large collection. Still, it is a matter of interest to know what books he actually did read at this formative period. Some of them certainly were worth reading, such as *Aesop's Fables, Robinson Crusoe, Pilgrim's Progress, a History of the United States,* and Weems's *Life of Washington.* The last book Abe borrowed from a neighbor, old Josiah Crawford (I follow the statement of Mr. Lamon, rather than of Dr. Holland, who says it was Master Crawford, his teacher). When not reading it, he laid it away in a part of the cabin where he thought it would be free from harm, but it so happened that just behind the shelf on which he placed it was a great crack between the logs of the wall. One night a storm came up suddenly, the rain beat in through the crevice, and soaked the borrowed book through and through. The book was almost utterly spoiled. Abe felt very uneasy, for a book was valuable in his eyes, as well as in the eyes of its owner.

He took the damaged volume and trudged over to Mr. Crawford's in some perplexity and mortification.

"Well, Abe, what brings you over so early?" said Mr. Crawford.

"I've got some bad news for you," answered Abe, with lengthened face.

"Bad news! What is it?"

"You know the book you lent me—*The Life of Washington?*"

"Yes, yes."

"Well, the rain last night spoiled it." And Abe showed the book, wet to a pulp inside, at the same time explaining how it had been injured.

"It's too bad, I vum! You'd ought to pay for it, Abe. You must have been dreadful careless!"

"I'd pay for it if I had any money, Mr. Crawford."

"If you've got no money, you can work it out," said Crawford.

"I'll do whatever you think right."

So it was arranged that Abe should work three days for Crawford, "pulling fodder," the value of his labor being rated at twenty-five cents a day. As the book had cost seventy-five cents this would be regarded as satisfactory. So Abe worked his three days, and discharged the debt. Mr. Lamon is disposed to find fault with Crawford for exacting this penalty, but it appears to me only equitable, and I am glad to think that Abe was willing to act honorably in the matter.

The Character of a Happy Life

HENRY WOTTEN

Honesty is armor for the soul.

How happy is he born and taught,
    That serveth not another's will;
Whose armor is his honest thought,
    And simple truth his utmost skill!
Whose passions not his masters are,

Whose soul is still prepared for death,
Untied unto the worldly care
　　Of public fame, or private breath;

Who envies none that chance doth raise,
　　Or vice; who never understood
How deepest wounds are given by praise;
　　Nor rules of state, but rules of good:

Who hath his life from rumors freed,
　　Whose conscience is his strong retreat;
Whose state can neither flatterers feed,
　　Nor ruin make oppressors great;

Who God doth late and early pray,
　　More of his grace than gifts to lend;
And entertains the harmless day
　　With a religious book or friend.

This man is freed from servile bands,
　　Or hope to rise, or fear to fall;
Lord of himself, though not of lands;
　　And having nothing, yet hath all.

The Emperor and the Peasant Boy

This old tale from Mexico reminds us that one heart's honesty has the power to turn others in the right direction.

Long ago, during the days of the Aztec empire in what we now call Mexico, there ruled an emperor who sometimes liked to disguise himself and walk the city streets and country footpaths alone. He knew his subjects would speak far more openly and fearlessly to a common stranger than to their own emperor, and he was able to learn much about his people he would not have known had he always stayed on his throne.

One day the disguised emperor was wandering the countryside when he came upon a little peasant boy gathering a few sticks of firewood so his family might cook their dinner.

"You are working hard, my little friend," the emperor said, "but there's barely enough wood here to start a fire. Why don't you go into that thick forest on the hillside? There are plenty of sticks to be picked up there."

The boy shook his head.

"That hillside is part of the emperor's forest. He has set it aside for his hunting parties. No one may enter without his permission, and to pick up sticks there would mean instant death."

"Only if you were caught," the emperor smiled. "The forest is deserted now, and you could slip in and out easily. No one will see you, and I promise I will keep quiet."

"Thanks for the advice," the boy replied coldly, "but I think I'll just gather what I find here."

"But think of all that wood going to waste on the forest

floor! Surely your emperor must be a selfish, unkind ruler not to share it with you."

"It's true this law is harsh and unfair," the boy said angrily. "The emperor has no use for the sticks in the forest, and yet he denies them to many in need. But should I do wrong because the law is unjust? No, I will not enter the forest, not as long as there is a better way."

The boy picked up his meager bundle of sticks and turned for home with tears in his eyes.

The next day a royal messenger appeared at the peasant boy's home and commanded his whole family to come to the palace at once. They set out in fear and trembling, unable to imagine why they were being summoned.

They were led before the emperor himself, sitting on his throne in all his royal garb. The peasant boy recognized his face at once, and he paled with terror.

"You were the one who urged me to enter the royal forest!" he cried.

"Don't be afraid," the emperor said. "You've done no wrong. You refused to steal when you had the chance, and you insisted on obeying your emperor's law. I want to meet your parents. They have raised you well, and will be rewarded."

He pointed to a chest of gold, enough to keep want from their humble door for the rest of their lives.

"But there is something more important," the emperor went on. "You were right about my law. It is unjust. From now on, the royal forest is open to all."

He took the peasant boy by the arm.

"You wondered if there were not a better way," he said. "There was. Your virtue has reached the heart of your emperor."

⚛ The Good Bishop
ADAPTED FROM VICTOR HUGO

In this story from Victor Hugo's Les Misérables, *we see a lie told to help another. This is one of those rare occasions when lying makes sense.*

Jean Valjean was a wood-chopper's son, who, while very young, was left an orphan. His older sister brought him up, but when he was seventeen years of age, his sister's husband died, and upon Jean came the labor of supporting her seven little children. Although a man of great strength, he found it very difficult to provide food for them at the poor trade he followed.

One winter day he was without work, and the children were crying for bread. They were nearly starved. And, when he could withstand their entreaties no longer, he went out in the night, and, breaking a baker's window with his fist, carried home a loaf of bread for the famished children. The next morning he was arrested for stealing, his bleeding hand convicting him.

For this crime he was sent to the galleys with an iron collar riveted around his neck, with a chain attached, which bound him to his galley seat. Here he remained four years, then he tried to escape, but was caught, and three years were added to his sentence. Then he made a second attempt, and also failed, the result of which was that he remained nineteen years as a galley slave for stealing a single loaf of bread.

When Jean left the prison, his heart was hardened. He felt like a wolf. His wrongs had embittered him, and he was more like an animal than a man. He came with every man's hand raised against him to the town where the good bishop lived.

At the inn they would not receive him because they knew him to be an ex-convict and a dangerous man. Wherever he went, the knowledge of him went before, and everyone drove him away. They would not even allow him to sleep in a dog kennel or give him the food they had saved for the dog. Everywhere he went they cried: "Be off! Go away, or you will get a charge of shot." Finally, he wandered to the house of the good bishop, and a good man he was.

For his duties as a bishop, he received from the state 3,000 francs a year; but he gave away to the poor 2,800 francs of it. He was a simple, loving man, with a great heart, who thought nothing of himself, but loved everybody. And everybody loved him.

Jean, when he entered the bishop's house, was a most forbidding and dangerous character. He shouted in a harsh loud voice: "Look here, I am a galley slave. Here is my yellow passport. It says: 'Five year for robbery and fourteen years for trying to escape. The man is very dangerous.' Now that you know who I am, will you give me a little food, and let me sleep in the stable?"

The good bishop said: "Sit down and warm yourself. You will take supper with me, and after that sleep here."

Jean could hardly believe his senses. He was dumb with joy. He told the bishop that he had money, and would pay for his supper and lodging.

But the priest said: "You are welcome. This is not my house, but the house of Christ. Your name was known to me before you showed me your passport. You are my brother."

After supper the bishop took one of the silver candlesticks that he had received as a Christmas present, and, giving Jean the other, led him to his room, where a good bed was provided. In the middle of the night Jean awoke with a hardened heart. He felt that the time had come to get revenge for all his wrongs. He remembered the silver knives and forks that had been used for supper, and made up his mind to steal them, and go away in the night. So he took what he could find, sprang into the garden, and disappeared.

When the bishop awoke, and saw his silver gone, he said: "I have been thinking for a long time that I ought not to keep the silver. I should have given it to the poor, and certainly this man was poor."

At breakfast time five soldiers brought Jean back to the bishop's house. When they entered, the bishop, looking at him, said: "Oh, you are back again! I am glad to see you. I gave you the candlesticks, too, which are silver also, and will bring forty francs. Why did you not take them?"

Jean was stunned indeed by these words. So were the soldiers. "This man told us the truth, did he?" they cried. "We thought he had stolen the silver and was running away. So we quickly arrested him."

But the good bishop only said: "It was a mistake to have him brought back. Let him go. The silver is his. I gave it to him."

So the officers went away.

"Is it true," Jean whispered to the bishop, "that I am free? I may go?"

"Yes," he replied, "but before you go take your candlesticks."

Jean trembled in every limb, and took the candlesticks like one in a dream.

"Now," said the bishop, "depart in peace, but do not go through the garden, for the front door is always open to you day and night."

Jean looked as though he would faint.

Then the bishop took his hand, and said: "Never forget you have promised me you would use the money to become an honest man."

He did not remember having promised anything, but stood silent while the bishop continued solemnly:

"Jean Valjean, my brother, you no longer belong to evil, but to good. I have bought your soul for you. I withdrew it from black thoughts and the spirit of hate, and gave it to God."

❧ The Indian Cinderella

RETOLD BY CYRUS MACMILLAN

This North American Indian tale is about how honesty is rewarded and dishonesty punished. Glooskap, mentioned in the opening paragraph, was a god of the Eastern Woodlands Indians.

On the shores of a wide bay on the Atlantic coast there dwelt in old times a great Indian warrior. It was said that he had been one of Glooskap's best helpers and friends, and that he had done for him many wonderful deeds. But that, no man knows. He had, however, a very wonderful and strange power: he could make himself invisible. He could thus mingle unseen with his enemies and listen to their plots. He was known among the people as Strong Wind, the Invisible. He dwelt with his sister in a tent near the sea, and his sister helped him greatly in his work. Many maidens would have been glad to marry him, and he was much sought after because of his mighty deeds; and it was known that Strong Wind would marry the first maiden who could see him as he came home at night. Many made the trial, but it was a long time before one succeeded.

Strong Wind used a clever trick to test the truthfulness of all who sought to win him. Each evening as the day went down, his sister walked on the beach with any girl who wished to make the trial. His sister could always see him, but no one else could see him. And as he came home from work in the twilight, his sister as she saw him drawing near would ask the girl who sought him, "Do you see him?" And each girl would falsely answer "Yes." And his sister would ask, "With what does he draw his sled?" And each girl would answer, "With the hide of a moose," or "With a pole," or "With a great cord." And then his sister would know that they all had lied, for their answers were mere guesses. And many tried and lied and failed, for Strong Wind would not marry any who were untruthful.

There lived in the village a great chief who had three daughters. Their mother had long been dead. One of these was much younger than the others. She was very beautiful and gentle and well beloved by all, and for that reason her older sisters were very jealous of her charms and treated her very cruelly. They clothed her in rags that she might be ugly; and they cut off her long black hair; and they burned her face with coals from the fire that she might be scarred and disfigured. And they lied to their father, telling him that she had done these things herself. But the girl was patient and kept her gentle heart and went gladly about her work.

Like other girls, the chief's two eldest daughters tried to win Strong Wind. One evening, as the day went down, they walked on the shore with Strong Wind's sister and waited for his coming. Soon he came home from his day's work, drawing his sled. And his sister asked as usual, "Do you see him?" And each one, lying, answered "Yes." And she asked, "Of what is his shoulder strap made?" And each, guessing, said "Of rawhide." Then they entered the tent where they hoped to see Strong Wind eating his supper; and when he took off his coat and his moccasins they could see them, but more than these they saw nothing. And Strong Wind knew that they had lied, and he kept himself from their sight, and they went home dismayed.

One day the chief's youngest daughter with her rags and her burned face resolved to seek Strong Wind. She patched her clothes with bits of birch bark from the trees, and put on the few little ornaments she possessed, and went forth to try to see the Invisible One as all the other girls of the village had done before. And her sisters laughed at her and called her "fool." And as she passed along the road all the people laughed at her because of her tattered frock and her burned face, but silently she went her way.

Strong Wind's sister received the little girl kindly, and at twilight she took her to the beach. Soon Strong Wind came home drawing his sled. And his sister asked, "Do you see him?" And the girl answered "No," and his sister wondered greatly because she spoke the truth. And again she asked, "Do you see him now?" And the girl answered, "Yes, and he is very wonderful." And she asked, "With what does he draw his sled?" And the girl answered, "With the Rainbow," and she was much afraid. And she asked further, "Of what is his bowstring?" And the girl answered, "His bowstring is the Milky Way."

Then Strong Wind's sister knew that because the girl

had spoken the truth at first her brother had made himself visible to her. And she said, "Truly, you have seen him." And she took her home and bathed her, and all the scars disappeared from her face and body; and her hair grew long and black again like the raven's wing; and she gave her fine clothes to wear and many rich ornaments. Then she bade her take the wife's seat in the tent. Soon Strong Wind entered and sat beside her, and called her his bride. The very next day she became his wife, and ever afterward she helped him to do great deeds. The girl's two elder sisters were very cross and they wondered greatly at what had taken place. But Strong Wind, who knew of their cruelty, resolved to punish them. Using his great power, he changed them both into aspen trees and rooted them in the earth. And since that day the leaves of the aspen have always trembled, and they shiver in fear at the approach of Strong Wind, it matters not how softly he comes, for they are still mindful of his great power and anger because of their lies and their cruelty to their sister long ago.

The Lie That Deserved Another

Exaggerations seldom go unnoticed, as this tale from Southeast Asia shows us.

A man returned home after traveling abroad, eager to brag about his adventures.

"I've seen things you've never imagined, not even in your dreams," he told his friends. "Once I saw the longest ship afloat. The captain was standing at the stern, and he gave the cabin boy a message to take to the first mate, who stood at the bow. The lad was only ten when he started; his white beard swabbed the deck by the time he'd reached the mast. I didn't wait to see if he lived long enough to make it the rest of the way."

His friends looked at each other. One said:

"That's nothing. You didn't need to leave home to find sights like that. Why, in the forest just over that ridge, I've seen a tree so tall that it poked a hole in the sky. Once a bird tried to fly over the top, but by the time it reached just the third branch from the bottom, it was too old to go any further. So it stopped and laid an egg, and told its chick to continue the journey. Seven generations of birds have been flying toward the top, and they're not halfway yet."

"That's ridiculous," the traveler scoffed. "I've never heard such a lie in my life."

"If that's the case," asked his friend, "where did you get the tree to make the mast for your ship?"

The Piece of String
GUY DE MAUPASSANT

This story reminds us that a lie—even a little one—can kill.

Along all the roads around Goderville, peasants and their wives were coming in toward the town for it was market day.

There was a crowd in Goderville marketplace, a confusion of men and beasts. Horns of oxen, long-napped tall hats of the richer peasants, and the women's headdresses rose above the surface of the throng. Voices, bawling, sharp, and squeaky, were mingled in barbarous never-ending clamor, dominated at times by the mighty guffaw of some broad-chested countryman having his joke, or by the long-drawn lowing of a cow tied up to the wall of a house.

It all smelled of stables, milk and manure, of hay and sweat; gave off, in fact, that terribly sour savor, human, yet bestial, characteristic of workers in the fields.

Master Hauchecorne, of Breauté, coming in to Goderville, was making his way toward the marketplace when he perceived on the ground a short piece of string. Master Hauchecorne, thrifty like every true Norman, thought that anything was worth picking up that could be put to any use; so, stooping painfully, for he suffered from rheumatism, he picked up the bit of thin cord, and was carefully rolling it up when he observed Master Malandain, the saddler, standing in his doorway, looking at him. They had once had a difference about a halter, and owed each other a grudge, for both were by nature inclined to bear malice. Master Hauchecorne was seized with a sort of shame at being thus seen by his enemy, grubbing in the mud for a bit of string. He abruptly hid his spoil under his blouse, then put it in his trouser pocket, and pretended to be still looking on the ground for something he could not find. Finally he went off toward the market, with his head poked forward, bent nearly double by his rheumatism.

He was swallowed up at once in the slow-moving, noisy crowd, disputing over its interminable bargainings. Peasants were punching the cows, moving hither and thither, in perpetual fear of being taken in, and not daring to make up their minds; scrutinizing the seller's eye, to try and discover the deceit in the man and the blemish in his beast.

The women, placing their great baskets at their feet, had

taken out their fowls, which lay on the ground with legs tied together, eyes wild with fright, and crests all scarlet.

They listened to the offers made, and held out for their prices with wooden, impassive faces; then, suddenly deciding to take the bid, would scream after the customer as he slowly walked away:

"Done with you, Master Anthime. You shall have it."

Then, little by little, the marketplace emptied, and, the Angelus ringing midday, those who lived too far away straggled into the inns.

At Jourdain's the big dining room was crowded with guests, just as the huge courtyard was crowded with vehicles of every breed, carts, cabriolets, wagonettes, tilburys, covered carts innumerable, yellow with mud, out of trim and patched, some raising their two shafts, like arms, to the sky, some with nose on the ground and tail in the air.

Right up against the diners the immense fireplace, flaming brightly, threw a mighty heat onto the backs of the right-hand row seated at table. Three jacks were turning, garnished with chickens, pigeons, and legs of mutton, and a delectable odor of roast meat and of gravy streaming over the well-browned crackling rose from the hearth, bringing joy to the heart and water to the mouth.

All the aristocracy of the plow dined at M. Jourdain's, innkeeper and horse-dealer, a shrewd fellow, and a "warm man."

The dishes were passed, and emptied, together with mugs of golden cider. Everyone told the story of his bargains, and asked his neighbor about the crops. The weather was good for green stuff, but a little damp for corn.

Suddenly, from the courtyard in front of the house, came the roll of a drum.

All but a few, too lazy to move, jumped up at once, and flew to the doors and windows, their mouths still full and their napkins in their hands.

Finishing off the roll of his drum, the town crier shouted in staccato tones, with a scansion of phrase peculiarly out of rhythm:

"This is to inform the inhabitants of Goderville, and all others—present at the market, that there was lost this morning on the Beuzeville road between nine and ten o'clock, a black leather pocketbook, containing five hundred francs and some business papers. It should be returned—to the Town Hall immediately, or to Master Fortuné Houlbrèque at Manneville. A reward of twenty francs is offered."

The man went by, and presently the dull rumble of the drum was heard again, and then the crier's voice, fainter in the distance.

Everyone began discussing the event, calculating the chances of Master Houlbrèque's recovering or not recovering his pocketbook.

And so the meal came to an end.

They were finishing their coffee when the brigadier of gendarmes appeared at the door, and asked:

"Is Master Hauchecorne, of Breauté, here?"

Master Hauchecorne, seated at the far end of the table, answered:

"Here!"

"Master Hauchecorne," proceeded the officer, "will you be so good as to come with me to the Town Hall? The mayor would like to speak to you."

Surprised and uneasy, the peasant gulped down his cognac, rose, and stooping even more than in the morning (for the first steps after resting were always particularly painful), got himself started, repeating:

"All right! I'm coming!" and following the sergeant.

The mayor was awaiting him, seated in an armchair. He was the notary of the district, a stout, serious man, full of pompous phrases.

"Master Hauchecorne," said he, "you were seen this morning to pick up, on the Beuzeville road, the pocketbook lost by Master Houbrèque, of Manneville."

The peasant, in stupefaction, gazed at the mayor, intimidated at once by this suspicion which lay heavy upon him without his comprehending it.

"Me? Me—me pick up that pocketbook?"

"Yes, you."

"On my word of honor, I didn't! Why, I didn't even know about it!"

"You were seen."

"Seen? I? Who saw me?"

"M. Malandain, the saddler."

Then the old man remembered, and understood. Reddening with anger, he said:

"Ah! He saw me, that animal! Well, what he saw me pick up was this string, look here, M. le Maire!"

And rummaging in his pocket, he pulled out the little piece of string.

But the mayor shook his head incredulously.

"You won't make me believe, Master Hauchecorne, that M. Malandain, a trustworthy man, took that piece of string for a pocketbook."

The enraged peasant raised his hand, spat solemnly to show his good faith, and repeated:

"It's God's truth, all the same, the sacred truth, M. le

Maire. There, on my soul and honor, I say it again."

The mayor proceeded.

"After having picked up the article in question, you even went on searching in the mud, to make sure a coin or two mightn't have fallen out."

The poor old fellow choked with indignation and fear.

"To say such things! . . . How can anyone . . . telling lies like that, to undo an honest man! How can anyone?"

Protest as he would, he was not believed.

They confronted him with M. Malandain, who repeated and substantiated his story. The two abused each other for a whole hour. By his own request, Master Hauchecorne was searched. Nothing was found on him.

At last the mayor, thoroughly puzzled, dismissed him, warning him that he was going to give notice to the public prosecutor and take his instructions.

The news had spread. As he went out of the Town Hall the old man was surrounded, and all sorts of serious or mocking questions were put to him, but no one showed the slightest indignation. He began to tell the story of the piece of string. They did not believe him. Everybody laughed.

He went on, stopped by everyone, stopping everyone he knew, to tell his story over and over again, protesting, showing his pockets turned inside out, to prove that he had nothing on him. The only answer he got was:

"Get along, you sly old dog!"

He began to feel angry, worrying himself into a fever of irritation, miserable at not being believed, at a loss what to do, and continually repeating his story. Night came on. It was time to go home. He set out with three neighbors, to whom he showed the spot where he had picked up the piece of string; and the whole way home he kept talking of his misadventure.

In the evening he made a round of the village of Breauté, to tell everybody all about it. He came across unbelievers only.

He was ill all night.

The next day, about one o'clock, Marius Paumelle, a laborer at Master Breton's, a farmer at Ymauville, restored the pocketbook and its contents to Master Houlbrèque, of Manneville.

The man declared that he found the object on the road; but not being able to read, he had taken it home and given it to his master.

The news spread through the neighborhood. Master Hauchecorne was informed of it, and started off at once on a round, to tell his story all over again, with its proper ending. It was a triumph.

"What knocked me over," he said, "was not so much the thing itself, you know, but that charge of lying. There's nothing hurts a man so much as being thought a liar."

The whole day long he talked of his adventure, telling it to people he met on the roads, to people drinking at the inns, and even at the church door on the following Sunday. He stopped perfect strangers to tell [them] about it. He was easy in his mind now, and yet—there was something that bothered him, though he could not exactly arrive at what it was. People had an amused look while they were listening to him. They did not seem convinced. He felt as if a lot of tattle was going on behind his back.

On the Tuesday of the following week he went off to Goderville market, urged thereto solely by the desire to tell his story. Malandain, standing at his door, began to laugh as he went past. Why?

He began his story to a farmer of Criquetot, who did not let him finish, but, giving him a dig in the pit of the stomach, shouted in his face: "Get along, you old rogue!" and turned his back.

Master Hauchecorne stopped short, confused, and more and more uneasy. Why was he being called an "old rogue?"

When he was seated at the table at Jourdain's inn he began again to explain the whole affair.

A horse-dealer from Montvillier called out:

"Come, come, that's an old trick; I know all about your piece of string!"

Hauchecorne stammered:

"But it's been found, that pocketbook!"

But the other went on:

"Oh! shut up, old boy, there's one who finds, and another who brings back. All on the strict QT."

The peasant was thunderstruck. He understood at last. It was insinuated that he had caused the pocketbook to be taken by someone else, an accomplice.

He tried to protest, but the whole table began laughing.

He could not finish his dinner, and went away, with every one jeering at him.

He returned home, ashamed and indignant, choking with anger and bewilderment, and all the more overwhelmed because, in his artful Norman brain, he knew himself capable of having done what they accused him of, and of even boasting about it afterward, as though it were a feat. He realized confusedly that it would be impossible to prove his innocence, his tricky nature being known to all. And he felt wounded to the heart by the injustice of this suspicion.

Then he began again to tell his story, making the tale a little longer every day, adding new reasons every time, more energetic protestations, most solemn oaths which he thought out and prepared in his solitary moments, for his mind was solely occupied by the story of the piece of string. They believed him less and less as his defense became more and more elaborate, his arguments more subtle.

"H'm! That's only to cover up his tracks," the hearers would say behind his back.

He was conscious of all this, but went on eating his heart out, exhausting himself in fruitless efforts.

Before the very eyes of people, he wasted away.

Jokers now would make him tell them the "piece of string" to amuse them, as one makes old soldiers tell about their battles. His spirit, undetermined, grew feebler and feebler.

Toward the end of December he took to his bed.

He died at the beginning of January, and in his last delirium still protested his innocence, repeating:

"A little piece of string . . . a little piece of string . . . look, here it is, M. le Maire!"

﹋ The Question

*Look for honesty in yourself before you seek it in
your neighbors.*

Were the whole world good as you—
            not an atom better—
     Were it just as pure and true,
     Just as pure and true as you;
     Just as strong in faith and works;
     Just as free from crafty quirks;
     All extortion, all deceit;
     Schemes its neighbors to defeat;
     Schemes its neighbors to defraud;
     Schemes some culprit to applaud—
Would this world be better?

If the whole world followed you—
            followed to the letter—
     Would it be a nobler world,
     All deceit and falsehood hurled
     From it altogether;
     Malice, selfishness, and lust,
     Banished from beneath the crust,
     Covering human hearts from view—
     Tell me, if it followed you,
Would the world be better?

The Story of Regulus

RETOLD BY JAMES BALDWIN

This ancient story is about the Roman general and statesman Marcus Atilius Regulus. It takes place in the third century B.C. during the First Punic War between Rome and Carthage. The legend of how Regulus kept his word made him famous in Roman history.

On the other side of the sea from Rome there was once a great city named Carthage. The Roman people were never very friendly to the people of Carthage, and at last a war began between them. For a long time it was hard to tell which would prove the stronger. First the Romans would gain a battle, and then the men of Carthage would gain a battle; and so the war went on for many years.

Among the Romans there was a brave general named Regulus—a man of whom it was said that he never broke his word. It so happened after a while that Regulus was taken prisoner and carried to Carthage. Ill and very lonely, he dreamed of his wife and little children so far away beyond the sea; and he had but little hope of ever seeing them again. He loved his home dearly, but he believed that his first duty was to his country; and so he had left all to fight in this cruel war.

He had lost a battle, it is true, and had been taken prisoner. Yet he knew that the Romans were gaining ground, and the people of Carthage were afraid of being beaten in the end. They had sent into other countries to hire soldiers to help them. But even with these they would not be able to fight much longer against Rome.

One day some of the rulers of Carthage came to the prison to talk with Regulus.

"We should like to make peace with the Roman people," they said, "and we are sure that, if your rulers at home knew how the war is going, they would be glad to make peace with us. We will set you free and let you go home, if you will agree to do as we say."

"What is that?" asked Regulus.

"In the first place," they said, "you must tell the Romans about the battles which you have lost, and you must make it plain to them that they have not gained anything by the war. In the second place, you must promise us that, if they will not make peace, you will come back to your prison."

"Very well," said Regulus. "I promise you that if they will not make peace, I will come back to prison."

And so they let him go, for they knew that a great Roman would keep his word.

When he came to Rome, all the people greeted him gladly. His wife and children were very happy, for they thought that now they would not be parted again. The white-haired Fathers who made the laws for the city came to see him. They asked him about the war.

"I was sent from Carthage to ask you to make peace," he said. "But it will not be wise to make peace. True, we have been beaten in a few battles, but our army is gaining ground every day. The people of Carthage are afraid, and well they may be. Keep on with the war a little while longer, and Carthage shall be yours. As for me, I have come to bid my wife and children and Rome farewell. Tomorrow I will start back to Carthage and to prison, for I have promised."

Then the Fathers tried to persuade him to stay.

"Let us send another man in your place," they said.

"Shall a Roman not keep his word?" answered Regulus. "I am ill, and at the best have not long to live. I will go back as I promised."

His wife and little children wept, and his sons begged him not to leave them again.

"I have given my word," said Regulus. "The rest will be taken care of."

Then he bade them goodbye, and went bravely back to the prison and the cruel death which he expected.

This was the kind of courage that made Rome the greatest city in the world.

ᕦ Truth and Falsehood

As this folktale from Greece points out, the virtuous soul not only loves truth for its own sake, it loathes the actions of falsehood. Deceit is far more painful for that soul than bearing the hardships that sometimes accompany honesty.

Once upon a time Truth and Falsehood met each other on the road.

"Good afternoon," said Truth.

"Good afternoon," returned Falsehood. "And how are you doing these days?"

"Not very well at all, I'm afraid," sighed Truth. "The times are tough for a fellow like me, you know."

"Yes, I can see that," said Falsehood, glancing up and down at Truth's ragged clothes. "You look like you haven't had a bite to eat in quite some time."

"To be honest, I haven't," admitted Truth. "No one seems to want to employ me nowadays. Wherever I go, most people ignore me or mock me. It's getting discouraging, I can tell you. I'm beginning to ask myself why I put up with it."

"And why the devil do you? Come with me, and I'll show you how to get along. There's no reason in the world why you can't stuff yourself with as much as you want to eat, like me, and dress in the finest clothes, like me. But you must promise not to say a word against me while we're together."

So Truth promised and agreed to go along with Falsehood for a while, not because he liked his company so much, but because he was so hungry he thought he'd faint soon if he didn't get something into his stomach. They walked down the road until they came to a city, and Falsehood at once led the way to the very best table at the very best restaurant.

"Waiter, bring us your choicest meats, your sweetest sweets, your finest wine!" he called, and they ate and drank all afternoon. At last, when they could hold no more, Falsehood began banging his fist on the table and calling for the manager, who came running at once.

"What the devil kind of place is this?" Falsehood snapped. "I gave that waiter a gold piece nearly an hour ago, and he still hasn't brought our change."

The manager summoned the waiter, who said he'd never even seen a penny out of the gentleman.

"What?" Falsehood shouted, so that everyone in the place turned and looked. "I can't believe this place! Innocent, law-abiding citizens come in to eat, and you rob them of their hard-earned money! You're a pack of thieves and liars! You may have fooled me once, but you'll never see me again! Here!" He threw a gold piece at the manager. "Now this time bring me my change!"

But the manager, fearing his restaurant's reputation would suffer, refused to take the gold piece, and instead brought Falsehood change for the first gold piece he claimed to have spent. Then he took the waiter aside and called him a scoundrel, and said he had a mind to fire him. And as much as the waiter protested that he'd never collected a cent from the man, the manager refused to believe him.

"Oh, Truth, where have you hidden yourself?" the waiter sighed. "Have you now deserted even us hard-working souls?"

"No, I'm here," Truth groaned to himself, "but my judgment gave way to my hunger, and now I can't speak up without breaking my promise to Falsehood."

As soon as they were on the street, Falsehood gave a hearty laugh and slapped Truth on the back. "You see how the world works?" he cried. "I managed it all quite well, don't you think?"

But Truth slipped from his side.

"I'd rather starve than live as you do," he said.

And so Truth and Falsehood went their separate ways, and never traveled together again.

Ꮼ Truth, Falsehood, Fire, and Water

This tale about the eternal struggle between truth and falsehood is told in Ethiopia and other eastern African nations.

Long ago Truth, Falsehood, Fire, and Water were journeying together and came upon a herd of cattle. They talked it over and decided it would be fairest to divide the herd into four parts, so each could take home an equal share.

But Falsehood was greedy and schemed to get more for himself.

"Listen to my warning," he whispered, pulling Water to one side. "Fire plans to burn all the grass and trees along your banks and drive your cattle away across the plains so he can have them for himself. If I were you, I'd extinguish him now, and then we can have his share of the cattle for ourselves."

Water was foolish enough to listen to Falsehood, and he dashed himself upon Fire and put him out.

Next Falsehood crept toward Truth.

"Look what Water has done," he whispered. "He has murdered Fire and taken his cattle. We should not consort with the likes of him. We should take all the cattle and go to the mountains."

Truth believed Falsehood and agreed to his plan. Together they drove the cattle into the mountains.

"Wait for me!" Water called, and he hurried after them, but of course he could not run uphill. So he was left all alone in the valley below.

When they reached the top of the highest mountain, Falsehood turned to Truth and laughed.

"I've tricked you, stupid fool," he shrieked. "Now you must give me all the cattle and be my servant, or I'll destroy you."

"Yes, you have tricked me," Truth admitted, "but I will never be your servant."

And so they fought, and when they clashed the thunder rolled back and forth across the mountain tops. Again and again they threw themselves together, but neither could destroy the other.

Finally they decided to call upon the Wind to declare a winner of the contest. So Wind came rushing up the mountain slopes, and he listened to what they had to say.

"It is not for me to declare a winner in this fight," he told them. "Truth and Falsehood are destined to struggle. Sometimes Truth will win, but other times Falsehood will prevail, and then Truth must rise up and fight again. Until the end of the world. Truth must battle Falsehood, and must never rest or let down his guard, or he will be finished once and for all."

And so Truth and Falsehood are fighting to this day.

LOYALTY

Loyalty

The great Jewish teacher Rabbi Hillel once asked: "If I am not for myself, who is for me? But if I am only for myself, what am I?"

You should ask yourself those same questions when thinking about loyalty. It is certainly important to care about yourself, to think of your own needs, to "look out for number one." But if that is *all* you care about, or if that is what you care about the *most,* what kind of person does that make you?

Loyalty means caring in a serious way about your relationships with others and being willing to show it through your actions. You can have loyalty to many people or groups—to family, to friends, to your school, to your church, to your country. In all these cases, loyalty means looking past your own needs. It means putting yourself in second place, if necessary. It requires that you do the right thing at the right time for those you care about.

We often say that we "owe our loyalty" to someone or something. That's because relationships are a two-way street. We want to show we care about certain people in part because they have shown they care about us. Eleanor

Roosevelt put it this way: "Up to a certain point it is good for us to know that there are people in the world who will give us love and unquestioned loyalty to the limit of their ability. I doubt, however, if it is good for us to feel assured of this without the accompanying obligation of having to justify this devotion by our behavior."

Children can show loyalty to their parents, for example, by behaving with respect and obedience. Parents, in return, do everything they can to take care of their children and act in their best interests.

Husbands and wives show loyalty to each other in part through their faithfulness to one another. Fidelity in marriage is an expression of love. It is a kind of loyalty that helps make a marriage a sacred relationship.

Friends show loyalty by being honest and dependable with each other. Loyalty to a friend, by the way, does not mean doing whatever your friend asks you to do. It means, rather, doing what will help your friend become a better person.

Loyalty to team means showing up for practice on time and giving your best efforts. And, in return, you expect your teammates to do the same.

Loyalty to country—patriotism—involves obeying its laws, upholding its principles, and even defending those principles if necessary. Citizens owe such loyalty in return for the protection of their rights and privileges as well as for the many opportunities that their country has offered them.

When you say the Pledge of Allegiance to the flag, you are literally giving an oath of loyalty, not to a piece of cloth but to a symbol. For your pledge to mean anything, you need to know a few things about "the Republic for which it stands." For example, you need to know something about its Constitution, its government, its history, and its traditions. Otherwise, you are simply swearing blind allegiance.

In all of these cases, loyalty means that you are ready to put another before yourself. In an age when people are told to "do what feels good," or "do your own thing," loyalty reminds us that often we should be doing something for someone else. As Woodrow Wilson said, "Loyalty means nothing unless it has at its heart the absolute principle of self-sacrifice." That self-sacrifice is, in the end, what gives serious meaning to our relationships.

A Brother in Need

Loyalty begins at home, as this Vietnamese tale reminds us.

There were once two brothers, Gan and Duc, whose father died suddenly, without leaving a will. Gan, the older brother, took all the land and property for himself except for one small shack and one miserable patch of acreage, which he allowed Duc to have. Duc's field was so tiny it could produce barely enough for him to eat, and year after year he grew poorer and thinner despite his hard work. Gan's green field, meanwhile, flourished every year until he was the wealthiest man in the province.

The richer Gan grew, the more friends he discovered. They came to see him night and day, and he never hesitated to serve lavish meals, pour his best wines, and give away expensive tokens of affection. "I'll do anything for a friend in need," Gan was fond of saying.

Now, Gan had a kind-hearted wife named Hanh who could not understand why her husband treated his own brother so cruelly.

"You say there's nothing you wouldn't do for your friends," she pointed out, "and yet look at the way you let your brother live."

"I have nothing to do with the way he lives," Gan snapped. "He can fend for himself, just as I have. Besides, my friends rank among the finest people in the province. It's only fitting that I treat them according to what they deserved."

"Nevertheless, he is your brother. And I'm sure if you

treated him as your friend, you'd find more devotion in him than in these friends you treat as brothers."

But this conversation took place many times, and Gan never listened.

One evening Gan came home to find his wife in tears.

"What's happened?" he asked.

"Something horrible," she sobbed. "This afternoon a beggar came to the door and asked for something to eat. He looked so weak and pale, I couldn't say no. So I told him to step inside while I got something from the kitchen. But no sooner did the poor man cross our threshold than he fainted from hunger. He struck his head on the table and fell dead on the floor. I was so frightened, I wrapped his body in a blanket and dragged it into the garden."

"But there's nothing to worry about," Gan assured her. "You did nothing wrong. We'll explain the situation to the mandarin. You were just trying to help."

"You're wrong," Hanh cried. "The mandarin has never liked you. He's jealous of your riches and popularity. He'll use this chance to ruin us, if he can."

At this Gan turned pale himself. He remembered how stern and cold the mandarin had always been, and how he never accepted Gan's invitations to come dine.

"What will we do then?" he asked, ringing his hands.

"I've thought of a plan," Hanh whispered. "Tonight you must bury the beggar deep in the forest, where no one will find him. Choose your most devoted friend to help you and swear him to secrecy."

So Gan hurried to the home of the man who had dined most at his table. His friend greeted him with a warm embrace and an eager smile. But when Gan explained in low tones how he needed help, his friend shook his head and backed away. He was sorry, he'd love more than anything to help, but his back was giving him problems, and he couldn't possibly carry the load of a dead man through the forest.

Gan hurried to another friend's house, where once again he was warmly received.

"It's been too long!" the friend gushed. "Tell me now, how can I help you?"

"I knew I could count on you," Gan sighed. "You were always the best of friends. Something horrible has happened." But as he told his story, his friend's expression changed.

"I wish I could help, Gan, you know I do," he lamented. "But the fact is, my poor old grandmother is ill tonight and may even be on her deathbed. I can't possibly leave her. I knew you'd understand."

And so it went, from door to door, from friend to friend. Some had sick relatives, some were ill themselves, others had pressing engagements. None were able to help, and Gan trudged home alone, trembling with fear and disappointment.

His wife listened to what happened and said:

"There's no time to lose. You don't have a choice. You must go ask your brother for help."

Gan knew she was right—there was no one else now. He hurried into the night again and found his brother's humble house.

Duc could not conceal his surprise when he opened his door. Then he saw the anguish on his brother's face.

"What's wrong?" he asked at once. "You look half-dead. Are you sick? Is Hanh all right?"

In faltering words, Gan told why he had come. Before he had finished, Duc was putting on his jacket. The two brothers rushed back to Gan's house, found the shrouded body in the garden, and hauled it into the woods. The sun was rising by the time they'd buried the secret burden and staggered home again.

They were stunned to find one of the mandarin's men waiting for them.

"You are to come with me," he ordered Gan, "along with your wife and brother."

They were taken to the mandarin's house, and there they found gathered all the friends whose help Gan had begged. One by one the informers stepped forward and told how they had refused to take part in the brothers' foul crime.

"Not only are you murderers," the mandarin said, "you tried to talk your friends into concealing your misdeed. Thankfully, your friends are better men than you. They are honest, and they are loyal to me. They followed you into the forest and then came to report your crime. So there's no use in denying it. We'll go retrieve the body, and then you'll get what is due."

The entire crowd trooped into the forest, and the hastily dug grave was uncovered. There was a gasp when the blanket was unwrapped and the corpse of an old ram, not a beggar, fell out.

"What is the meaning of this?" the mandarin demanded.

Gan and Duc stood as confused as the rest. Their accusers glanced at each other nervously.

Then Hanh stepped forward.

"This is my doing," she confessed. "For a long time I've watched my husband treat his brother like a stranger while he spared nothing on his friends. I could see how those friends hung on to him only because of the food and wine they could have at his expense. I wanted to prove to him that there can be no loyalty greater than a brother's. So yesterday, when this old ram of ours died, I invented a plan to open my husband's eyes. And here we are."

Gan's accusers looked at their feet, while the mandarin stood silent for a moment.

"You are a wise woman," he said at last. "This lesson is worth a night's inconvenience."

From then on, Gan and Duc lived as brothers should.

America the Beautiful
KATHARINE LEE BATES

Massachusetts educator and author Katharine Lee Bates wrote "America the Beautiful" in 1893 after being inspired by the view from Pikes Peak in Colorado. She revised the lyrics to their final form in 1911. They are set to the music of Samuel A. Ward's "Materna."

> O beautiful for spacious skies,
>   For amber waves of grain,
> For purple mountain majesties
>   Above the fruited plain!
> America! America!
>   God shed His grace on thee
> And crown thy good with brotherhood
>   From sea to shining sea!

O beautiful for Pilgrim feet,
  Whose stern, impassioned stress
A thoroughfare for freedom beat
  Across the wilderness!
America! America!
  God mend thine every flaw,
Confirm thy soul in self-control,
  Thy liberty in law!

O beautiful for heroes proved
  In liberating strife,
Who more than self their country loved,
  And mercy more than life!
America! America!
  May God thy gold refine,
Till all success be nobleness
  And every gain divine!

O beautiful for patriot dream
  That sees beyond the years
Thine alabaster cities gleam
  Undimmed by human tears!
America! America!
  God shed His grace on thee,
And crown thy good with brotherhood
  From sea to shining sea!

Barbara Frietchie

JOHN GREENLEAF WHITTIER

Sometimes our sense of loyalty demands that we show the flag even in the enemy's midst. John Greenleaf Whittier (1807–1892) wrote this poem in 1863, during the Civil War, and claimed its story is true.

Up from the meadows rich with corn,
Clear in the cool September morn,

The clustered spires of Frederick stand
Green-walled by the hills of Maryland.

Round about them orchards sweep,
Apple and peach tree fruited deep,

Fair as the garden of the Lord
To the eyes of the famished rebel horde,

On that pleasant morn of the early fall
When Lee marched over the mountain wall;

Over the mountains winding down,
Horse and foot, into Frederick town.

Forty flags with their silver stars,
Forty flags with their crimson bars,

Flapped in the morning wind: the sun
Of noon looked down, and saw not one.

Up rose old Barbara Frietchie then,
Bowed with her fourscore years and ten;

Bravest of all in Frederick town,
She took up the flag the men hauled down;

In her attic window the staff she set,
To show that one heart was loyal yet.

Up the street came the rebel tread,
Stonewall Jackson riding ahead.

Under his slouched hat left and right
He glanced; the old flag met his sight.

"Halt"—the dust-brown ranks stood fast.
"Fire"—out blazed the rifle blast.

It shivered the window, pane and sash;
It rent the banner with seam and gash.

Quick, as it fell, from the broken staff
Dame Barbara snatched the silken scarf.

She leaned far out on the windowsill,
And shook it forth with a royal will.

"Shoot, if you must, this old gray head,
But spare your country's flag," she said.

A shade of sadness, a blush of shame,
Over the face of the leader came;

The nobler nature within him stirred
To life at that woman's deed and word;

"Who touches a hair on yon gray head
Dies like a dog! March on!" he said.

All day long through Frederick street
Sounded the tread of marching feet:

All day long that free flag tost
Over the heads of the rebel host.

Even its torn folds rose and fell
On the loyal winds that loved it well;

And through the hill gaps sunset light
Shone over it with a warm good night.

Barbara Frietchie's work is o'er,
And the Rebel rides on his raids no more.

Honor to her! and let a tear
Fall, for her sake, on Stonewall's bier.

Over Barbara Frietchie's grave
Flag of Freedom and Union, wave!

Peace and order and beauty draw
Round thy symbol of light and law;

And ever the stars above look down
On thy stars below in Frederick town!

‿ Castor and Pollux

The Greek writer Menander said that to live is not to live for one's self alone. The story of Castor and Pollux helps us understand this meaning of the word brotherhood.

On winter nights the constellation Gemini lies high overhead, and its two principal stars, Castor and Pollux, are among the brightest in the heavens. We know them as the Twins, but old myths from the days of Greek heroes say they were really half brothers. Leda was the mother of both, while Castor's father was Tyndareus, the king of Sparta, and Pollux's father was Zeus, king of the gods. So the span of Castor's life was fixed, but Pollux was immortal.

By all accounts, the brothers were never apart, so great was their devotion to each other, and they shared many adventures. They sailed with Jason and the Argonauts on the quest for the Golden Fleece, and they rescued their sister Helen when she was kidnapped by Theseus, the same beautiful Helen whose face later "launched a thousand ships" and brought about the Trojan War. They also took part in the famous Calydonian hunt, in which many of Greece's bravest heroes gathered to rid the land of a monstrous boar.

The most famous legend about Castor and Pollux is about how they ended their earthly lives. The Greek poet Pindar tells us that Castor was wounded in battle. His brother rushed to his side, only to find him almost dead, gasping out his life with short-drawn breath. Pollux did everything he could to save him, but there was no hope.

"Oh father Zeus," Pollux cried, "take my life instead of

my brother's! Or if not that, let me die also! Without him, I will know nothing but grief for the rest of my days."

As he spoke, Zeus approached and answered. "You are my son, Pollux, and therefore enjoy eternal life. Your brother was born of mortal seed, and destined like all humans to taste death. But I will give you a choice. You may come to Olympus, as is your right, and dwell with Athena and Ares and the rest of the gods. Or, if you wish to share your immortality with your brother, then half the time you must spend beneath the earth, and the other half in the golden home of heaven."

Pollux did not for an instant waver, but gave up his life in Olympus, and chose to share light and darkness forever with his brother. So Zeus unclosed Castor's eyes and restored his breath. And even now we see them as the constellation Gemini. They spend half their time fixed in the starry heavens, and the other half sunk beneath the horizon.

⟣ Fading Favor

This Chinese tale reminds us that our fidelities should not change because another's physical appearance changes. In many marriage vows, people say "til death do us part," not "til age do us part."

In olden days there was a king who liked to keep his court filled with ladies from all over the land. His favorite was a beautiful young maiden named Hua.

"Ah, Hua," he used to say, "you are the most wondrous creature under the blue heavens. Someday you shall be my queen."

This king kept a stern law that anyone who rode his horse without his permission would be punished by death. One day, when Hua suddenly learned her mother was ill, she jumped on the horse and rode off to the old woman's bedside.

"What devotion!" the king sighed. "To think she risked her own life to tend to her poor mother!"

Another time, Hua and the king were strolling in the royal garden. Hua picked a plum and took a bite; its flavor was so splendid, she handed it to the king to taste.

"What loyalty," he thought. "She discovers this perfect fruit and would rather give it to me to enjoy than finish it herself!"

But eventually Hua's beauty began to fade, and with it the king's affections.

"Didn't she once take my horse, even though she knew it was a crime?" he remembered. "And another time she handed me the remains of a plum after chewing on it herself!"

He decided to choose a younger woman as his queen.

How Queen Esther Saved Her People

RETOLD BY WALTER RUSSELL BOWIE

The events of the book of Esther in the Bible are reported to have occurred during the reign of the Persian king Ahasuerus, whom biblical scholars usually identify with Xerxes (c. 519–465 B.C.). Esther and her kinsman Mordecai were members of the Jewish population remaining in the East after many other Jews had returned to Jerusalem from the

Babylonian exile. The story is one of a young queen who must face danger alone to save her people.

The story of the book of Esther begins with one of the kings of Persia, who is called Ahasuerus. According to the story, Ahasuerus decided one day to have a great feast in the garden of his palace. He invited all the chief men of the kingdom to come. The garden court was a beautiful place within the palace walls. It had marble pillars and a pavement of red, blue, white, and black marble. There were hangings of white and green and blue, fastened on silver rings. The goblets in which the wine was served were gold.

The feasting went on for seven days. By that time everyone, including the king, had eaten and drunk a great deal too much. The queen, whose name was Vashti, was very beautiful. Suddenly the king had a notion that he would show her off to his guests. She was in her rooms with her maids. The king sent seven of his servants to tell the queen to come to the feast.

Vashti was ashamed and indignant that the king had sent her such a message. She had no intention of appearing before a large company of half-drunken men. She told the servants to tell the king that she would not come.

When the king heard that, he was furious. He had boasted of the queen's beauty. Now he would seem foolish in the sight of his guests. He asked some of them what they thought he ought to do. These men did not have much respect for women. They began to think that if their wives heard that the queen had disobeyed the king, they would disobey their husbands. The men told the king that he ought to get rid of Vashti and find a new queen.

That was exactly what Ahasuerus decided to do. He

sent Vashti away. Then came the question of choosing a new queen. The king's servants looked everywhere in the kingdom, and brought to the palace the most beautiful maidens they could find. Among them was a maiden from a Jewish family, whose name was Esther. She was young and innocent and lovely, and could never have dreamed that she might become the queen of Persia. When the king saw Esther, he preferred her to everyone else, and he made her his wife, But he did not know that she had come from among the Jews.

Now Esther had a cousin named Mordecai. Mordecai, who was older than Esther, had brought her up like a daughter because her own father was dead. Esther trusted him in everything, and whatever he advised her to do, she did. Mordecai told her not to tell the king that she was a Jew.

Mordecai came often to the palace, to speak with Esther. Often he would sit in the gate where people went in and out and where they stood together talking. One day he saw two men who were plainly very angry. They talked excitedly, and Mordecai overheard what they were saying. They were plotting together to kill the king.

Mordecai sent word of that to Esther, and Esther warned the king. The king had the two men arrested and put to death. By his warning, Mordecai had saved the king's life. The king should have been very grateful, but he was more interested in himself than in anyone else. Although he had been told that it was Mordecai who had brought the warning, he soon forgot it.

Meanwhile there was another man who was becoming the king's favorite. His name was Haman. The king's servants had to bow to Haman whenever he passed by. But Mordecai would not bow to Haman or give any sign that he noticed him at all. Every day Mordecai was warned that he would find himself in trouble if he did not do as the king's servants did, but Mordecai paid no attention. After a while someone asked Haman if he had noticed that Mordecai, the Jew, never bowed to him when he went by. The very idea made Haman angry, for he was proud and jealous. To hear that anybody had dared not show respect to him was more than he would stand. He began to consider what would be the worst thing he would do to Mordecai. He thought about it for some time. Finally he decided that there was something worse than having Mordecai punished alone. Since Mordecai was a Jew, Haman would make all the Jewish people suffer.

So one day Haman went to the king and poured into his ears all the ugly tales he could think of about the Jews. He reminded Ahasuerus that the Jews were scattered all through the kingdom. He said there were entirely too many of them for the kingdom's good. Had the king stopped to remember that the Jews were different from the people of Persia, and had different laws? He suggested getting rid of these Jewish people who might turn out to be enemies of Persia. And Haman said that he would put ten thousand talents of silver, a huge amount of money, into the king's treasury if the king would sign an order that all the Jews should be destroyed.

Ahasuerus not only had a quick temper but he was stupid, too. He believed everything that Haman told him. He flew into a rage against the Jews and told Haman to have them killed.

Haman heard that with wicked pleasure. He lost no time in making sure that what he had planned should happen. He sent out orders, in the king's name and with the king's seal, to the governors of all the parts of the kingdom. These orders commanded that on a certain day every Jewish person—man, woman, and child—should be put to death. Then Haman went in and sat down to drink wine with the king, and to rejoice.

Out in the city the people who had begun to hear the news were shocked and troubled. Before long the news reached Mordecai. He dressed himself in rough sackcloth and poured ashes on his head as a sign of distress. Then he went to the gate of the palace to weep and mourn.

One of the palace maids told Esther of this. Esther was greatly troubled. She sent to Mordecai to beg him to take off his sackcloth, and to let her know quickly what was wrong. Mordecai told the messenger the terrible truth— that all the Jews in the kingdom were in danger of death. Only she might save them by going to the king and begging him to change the order.

Esther seemed to be faced with more than a woman could bear. She was the queen, but she knew only too well the cruel laws of the Persian court. She knew that no one, least of all a woman, might dare to cross the king. Esther sent the messenger back to Mordecai. Did he not know that if anyone went to the king uninvited, he might be put to death? This would certainly happen unless the king was in good humor and held out his golden scepter as a sign of permission to come near. Esther had no reason to think that the king would treat her so kindly. It had been many days since he had sent for her and since she had seen him.

Mordecai sent back word that there was only one hope for the Jews in Persia; only one person could do anything, and that person was Esther. She must not think, Mordecai added, that if the king's order for the killing of Jews was carried out she would escape. It would be found out that she too was a Jew, and she would be treated like the rest. But she alone might be able to do what everyone else put together could not do. Perhaps this was her chance to show a kind of courage that few would dare to show. "Who knows," said Mordecai, "but that you have come to the kingdom for such a time as this?"

When Esther received Mordecai's message, all her heart rose bravely to answer. So much depended on her that she could not be timid anymore. She sent word back to Mordecai that he should gather the Jews together to fast and pray. She and her maids in the palace would do the same. Then she would go to the king and try to persuade him. "And if I perish," she said, "I perish."

The moment came when she must take the great and final risk. Ahasuerus, in all his pomp and power, was sitting on his royal throne. Esther dressed herself in her queenliest robes. She went to the door of the throne room. The door was opened, and she stood there, beautiful and silent, waiting, looking at the king. If he were angry, that would be the end.

But the king stretched out the golden scepter toward her. "Queen Esther!" he said. "What will you have? What is your request? It shall be given you, even if it be half of the kingdom!"

So the king was not angry! He was fond of her, and perhaps he would listen to her more than he had listened to the wicked Haman. But she would not tell her real wish now. Instead, she said, "If it seems good to the king, will he, and Haman also, come to a banquet which I have made ready today?"

The king said that he would come, and that Haman should come, too.

When they were seated at the table, the king told Esther again that he would give her anything she wanted, no matter what it might be. But she begged him not to have her tell him then what she wanted. Would he wait until tomorrow? And would he and Haman come to another banquet the next day? Yes, the king said, they would come.

Haman went out, proud and pleased. He had been invited to a banquet alone with the king and queen, and he was invited again tomorrow! But as he left the palace, there, sitting at the gate, was Mordecai. Mordecai did not stand up or bow, or even notice him. That spoiled everything. Haman snapped his lips shut and walked by Mordecai without a word. When he reached home he called his wife and some of his friends, and broke into a storm of complaining. He told them all of the honors the king had given him, and that anybody could see how great a man he was, but that this Mordecai still despised him.

Haman's wife and friends were as bad-tempered as Haman. Why did he not go at once and ask the king's permission to hang Mordecai? "Ask the king to make a gallows fifty cubits high," they said. That seemed to Haman a good idea. Without asking the king, he had the gallows built to hang Mordecai on.

Then things began to happen in a way Haman had not expected. That night the king could not sleep. He tossed about impatiently. Finally he decided he would read awhile, and he told one of his servants to bring him a book. The book the servant happened to bring was a history of the events of the king's court during the last few years. The king commanded that the book be read aloud to him. As he listened, he heard about the two men who had plotted to kill him, and how Mordecai had overheard them and had given warning.

Suddenly the king remembered that he had never rewarded Mordecai for this. It annoyed him to think that he had forgotten about it all this time. He asked his servants, "What about this Mordecai? What has been done for him?"

They told him, "Nothing."

"Who is in the court right now?" the king asked.

It happened that at just that moment Haman had come to the palace to tell the king about the gallows he had had built for Mordecai. The servants told the king that Haman was outside.

"Let him come in," said the king.

So Haman came in. The king's mind was full of what he had been hearing. "Haman," he asked, "what ought to be done to a man whom the king wants very much to honor?"

He means me! thought Haman. He tried not to look excited.

"What ought to be done for a man whom the king wants very much to honor?" Haman repeated. "Let royal robes be brought like those which the king wears, and the king's horse, too, and the king's own crown. Let these be put in charge of one of the noblest of the princes. Let the prince put the royal robes on the man the king has chosen to honor. Then the prince shall lead this man, on horseback, through the city and proclaim to the people that he is the man whom the king delights to honor."

"Good!" said the king. "Now hurry and do exactly as you have said. Take one of my royal robes and have the king's horse brought. Find Mordecai the Jew and lead him through the city."

If the king had struck Haman with a hammer between the eyes, Haman could not have been more stunned. But there was no escape from what the king had commanded, and Haman did not dare even to look surprised. In a black and bitter fury he had to go out and give Mordecai the honors he had supposed were meant for him. He held the bridle of the king's horse, with Mordecai riding on it, dressed in a royal robe. And he had to cry to the people who crowded the streets, "This is the man whom the king delights to honor!"

But that was not all. The banquet with the king and queen was still to come.

When the three of them were sitting there together, Ahasuerus asked Esther again what she wanted him to do for her. This time she really told him. She reminded him of the order that had gone out in his name that all the Jews in the kingdom should be killed. Then she told him that she herself belonged to the Jewish people. She pleaded that he would take back that dreadful order and spare them. "If I have found favor in your sight," she said, "grant me this petition!"

When the king looked at Esther, so lovely and so distressed, he was angry to think that he had been tricked by someone, he had almost forgotten who, into giving that order. "Who has done this?" he demanded. "Where is he?"

Then Esther the queen looked straight at Haman. "It is this wicked Haman," she said.

The king was so full of rage that he got up and strode out into the garden. Haman was terrified, and he fell down on the couch where the queen was sitting. In came the king again at that moment, and he thought Haman was trying to hurt the queen. "What!" he cried. "Will he attack the queen here in my own palace?" He called his servants, and they took Haman out.

One of the king's officers came and asked the king if he knew that Haman had built a gallows near his own house, a gallows nearly a hundred feet high. No, the king had not known it, but now that he knew, he knew also what should be done with it. "Take Haman and hang him on it," he commanded. So on the very gallows which he had intended for Mordecai, Haman himself was hanged.

That is the story of the book of Esther. And from that day the Jewish people, who had suffered a great deal, were glad to remember the truthful Mordecai and the young queen who, all alone, carried through a dangerous duty.

ᕈ Loyalty to a Brother
WALTER MACPEEK

Family loyalties involve certain obligations. They are duties we perform out of love, as this simple story from an old Boy Scout book reminds us.

One of two brothers fighting in the same company in France fell by a German bullet. The one who escaped asked permission of his officer to go and bring his brother in.

"He is probably dead," said the officer, "and there is no use in your risking your life to bring in his body."

But after further pleading the officer consented. Just as the soldier reached the lines with his brother on his shoulders, the wounded man died.

"There, you see," said the officer, "you risked your life for nothing."

"No," replied Tom. "I did what he expected of me, and I have my reward. When I crept up to him and took him in my arms, he said, 'Tom, I knew you would come—I just felt you would come.'"

There you have the gist of it all; somebody expects something fine and noble and unselfish of us; someone expects us to be faithful.

Nathan Hale
FROM *AMERICAN HERITAGE* MAGAZINE

Americans look to the Revolutionary War to find the two names that mark the extremes of loyalty to country. On one end of the spectrum we find Benedict Arnold, perhaps the most despised name in the nation's history. At the other end stands Nathan Hale.

Ever since he was executed by the British on the morning of September 22, 1776, the death of Nathan Hale has been recognized as one of the great moments of American patriotism. Some years ago the late George Dudley Seymour gathered all the contemporary descriptions of the young hero's career that he could find, and had them privately printed in a *Documentary Life of Nathan Hale*. In the selections below we can read at first hand, in the words of both his friends and his foes, a story that has inspired generations of Hale's countrymen.

Following his graduation from Yale in 1773 at the age of eighteen, Hale taught school for a time in his native

Connecticut. Then, on July 1, 1775—two months after Lexington and Concord—he was commissioned a lieutenant in the Continental Army, and closed his one-room school in New London, a building still proudly preserved by the town. We see him first in the reminiscences of a comrade-in-arms, Lieutenant Elisha Bostwick:

> I can now in imagination see his person and hear his voice—his person, I should say, was a little above the common stature in height, his shoulders of a moderate breadth, his limbs strait and very plump: regular features—very fair skin—blue eyes—flaxen or very light hair which was always kept short—his eyebrows a shade darker than his hair and his voice rather sharp or piercing—his bodily agility was remarkable. I have seen him follow a football and kick it over the tops of the trees in the Bowery at New York (an exercise which he was fond of)—his mental powers seemed to be above the common sort—his mind of a sedate and sober cast, and he was undoubtedly pious; for it was remarked that when any of the soldiers of his company were sick he always visited them and usually prayed for and with them in their sickness.

Early in the fall of 1776, after being disastrously defeated on Long Island, Washington needed to know the dispositions and the intentions of the British forces. Hale and the other officers of the picked regiment known as Knowlton's Rangers, were asked to volunteer for an intelligence mission behind enemy lines. On the first call, none responded; on the second, Nathan Hale alone stepped forward. A little later he told his friend Captain (afterward General) William Hull what he had done:

> [Hale] asked my candid opinion [says Hull's memoir]. I replied, that it was an action which involved serious consequences, and the propriety of it was doubtful

. . . Stratagems are resorted to in war; they are feints and evasions, performed under no disguise . . . and, considered in a military view, lawful and advantageous . . . But who respects the character of a spy, assuming the garb of friendship but to betray? . . . I ended by saying, that should he undertake the enterprise, his short, bright career would close with an ignominious death.

He replied, "I am fully sensible of the consequences of discovery and capture in such a situation . . . Yet . . . I wish to be useful, and every kind of service, necessary to the public good, becomes honorable by being necessary. If the exigencies of my country demand a peculiar service, its claims to perform that service are imperious."

Sergeant Stephen Hempstead of New London accompanied him as he set out on his mission from Norwalk, Connecticut:

Captain Hale had a general order to all armed vessels to take him to anyplace he should designate: he was set across the Sound . . . at Huntington (Long Island) . . . Captain Hale had changed his uniform for a plain suit of citizen's brown clothes, with a round broad-brimmed hat, assuming the character of a Dutch schoolmaster, leaving all his other clothes, commission, public and private papers, with me, and also his silver shoe buckles, saying they would not comport with his character of schoolmaster, and retaining nothing but his college diploma, as an introduction to his assumed calling. Thus equipped, we parted.

Hale's servant, Asher Wright, who had remained behind, told what happened next:

He passed all their guards on Long Island, went over to New York in a ferryboat and got by all the guards but the last. They stopped him, searched and found drawings of the works, with descriptions in Latin, under the inner sole of the pumps which he wore. Some say his cousin, Samuel Hale, a Tory, betrayed him. I don't know; guess he did.

"Betrayed" is probably too strong; "identified" is closer to the truth. A surviving letter from Samuel, a Harvard man (1766), seems to deny any misdeed, or at least any guilt, as the story was spread in a Newburyport newspaper—but he thereafter fled to England and never returned to America, even after the war, for his wife and son.

The next day a kindhearted British officer, Captain John Montresor, approached the American lines under a flag of truce to report the inevitable denouement. Captain Hull recorded Montresor's words:

> Hale at once declared his name, his rank in the American army, and his object in coming within the British lines.
>
> Sir William Howe, without the form of a trial, gave orders for his execution the following morning. He was placed in the custody of the provost marshal, who was . . . hardened to human suffering and every softening sentiment of the heart. Captain Hale, alone, without sympathy or support, save that from above, on the near approach of death asked for a clergyman to attend him. It was refused. He then requested a Bible; that too was refused by his inhuman jailer.
>
> On the morning of his execution . . . my station was near the fatal spot, and I requested the provost marshal to permit the prisoner to sit in my marquee, while he was making the necessary preparations. Captain Hale entered: he was calm, and bore himself with gentle dignity, in the consciousness of rectitude and high intentions. He asked for writing materials, which I furnished him: he

wrote two letters . . . He was shortly after summoned to the gallows. But a few persons were around him, yet his characteristic dying words were remembered. He said, "I only regret, that I have but one life to lose for my country."

A brief excerpt from a letter written at Coventry, Connecticut, the following spring by Nathan Hale's father, Richard, who had six sons altogether in the Revolution, betrays the deep grief of this unlettered man:

> You desired me to inform you about my son Nathan. . . . He was executed about the twenty-second of September last by the accounts we have had. A child I sot much by but he is gone. . . .

This letter, addressed to Richard Hale's brother, Major Samuel Hale, in Portsmouth, New Hampshire, on March 28, 1777, was put away in a secret drawer of the major's desk. In 1908, the old desk was sold at auction as an antique, and three years later the new owner, the Honorable Frank L. Howe of Barrington, New Hampshire, chanced upon it. Such is the thrill of historical discovery.

Only a Dad
EDGAR GUEST

We should not forget to sing praises for devoted fathers—especially our own. This Edgar Guest poem may help us remember that the only reward a devoted father seeks is his family's flourishing.

Only a dad with a tired face,
Coming home from the daily race,
Bringing little of gold or fame
To show how well he has played the game;
But glad in his heart that his own rejoice
To see him come and to hear his voice.

Only a dad with a brood of four,
One of ten million men or more
Plodding along in the daily strife,
Bearing the whips and the scorns of life,
With never a whimper of pain or hate,
For the sake of those who at home await.

Only a dad, neither rich nor proud,
Merely one of the surging crowd,
Toiling, striving from day to day,
Facing whatever may come his way,
silent whenever the harsh condemn,
And bearing it all for the love of them.

Only a dad but he gives his all,
To smooth the way for his children small,
Doing with courage stern and grim
The deeds that his father did for him.
This is the line that for him I pen:
Only a dad, but the best of men.

≈ Penelope's Web

ADAPTED FROM JAMES BALDWIN

Penelope's long wait for her husband's return from the Trojan War is one of our greatest stories of loyalty. The queen's patience and love make her one of Greek mythology's most memorable characters. The story comes from Homer's Odyssey. *In this retelling, Odysseus is called by his Latin name, Ulysses.*

Of all the heroes who fought against Troy, the wisest and shrewdest was Ulysses, king of Ithaca. Yet, he went unwillingly to war. He longed to stay at home with his wife, Penelope, and their baby boy, Telemachus. But the princes of Greece demanded that he help them, and at last he consented.

"Go, Ulysses," said Penelope, "and I will keep your home and kingdom safe until you return."

"Do your duty, Ulysses," said his old father, Laertes. "Go, and may wise Athena speed your coming back."

And so, bidding farewell to Ithaca and all he held dear, he sailed away to the Trojan War.

Ten long years passed, and then news reached Ithaca that the weary siege of Troy was ended, the city lay in ashes, and the Greek kings were returning to their native lands. One by one, all the heroes reached their homes, but of Ulysses and his companions there came no word. Every day, Penelope and young Telemachus and feeble old Laertes stood by the shore and gazed with aching eyes far over the waves. But no sign of sail or glinting oars could they discern. Months passed by, and then years, and still no word.

"His ships are wrecked, and he lies at the bottom of the

sea," sighed old Laertes, and after that he shut himself up in his narrow room and went no more to the shore.

But Penelope still hoped and hoped. "He is not dead," she said. "And until he comes home, I will hold this fair kingdom for him."

Every day his seat was placed for him at the table. His coat was hung by his chair, his chamber was dusted, and his great bow that hung in the hall was polished.

Ten more years passed with constant watching. Telemachus became a tall, gentle-mannered young man. And throughout all Greece, men began to talk of nothing but Penelope's great nobility and beauty.

"How foolish of her," the Greek princes and chiefs said, "to be forever looking for Ulysses. Everyone knows he is dead. She ought to marry one of us now."

So one after another, the chiefs and princes who were looking for wives sailed to Ithaca, hoping to win Penelope's love. They were haughty and overbearing fellows, glorying in their own importance and wealth. Straight to the palace they went, not waiting for an invitation, for they knew they would be treated as honored guests, whether they were welcome or not.

"Come now, Penelope," they said, "we all know Ulysses is dead. We have come as suitors for your hand, and you dare not turn us away. Choose one of us, and the rest will depart."

But Penelope answered sadly, "Princes and heroes, this cannot be. I am quite sure Ulysses lives, and I must hold his kingdom for him till he returns."

"Return he never will," said the suitors. "Make your choice now."

"Give me a month longer to wait for him," she pleaded. "In my loom I have a half-finished web of soft linen. I am weaving it for the shroud of our father, Laertes, who is very old and cannot live much longer. If Ulysses fails to return by the time this web is finished, then I will choose, though unwillingly."

The suitors agreed and made themselves at home in the palace. They seized the best of everything. They feasted daily in the great dining hall, wasting much, and helped themselves to all the wine in the cellar. They were rude and uproarious in the once quiet chambers of the palace, and insulting to the people of Ithaca.

Every day Penelope sat at her loom and wove. "See how much I have added to the length of the web?" she would say when evening came. But at night, when the suitors were asleep, she raveled out all the threads she had woven during the day. Thus although she was always at work, the web was never finished.

As the weeks passed, however, the suitors began to grow weary of waiting.

"When will that web be finished?" they impatiently asked.

"I am busy with it every day," Penelope answered, "but it grows very slowly. Such a delicate piece of work cannot be completed so quickly."

But one of the suitors, a man named Agelaus, was not satisfied. That night he crept quietly through the palace and peeped into the weaving room. There he saw Penelope busily unraveling the web by the light of a little lamp, while she whispered to herself the name of Ulysses.

The next morning the secret was known to every one of the unwelcome guests. "Fair queen," they said, "you are very cunning, but we have found you out. That web must be finished before the sun rises again, and then tomorrow you must make your choice. We shall wait no longer."

The following afternoon the unwelcome guests assembled in the great hall. The feast was set, and they ate and drank and sang and shouted as never before. They made such an uproar that the very timbers of the palace shook.

While the turmoil was at its height, Telemachus came in, followed by Eumaeus, his father's oldest and most faithful servant. Together they began to remove all the shields and swords that hung on the walls and rattled from so much commotion.

"What are you doing with those weapons?" shouted the suitors, who finally noticed the old man and the youth.

"They are becoming tarnished with smoke and dust," said Eumaeus, "and will keep much better in the treasure room."

"But we will leave my father's great bow that hangs at the head of the hall," added Telemachus. "My mother polishes it every day, and she would sadly miss it if it were removed."

"She won't be polishing it much longer," the suitors laughed. "Before this day is over, Ithaca will have a new king."

At that moment a strange beggar entered the courtyard. His feet were bare, his head was uncovered, his clothes were in rags. He approached the kitchen door, where an old greyhound, Argos, was lying on a heap of ashes. Twenty years before, Argos had been Ulysses' favorite and most loyal hunting dog. But now, grown toothless and almost blind, he was only abused by the suitors.

When he saw the beggar slowly moving through the yard, he raised his head to look. Then a strange look came suddenly into his old eyes. His tail wagged feebly, and he tried with all his failing strength to rise. He looked up lovingly into the beggar's face, and uttered a long but joyful howl like that which he once uttered in his youth when greeting his master.

The beggar stooped and patted his head. "Argos, old friend," he whispered.

The dog staggered to his feet, then fell, and was dead with the look of joy still in his eyes.

A moment later the beggar stood in the doorway of the great hall, where he was seen whispering a few words to Telemachus and faithful Eumaeus.

"What do you want here, Old Rags?" the suitors called, hurling crusts of bread at his head. "Get out! Be gone!"

But at that moment, down the stairs came Penelope, stately and beautiful, with her servants and maids around her.

"The queen! The queen!" cried the suitors. "She has come to choose one of us!"

"Telemachus, my son," said Penelope, "what poor man is this whom our guests treat so roughly?"

"Mother, he is a wandering beggar whom the waves cast upon our shores last night," answered the prince. "He says that he brings news of my father."

"Then he shall tell me of it," said the queen. "But first he must rest." At this she caused the beggar to be led to a seat at the farther side of the room, and gave orders that he be fed and refreshed.

An old woman, who had been Ulysses' nurse when he was a child, brought a great bowl of water and towels. Kneeling on the stones before the stranger, she began to wash his feet. Suddenly she sprang back, overturning the bowl in her confusion.

"O, master! The scar!" she muttered quietly.

"Dear nurse," whispered the beggar, "you were ever discreet and wise. You know me by the old scar I have carried on my knee since boyhood. Keep well the secret, for I bide my time, and the hour of vengeance is nigh."

This man in rags was indeed Ulysses, the king. Alone in a little boat he had been cast, that very morning, upon the shore of his own island. He had made himself known to Telemachus and old Eumaeus alone, and by his orders they had removed the weapons that hung on the wall of the great hall.

Meanwhile, the suitors had gathered again around the feast table and were more boisterous than before. "Come, fair Penelope!" they shouted. "This beggar can tell his tale tomorrow. It is time for you to choose a new husband! Choose now!"

"Chiefs and princes," said Penelope, in trembling tones, "let us leave this decision to the gods. Behold, there hangs the great bow of Ulysses, which he alone was able to string. Let each of you try his strength in bending it, and I will choose the one who can shoot an arrow from it the most skillfully."

"Well said!" cried all the suitors, and they lined up to try their strength. The first took the bow in his hands, and struggled long to bend it. Then, losing patience, he threw it on the ground and strode away. "None but a giant can string a bow like that," he said.

Then, one by one, the other suitors tried their strength, but all in vain.

"Perhaps the old beggar would like to take part in this contest," one said with a sneer.

Then Ulysses in his beggar's rags rose from his seat and

went with halting steps to the head of the hall. He fumbled with the great bow, gazing at its polished back and its long, well-shaped arms, stout as bars of iron. "Methinks," he said, "that in my younger days I once saw a bow like this."

"Enough! Enough!" shouted the suitors. "Get out, you old fool!"

Suddenly, a great change came over the stranger. Almost without effort, he bent the great bow and strung it. Then he rose to his full height, and even in his beggar's rags appeared every inch a king.

"Ulysses! Ulysses!" Penelope cried.

The suitors were speechless. Then, in the wildest alarm, they turned and tried to escape from the hall. But the arrows of Ulysses were swift and sure, and not one missed its mark. "Now I avenge myself upon those who have tried to destroy my home!" he cried. And thus, one after another, the lawless suitors perished.

The next day Ulysses sat in the great hall with Penelope and Telemachus and all the joyful members of the household, and he told the story of his long wanderings over the sea. And Penelope, in turn, related how she had faithfully kept the kingdom, as she had promised, though beset by insolent and wicked suitors. Then she brought from her chamber a roll of soft, white cloth of wonderful delicacy and beauty, and said, "This is the web, Ulysses. I promised that on the day of its completion I would choose a husband, and I choose you."

The Story of Cincinnatus

RETOLD BY JAMES BALDWIN

This story takes place in 458 B.C., when Rome was attacked by a tribe called the Aequi. It reminds us that the loyal citizen expects no great reward for coming to his country's aid.

There was a man named Cincinnatus who lived on a little farm not far from the city of Rome. He had once been rich, and had held the highest office in the land, but in one way or another he had lost all his wealth. He was now so poor that he had to do all the work on his farm with his own hands. But in those days it was thought to be a noble thing to till the soil.

Cincinnatus was so wise and just that everybody trusted him, and asked his advice. When anyone was in trouble, and did not know what to do, his neighbors would say,

"Go and tell Cincinnatus. He will help you."

Now there lived among the mountains, not far away, a tribe of fierce, half-wild men, who were at war with the Roman people. They persuaded another tribe of bold warriors to help them, and then marched toward the city, plundering and robbing as they came. They boasted that they would tear down the walls of Rome, and burn the houses, and kill all the men, and make slaves of the women and children.

At first the Romans, who were very proud and brave, did not think there was much danger. Every man in Rome was a soldier, and the army which went out to fight the robbers was the finest in the world. No one stayed at home but the white-haired "Fathers," as they were called, who made the laws for the city, and a small company of men who guarded the walls. Everybody thought that it would be an easy thing to drive the men of the mountains back to the place where they belonged.

But one morning five horsemen came riding down the road from the mountains. They rode with great speed, and both men and horses were covered with dust and blood. The watchman at the gate knew them and shouted to them as they galloped in. Why did they ride thus? And what had happened to the Roman army?

They did not answer him, but rode into the city and along the quiet streets. Everybody ran after them, eager to find out what was the matter. Rome was not a large city at that time, and soon they reached the marketplace where the white-haired Fathers were sitting. Then they leaped from their horses, and told their story.

"Only yesterday," they said, "our army was marching through a narrow valley between two steep mountains. All at once a thousand savage men sprang out from among the rocks before us and above us. They had blocked up the way, and the pass was so narrow that we could not fight. We tried to come back, but they had blocked up the way on this side of us, too. The fierce men of the mountains were before us and behind us, and they were throwing rocks down upon us from above. We had been caught in a trap. Then ten of us set spurs to our horses, and five of us forced our way through, but the other five fell before the spears of the mountain men. And now, O Roman Fathers! Send help to our army at once, or every man will be slain, and our city will be taken."

"What shall we do?" said the white-haired Fathers. "Whom can we send but the guards and the boys? And who is wise enough to lead them and thus save Rome?"

All shook their heads and were very grave, for it seemed as if there was no hope. Then one said, "Send for Cincinnatus. He will help us."

Cincinnatus was in the field plowing when the men who had been sent to him came in great haste. He stopped and greeted them kindly, and waited for them to speak.

"Put on your cloak, Cincinnatus," they said, "and hear the words of the Roman people."

Then Cincinnatus wondered what they could mean. "Is all well with Rome?" he asked. And he called to his wife to bring him his cloak.

She brought the cloak; and Cincinnatus wiped the dust from his hands and arms, and threw it over his shoulder. Then the men told their errand.

They told him how the army with all the noblest men of Rome had been entrapped in the mountain pass. They told him about the great danger the city was in. Then they said, "The people of Rome make you their ruler and the ruler of their city, to do with everything as you choose. And the Fathers bid you come at once and go out against our enemies, the fierce men of the mountains."

So Cincinnatus left his plow standing where it was, and hurried to the city. When he passed through the streets, and gave orders as to what should be done, some of the people were afraid, for they knew that he had all power in Rome to do what he pleased. But he armed the guards and the boys, and went out at their head to fight the fierce mountain men, and free the Roman army from the trap into which it had fallen.

A few days afterward there was great joy in Rome. There was good news from Cincinnatus. The men of the mountains had been beaten with great loss. They had been driven back into their own place.

And now the Roman army, with the boys and the guards, was coming home with banners flying, and shouts of victory. And at their head rode Cincinnatus. He had saved Rome.

Cincinnatus might then have made himself king, for his word was law, and no man dared lift a finger against him. But, before the people could thank him enough for what he had done, he gave back the power to the white-haired Roman Fathers, and went again to his little farm and his plow.

He had been the ruler of Rome for sixteen days.

Thunder Falls

RETOLD BY ALLAN MACFARLAN

This story comes from the Kickapoo Indians, a Midwestern tribe once noted for their frequent wanderings; their name comes from a word meaning "he who moves about, standing now here, now there."

The blanket of night had wrapped the Kickapoo village in darkness. The people were gathered around the story-fire, awaiting the tale which the storyteller would tell. The listeners knew that the tale would not be of braves on the war trail or warriors who risked their lives on raids into the country of their enemies. And yet the story which they were about to hear was one of high courage. It was of two brave women who were still honored in song and dance because of their great courage and their noble sacrifice made for their tribe. This is the story that the people heard.

A band of our men were hunting, when the green earth had come from beneath the snow and rivers were fat and fast. Women were with the men, to help skin the animals taken in the chase, and to strip and dry the meat. For three suns the party had hunted, and deer had fallen to their hunting arrows.

As they traveled in country distant from our territory, there was always danger of attack by enemies. Braves kept watch always, but they did not watch well enough. One day the chief said it would be a good thing to return to the tribe, and the party made ready to go back when the sun came. Some of the braves and women did not see the sun again. A big war party of Shawnee surrounded and attacked the camp when night was leaving to let morning come.

The Kickapoo who were not killed or badly wounded escaped down into the gorges. They had hunted there and found a great cave, beneath the thundering falls of a mighty river. The chief had decided that they would hide there if they saw a large war party of the enemy, so all of the Kickapoo knew the hiding place.

The savage Shawnee killed the wounded and took two of our women back to their camp, as prisoners. The women were young and would be made to work. The camp of the Shawnee was far above the place where they had attacked our party. Their lodges were on the banks of the wide, fast-flowing river.

For six suns after the attack, the Shawnee warriors searched for our people who had escaped the raid. Sentries were placed at distant points so that the Kickapoo could not escape without being seen. The big war party of the Shawnee would be told of their movements. The enemy searched well, but our people hid better and were not discovered. Our chief did not let his party leave the great cavern, nor did they need to, for they had dried meat and water in plenty.

After some suns had passed, the people begged the chief to let them leave the shelter of the big cave beneath the falls. They felt safe there, but the terrible noise of the falls hurt their ears, as it roared like a curtain of thunder before the cavern. Their minds were afraid too, for they feared that spirits of evil dwelt in the dark, rocky gorges which surrounded them.

The chief was brave, but he knew how his band felt. He too would be happy to leave the great roaring and rumbling far behind him, even if, in escaping, more of his band would fall to the arrows of the Shawnee. "Tomorrow, the day of the seventh sun since the attack, will be the last that we remain here," he told his band. "When darkness comes, we will try to escape from the enemy into our own territory. Be ready!"

Our chief knew that the chances of reaching safety were few, as the Shawnee were many and must be angry that any of our people had escaped the raid. "Their anger must be very great," the Kickapoo chief thought, "because though they could follow the trails in the forest, their best trailers could not see footprints on the rocky ground which formed the river gorges."

The medicine man of the Shawnee went to their chief on the morning of the seventh sun and told him of a dream which he had had. His totem bird, the red-tailed hawk, had come to him in a dream and flown around and around him in circles, giving shrill cries and tempting him to follow it. The medicine man could not refuse to follow his totem bird, so his spirit followed it as it flew swiftly before him, until the hawk reached a clearing in the forest. Here, in the dream, the medicine man saw a circle of Shadow People.

"Can I follow the Shadow People to where our enemies are hidden?" the medicine man asked the hawk. "Who among them knows where the band is hiding?"

The hawk flew straight to the two women who were the prisoners of the Shawnee and circled the head of each.

"These women must know," declared the medicine man, as he told his chief of the dream. "My hawk totem never leads me on a false trail."

The Shawnee chief had great faith in the medicine man and his totem bird; so he called a council of his warriors. He told them of the dream and had the two captive women brought before him. When questioned, they declared that they did not know where the band to which they belonged was hidden.

"They speak with a crooked tongue," shouted the medicine man, "but torture will make it straight."

The women were tortured and, under the bite of blazing twigs held to their wrists, they cried out that they would reveal the hiding place of their band. For a moment, they spoke softly together in their own dialect and then, by signs, showed that they were ready to lead the Shawnee war party to the hiding place.

When the Shawnee were armed and about to follow them, the two women pointed to the river, instead of leading the way into the forest. By signs they showed that our people were far away and could be reached quicker by the Shawnees if they went by canoe. When the chief pointed toward the forest and his braves pushed the women in that direction, they showed by sign talk that they could not lead the Shawnees by land. Only by water did they know the way to the hidden Kickapoo band.

The chief believed the women, and they were taken to the big canoes that lay on the riverbank. With hands and sounds, the women told that close to the falls there was a little branch of the main river which they must follow to reach the Kickapoo. The chief ordered the women into the leading canoe. He too sat in it, with his medicine man and six of his best warriors. The rest of the party followed close behind, in many canoes. Paddles flashed and the canoes went swift as a fish downstream.

After paddling far, the chief asked the women if they were not yet near the hiding place of his enemies. The women sign-talked that the place was near, and again the paddles rose and fell. The braves did not have to paddle so hard now because the current was becoming swifter and stronger, as the canoes sped along. Quicker and quicker the canoes traveled. From the distance came the thunder of the falls. Closer and closer came the earth-shaking roar.

The chief was brave, but even he feared the mighty force of the swift-rushing waters. He was directly behind the two captive women, who sat in the bow. He touched them on the shoulders, and they turned to him at once. The chief ceased to fear when he saw that both women were smiling. The elder of the two, with a wave of her arm toward the south bank, showed that in a moment they would reach the fork of the river, where the paddlers could swing the canoes from the rushing current into the calm water of the smaller stream.

Faster, ever faster, the canoes now dashed through the foaming torrent. Narrower grew the rushing river as it roared between solid walls of rock. No time to try to turn the canoes!

Too late, the chief and warriors knew that they had been tricked. The bravest had but time to sing a few notes of their death songs before the raging torrent swept the shattered canoes over the crest of the mighty waterfall. Proudly leading the band of enemy warriors to death on the jagged rocks below were the two brave women of the Kickapoo.

My story is done, but that of the two who saved our band of warriors from death will go on as long as grass grows and water runs.

Yudisthira at Heaven's Gate

This story is from the Mahabharata, *which, with the* Ramayana, *is one of the two great epic poems of India. Here loyalty is literally the test to gain entrance to heaven.*

Good King Yudisthira had ruled over the Pandava people for many years and had led them in a successful, but very long war against giant forces of evil. At the end of his labors, Yudisthira felt that he had had enough years on earth and it was time to go on to the kingdom of the Immortals. When all his plans were made, he set out for the high Mount Meru to go from there to the Celestial City. His beautiful wife, Drapaudi, went with him and also his four brothers. Very soon, they were joined by a dog which followed quietly behind him.

But the journey to the mountain was a long and sorrowful one. Yudisthira's four brothers died one by one along the way, and after that his wife, the beautiful Drapaudi. The King was all alone then, except for the dog, which continued to follow him faithfully up and up the steep, long road to the Celestial City.

At last the two, weak and exhausted, stopped before the gates of Heaven. Yudisthira bowed humbly there as he asked to be admitted.

Sky and earth were filled with a loud noise as the God Indra, God of a Thousand Eyes, arrived to meet and welcome the King to Paradise. But Yudisthira was not quite ready.

"Without my brothers and my beloved wife, my innocent Drapaudi, I do not wish to enter Heaven, O Lord of all the deities," he said.

"Have no fear," Indra answered. "You shall meet them all in Heaven. They came before you and are already there!"

But Yudisthira had yet another request to make.

"This dog has come all the way with me. He is devoted to me. Surely for his faithfulness I cannot leave him outside! And besides, my heart is full of love for him!"

Indra shook his great head and the earth quaked.

"You yourself may have immortality," he said, "and riches and success and all the joys of Heaven. You have won these by making this hard journey. But you cannot bring a dog into Heaven. Cast off the dog, Yudisthira! It is no sin!"

"But where would he go?" demanded the King. "And who would go with him? He has given up all the pleasures of earth to be my companion. I cannot desert him now."

The God was irritated at this.

"You must be pure to enter Paradise," he said firmly. "Just to touch a dog will take away all the merits of prayer. Consider what you are doing, Yudisthira. Let the dog go!"

But Yudisthira insisted. "O God of a Thousand Eyes, it is difficult for a person who has always tried to be righteous to do something that he knows is unrighteous—even in order to get into Heaven. I do not wish immortality if it means casting off one that is devoted to me."

Indra urged home once more.

"You left on the road behind you your four brothers and your wife. Why can't you also leave the dog?"

But Yudisthira said, "I abandoned those only because they had died already and I could no longer help them nor bring them back to life. As long as they lived I did not leave them."

"You are willing to abandon Heaven, then, for this dog's sake?" the God asked him.

"Great God of all Gods," Yudisthira replied, "I have steadily kept this vow—that I will never desert one that is frightened and seeks my protection, one that is afflicted and destitute, or one that is too weak to protect himself and desires to live. Now I add a fourth. I have promised never to forsake one that is devoted to me. I will not abandon my friend."

Yudisthira reached down to touch the dog and was about to turn sadly away from Heaven when suddenly before his very eyes a wonder happened. The faithful dog was changed into Dharma, the God of Righteousness and Justice.

Indra said, "You are a good man, King Yudisthira. You have shown faithfulness to the faithful, and compassion for all creatures. You have done this by renouncing the very Gods themselves instead of renouncing this humble dog that was your companion. You shall be honored in heaven, O King Yudisthira, for there is no act which is valued more highly and rewarded more richly than compassion for the humble."

So Yudisthira entered the Celestial City with the God of Righteousness beside him. He was reunited there with his brothers and his beloved wife to enjoy eternal happiness.

FAITH

✑ Faith

In this chapter you will find a poem entitled the "Landing of the Pilgrim Fathers" by Felicia Hemans. The lines "breaking waves dashed high," "woods against a stormy sky," and "the depths of the desert gloom" remind us that many of the first European settlers endured tremendous hardships to reach America. They came in no small part because they "sought a faith's pure shrine . . . Freedom to worship God." A century and a half later, Thomas Jefferson wrote in the Declaration of Independence that all men are "endowed by their Creator with certain unalienable Rights," words that transformed the Pilgrims' quest to worship freely into one of our nation's founding ideals.

That principle of toleration has helped make the people of the United States, in general, a very religious people. Millions have come to these shores from all parts of the earth to make a better life, not just in a material way but in a spiritual sense as well. They've come here to aspire to the decent, hard-working, compassionate lives their various faiths envision.

This does not mean, of course, that only people of faith

are good people. Some individuals live virtuous lives without any sort of faith in a Higher Power. And respecting their choice not to practice any faith is an important part of our tradition of religious freedom.

For most people of faith, however, their belief in God anchors their morality. It supports all of their other virtues and furnishes a context in which those virtues make sense. All the world's major religions are sources of discipline and power for living good lives and for helping others live good lives as well. They share common virtues as goals.

Take, for example, honesty. "Let your conduct be marked by truthfulness in word, deed and thought," Hinduism teaches. "Be honest like Heaven in conducting your affairs," Taoism advises. "Every day I examine myself . . . In my dealing with my friends, have I always been true to my words?" Confucianism asks.

On the subject of compassion, Muslims believe that "those who act kindly in this world will have kindness." Buddhists hold that "even if it were their last bite, their last morsel of food, they would not enjoy its use without sharing it, if there were anyone to receive it." And those of the Judaic and Christian faiths say, "Blessed is he who considers the poor."

There are, of course, very significant differences between different faiths. Each gives its own answers to the questions of human existence. But despite those differences, most faiths bring people to aim at the same shared set of virtues.

In this chapter you will find examples of faith supporting those virtues. You will read, for example, how Job's faith enabled him to persevere through a long series of hard trials. In "Our Lady's Juggler," you will see how faith helps some people find their life's work. In hymns and poems, you will find deep expressions of faith in response to life's great challenges as well as to everyday living. All of these works help us understand the power of faith.

A Mighty Fortress Is Our God

MARTIN LUTHER

This hymn, written by Martin Luther in 1529, is based on Psalm 46. It reminds us that many people rely not on their own strength to persevere, but on God's.

A mighty fortress is our God,
A bulwark never failing;
Our helper is he, amid the flock
Of mortal ills prevailing.
For still our ancient foe
Doth seek to work us woe;
His craft and pow'r are great,
And arm'd with cruel hate,
On earth is not his equal.

Did we in our own strength confide,
Our striving would be losing;
Were not the right man on our side,
The man of God's own choosing.
Dost ask who that may be?
Christ Jesus, it is he;
Lord Sabaoth his name,
From age to age the same,
And he must win the battle.

And though this world, with demons fill'd
Should threaten to undo us,
We will not fear, for God hath willed
His truth to triumph through us.

The Prince of darkness grim,
We tremble not for him;
His rage we can endure,
For lo, his doom is sure—
One little work shall fell him.

God's word above all earthly pow'rs,
No thanks to them, abideth;
The Spirit and the gifts are ours
Through him who with us sideth.
Let goods and kindred go,
This mortal life also;
The body they may kill
God's truth abideth still,
His kingdom is forever.

Amazing Grace
JOHN NEWTON

John Newton, the London-born author of this hymn, went to sea at age eleven, was later imprisoned on a man-of-war, escaped to work on a slave-trading vessel, and eventually became a slave ship captain. The hymn is a personal testimony to the "amazing grace" that turned Newton's life around (he later became an ardent abolitionist). After his ordination into the ministry of the Church of England in 1764, Newton and William Cowper produced the Olney Hymns, one of the greatest Anglican hymnals.

Amazing grace, how sweet the sound,
That save a wretch like me!
I once was lost, but now am found,
Was blind, but now I see.

'Twas grace that taught my heart to fear,
And grace my fears relieved;
How precious did that grace appear
The hour I first believed!

Through many dangers, toils, and snares
I have already come;
'Tis grace has brought me safe thus far,
And grace will lead me home.

The Lord has promised good to me,
His word my hope secures;
He will my shield and portion be
As long as life endures.

When we've been here ten thousand years,
Bright shining as the sun,
We've no less days to sing God's praise
Than when we'd first begun.

℘ Deucalion and Pyrrha

RETOLD BY THOMAS BULFINCH

*Greek mythology describes a Golden Age of inno-
cence and happiness, followed by the ages of Silver,
Bronze, and finally Iron. The latter was a savage*

time when "crime burst in like a flood" and "modesty, truth, and honor fled." War sprang up; the guest was not safe in his friend's house; brothers and sisters, husbands and wives could not trust one another. Reverence toward the gods was neglected, and one by one they abandoned the earth. Only the piety of one couple, Deucalion and Pyrrha, saved the human race.

Jupiter, seeing the wicked state of the world, burned with anger. He summoned the gods to council. They obeyed the call and took the road to the palace of heaven. The road, which anyone may see in a clear night, stretches across the face of the sky and is called the Milky Way. Along the road stand the palaces of the illustrious gods; the common people of the skies live apart, on either side. Jupiter addressed the assembly. He set forth the frightful condition of things on the earth, and closed by announcing his intention to destroy the whole of its inhabitants and provide a new race, unlike the first, who would be more worthy of life and much better worshippers of the gods.

So saying, he took a thunderbolt, and was about to launch it at the world and destroy it by burning; but recollecting the danger that such a conflagration might set heaven itself on fire, he changed his plan and resolved to drown . . . [the world]. The north wind, which scatters the clouds, was chained up; the south was sent out, and soon covered all the face of heaven with a cloak of pitchy darkness. The clouds, driven together, resound with a crash; torrents of rain fall; the crops are laid low; the year's labor of the husbandman perishes in an hour. Jupiter, not satisfied with his own waters, calls on his brother Neptune to aid him with his. He lets loose the rivers and pours them over the land. At the same time, he heaves the land with an earthquake and brings in the reflux of the ocean over the shores. Flocks, herds, men and houses are swept away, and temples, with their sacred enclosures, profaned. If any edifice remained standing, it was overwhelmed, and its turrets lay hidden beneath the waves.

Now all was sea, sea without shore. Here and there an individual remained on a projecting hilltop, and a few, in boats, pulled the oar where they had lately driven the plow. The fishes swim among the treetops; the anchor is let down into a garden. Where the graceful lambs played now unwieldy sea calves gambol. The wolf swims among the sheep, the yellow lions and tigers struggle in the water. The strength of the wild boar serves him not, nor his swiftness the stag. The birds fall with weary wing into the water, having found no land for a resting place. Those living beings whom the water spared fell prey to hunger.

Parnassus alone, of all the mountains, overtopped the waves; and there Deucalion, and his wife, Pyrrha, of the race of Prometheus, found refuge—he a just man, and she a faithful worshipper of the gods. Jupiter, when he saw none left alive but this pair, and remembered their harmless lives and pious demeanor, ordered the north winds to drive away the clouds, and disclose the skies to earth and earth to the skies. Neptune also directed Triton to blow on his shell and sound a retreat to the waters. The waters obeyed, and the sea returned to its shores and rivers to their channels.

Then Deucalion thus addressed Pyrrha: "O wife, only surviving woman, joined to me first by the ties of kindred and marriage and now by a common danger, would that we possessed the power of our ancestor Prometheus and could renew the race as he at first made it! But as we cannot, let us seek yonder temple and inquire of the gods what remains for us to do."

They entered the temple, deformed as it was with slime, and approached the altar, where no fire burned. There they fell prostrate on the earth and prayed the goddess to inform them how they might retrieve their miserable affairs. The oracle answered, "Depart from the temple with head veiled and garments unbound, and cast behind you the bones of your mother."

They heard the words with astonishment. Pyrrha first broke silence: "We cannot obey; we dare not profane the remains of our parents."

They sought the thickest of shades of the wood and revolved the oracle in their minds. At length Deucalion spoke: "Either my sagacity deceives me, or the command is one we may obey without impiety. The earth is the great parent of all; the stones are her bones; these we may cast behind us; and I think this is what the oracle means. At least, it will do no harm to try."

They veiled their faces, unbound their garments, and picked up stones and cast them behind them. The stones (wonderful to relate) began to grow soft and assume shape. By degrees, they put on a rude resemblance to the human form, like a block half finished in the hands of the sculptor. The moisture and slime that were about them became flesh; the stony part became bones; the veins remained veins, retaining their name, only changing their use. Those thrown by the hand of the man became men, and those by the woman became women. It was a hard race and well adapted to labor, as we find ourselves to be at this day, giving plain indications of our origin.

❧ Hanukkah Hymn

The Hanukkah festival of lights commemorates the rededication of the Temple in Jerusalem. This Hanukkah hymn expresses the praise, joy, and hope appropriate in commemorating that historic event.

Rock of Ages, let our song
Praise Thy saving power;
Thou, amidst the raging foes,
Wast our sheltering tower.
Furious, they assailed us,
But Thine arm availed us,
And Thy word
Broke their sword
When our own strength failed us.

Kindling new the holy lamps,
Priest approved in suffering,
Purified the nation's shrine,
Brought to God their offering,
And His courts surrounding,
Hear, in joy abounding,
Happy throngs
Singing songs
With a mighty sounding.

Children of the martyr race,
Whether free or fettered,
Wake the echoes of the songs
Where ye may be scattered.
Yours the message cheering

That the time is nearing
Which will see
All men free,
Tyrants disappearing.

I Never Saw a Moor

EMILY DICKINSON

Faith requires no proofs.

I never saw a moor,
I never saw the sea;
Yet know I how the heather looks,
And what a wave must be.

I never spoke with God,
Nor visited in heaven;
Yet certain am I of the spot
As if the chart were given.

Job

RETOLD BY JESSE LYMAN HURLBUT

The book of Job in the Bible is widely recognized as one of the world's great dramatic poems. Its main subject is: Why do righteous people suffer? The suffering of this "perfect and upright" man, his torment, his patience, and his final humility, have become a definition of faith. Here is a prose version of the events in the book of Job.

At some time in those early days—we do not know just at what time, whether in the days of Moses or later—there was living a good man named Job. His home was in the land of Uz, which may have been on the edge of the desert, east of the land of Israel. Job was a very rich man. He had sheep, and camels, and oxen, and asses, counted by the thousand. In all the east there was no other man so rich as Job.

And Job was a good man. He served the Lord God, and prayed to God every day, with an offering upon God's altar, as men worshipped in those times. He tried to live as God wished him to live, and was always kind and gentle. Every day, when his sons were out in the field, or were having a feast together in the house of any of them, Job went out to his altar, and offered a burnt offering for each one of his sons and his daughters, and prayed to God for them; for he said:

"It may be that my sons have sinned or have turned away from God in their hearts; and I will pray God to forgive them."

At one time, when the angels of God stood before the Lord, Satan the Evil One came also, and stood among them, as though he were one of God's angels. The Lord God saw Satan, and said to him, "Satan, from what place have you come?" "I have come," answered Satan, "from going up and down in the earth and looking at the people upon it."

Then the Lord said to Satan, "Have you looked at my servant Job? And have you seen that there is not another man like him in the earth, a good and a perfect man, one who fears God and does nothing evil?" Then Satan said to the Lord: "Does Job fear God for nothing? Hast thou not made a wall around him, and around his house, and around everything that he has? Thou hast given a blessing upon his work, and hast made him rich. But if thou wilt stretch forth thy hand, and take away from him all that he has, then he will turn away from thee and will curse thee to thy face."

Then the Lord said to the Evil One, "Satan, all that Job has is in your power; you can do to his sons, and his flocks, and his cattle, whatever you wish; only lay not your hand upon the man himself."

Then Satan went forth from before the Lord; and soon trouble began to come upon Job. One day, when all his sons and daughters were eating and drinking together in their oldest brother's house, a man came running to Job, and said:

"The oxen were plowing, and the asses were feeding beside them, when the wild men from the desert came upon them, and drove them all away; and the men who were working with the oxen and caring for the asses have all been killed; and I am the only one who has fled away alive!"

While this man was speaking, another man came rushing in; and he said:

"The lightning from the clouds has fallen on all the sheep, and on the men who were tending them; and I am the only one who has come away alive!"

Before this man had ended, another came in; and he said:

"The enemies from Chaldea have come in three bands, and have taken away all the camels. They have killed the men who were with them; and I am the only one left alive!"

Then at the same time, one more man came in, and said to Job:

"Your sons and your daughters were eating and drinking together in their oldest brother's house, when a sudden and terrible wind from the desert struck the house, and it fell upon them. All your sons and your daughters are dead, and I alone have lived to tell you of it."

Thus in one day, all that Job had—his flocks, and his cattle, and his sons and his daughters—all were taken away; and Job, from being rich, was suddenly made poor. Then Job fell down upon his face before the Lord, and he said:

"With nothing I came into the world, and with nothing I shall leave it. The Lord gave, and the Lord has taken away; blessed be the name of the Lord."

So even when all was taken from him Job did not turn away from God, nor did he find fault with God's doings.

And again the angels of God were before the Lord, and Satan, who had done all this harm to Job, was among them. The Lord said to Satan, "Have you looked at my servant Job? There is no other man in the world as good as he; a perfect man, one that fears God and does no wrong act. Do you see how he holds fast to his goodness, even after I have let you do him so great harm?" Then Satan answered the Lord, "All that a man has he will give for his life. But if thou wilt put thy hand upon him and touch his bone and his flesh, he will turn from thee, and will curse thee to thy face."

And the Lord said to Satan, "I will give Job into your hand; do to him whatever you please; only spare his life."

Then Satan went out and struck Job, and caused dreadful boils to come upon him, over all his body, from the soles of his feet to the crown of his head. And Job sat down in the ashes in great pain; but he would not speak one word against God. His wife said to him,

"What is the use of trying to serve God? You may as well curse God, and die!"

But Job said to her, "You speak as one of the foolish.

What? shall we take good things from the Lord? and shall we not take evil things also?" So Job would not speak against God. Then three friends of Job came to see him, and to try to comfort him in his sorrow and pain. Their names were Eliphaz, and Bildad, and Zophar. They sat down with Job, and wept, and spoke to him. But their words were not words of comfort. They believed that all these great troubles had come upon Job to punish him for some great sin, and they tried to persuade Job to tell what evil things he had done to make God so angry with him.

For in those times most people believed that trouble, and sickness, and the loss of friends, and the loss of what they had owned, came to men because God was angry with them on account of their sins. These men thought that Job must have been very wicked because they saw such evils coming upon him. They made long speeches to Job, urging him to confess his wickedness.

Job said that he had done no wrong, that he had tried to do right; and he did not know why these troubles had come; but he would not say that God had dealt unjustly in letting him suffer. Job did not understand God's ways, but he believed that God was good; and he left himself in God's hands. And at last God himself spoke to Job and to his friends, telling them that it is not for man to judge God, and that God will do right by every man. And the Lord said to the three friends of Job:

"You have not spoken of me what is right, as Job has. Now bring an offering to me; and Job shall pray for you, and for his sake I will forgive you."

So Job prayed for his friends, and God forgave them. And because in all his troubles Job had been faithful to God, the Lord blessed Job once more, and took away his boils from him, and made him well. Then the Lord gave to Job more than he had ever owned in the past, twice as many sheep, and oxen, and camels, and asses. And God gave again to Job seven sons and three daughters; and in all the land there were no women found so lovely as the daughters of Job. After his trouble, Job lived a long time, in riches, and honor, and goodness, under God's care.

Landing of the Pilgrim Fathers
FELICIA HEMANS

This poem helps us remember the bravery of those early settlers who came to these shores seeking religious freedom.

> The breaking waves dashed high,
>   On a stern and rock-bound coast,
> And the woods against a stormy sky,
>   Their giant branches tossed;
>
> And the heavy night hung dark,
>   The hills and waters o'er,
> When a band of exiles moored their bark
>   On the wild New England shore.
>
> Not as the conqueror comes,
>   They, the true-hearted came;
> Not with the roll of the stirring drums,
>   And the trumpet that sings of fame;
>
> Not as the flying come,
>   In silence and in fear—

They shook the depths of the desert gloom
     With their hymns of lofty cheer.

Amidst the storm they sang,
     And the stars heard, and the sea;
And the sounding aisles of the dim woods rang
     To the anthem of the free.

The ocean eagle soared
     From his nest by the white wave's foam;
And the rocking pines of the forest roared—
     This was their welcome home.

There were men with hoary hair
     Amidst that pilgrim band:
Why had they come to wither there,
     Away from their childhood's land?

There was a woman's fearless eye,
     Lit by her deep love's truth;
There was manhood's brow serenely high,
     And the fiery heart of youth.

What sought they thus afar?
     Bright jewels of the mine?
The wealth of seas, the spoils of war?
     They sought a faith's pure shrine!

Aye, call it holy ground,
     The soil where first they trod;
They have left unstained what there they found—
     Freedom to worship God.

ᕙ Our Lady's Juggler

ANATOLE FRANCE

Faith leads us to employ our God-given talents in God's service.

In the days of King Louis there was a poor juggler in France, a native of Compiègne, Barnaby by name, who went about from town to town performing feats of skill and strength.

On fair days he would unfold an old worn-out carpet in the public square, and when by means of a jovial address, which he had learned of a very ancient juggler, and which he never varied in the least, he had drawn together the children and loafers, he assumed extraordinary attitudes, and balanced a tin plate on the tip of his nose. At first the crowd would feign indifference.

But when, supporting himself on his hands face downward, he threw into the air six copper balls, which glittered in the sunshine, and caught them again with his feet; or when throwing himself backward until his heels and the nape of the neck met, giving his body the form of a perfect wheel, he would juggle in this posture with a dozen knives, a murmur of admiration would escape the spectators, and pieces of money rain down upon the carpet.

Nevertheless, like the majority of those who live by their wits, Barnaby of Compiègne had a great struggle to make a living.

Earning his bread in the sweat of his brow, he bore rather more than his share of the penalties consequent upon the misdoings of our father Adam.

Again, he was unable to work as constantly as he would have been willing to do. The warmth of the sun and the broad daylight were as necessary to enable him to display his brilliant parts as to the trees if flower and fruit should be expected of them. In wintertime he was nothing more than a tree stripped of its leaves, and as it were dead. The frozen ground was hard to the juggler, and, like the grasshopper of which Marie de France tells us, the inclement season caused him to suffer both cold and hunger. But as he was simple-natured he bore his ills patiently.

He had never meditated on the origin of wealth, nor upon the inequality of human conditions. He believed firmly that if this life should prove hard, the life to come could not fail to redress the balance, and this hope upheld him. He did not resemble those thievish and miscreant Merry Andrews who sell their souls to the devil. He never blasphemed God's name; he lived uprightly, and although he had no wife of his own, he did not covet his neighbor's, since woman is ever the enemy of the strong man, as it appears by the history of Samson recorded in the Scriptures.

In truth, his was not a nature much disposed to carnal delights, and it was a greater deprivation to him to forsake the tankard than the Hebe [goddess of youth who bore it]. For whilst not wanting in sobriety, he was fond of a drink when the weather waxed hot. He was a worthy man who feared God, and was very devoted to the Blessed Virgin.

Never did he fail on entering a church to fall upon his knees before the image of the Mother of God, and offer up this prayer to her:

"Blessed Lady, keep watch over my life until it shall

please God that I die, and when I am dead, ensure to me the possession of the joys of paradise."

Now on a certain evening after a dreary wet day, as Barnaby pursued his road, sad and bent, carrying under his arm his balls and knives wrapped up in his old carpet, on the watch for some barn where, though he might not sup, he might sleep, he perceived on the road, going in the same direction as himself, a monk, whom he saluted courteously. And as they walked at the same rate they fell into conversation with one another.

"Fellow traveler," said the monk, "how comes it about that you are clothed all in green? Is it perhaps in order to take the part of a jester in some mystery play?"

"Not at all, good father," replied Barnaby. "Such as you see me, I am called Barnaby, and for my calling I am a juggler. There would be no pleasanter calling in the world if it would always provide one with daily bread."

"Friend Barnaby," returned the monk, "be careful what you say. There is no calling more pleasant than the monastic life. Those who lead it are occupied with the praises of God, the Blessed Virgin, and the saints; and, indeed, the religious life is one ceaseless hymn to the Lord."

Barnaby replied—

"Good father, I own that I spoke like an ignorant man. Your calling cannot be in any respect compared to mine, and although there may be some merit in dancing with a penny balanced on a stick on the tip of one's nose, it is not a merit which comes within hail of your own. Gladly would I, like you, good father, sing my office day by day, and especially the office of the most Holy Virgin, to whom I have vowed a singular devotion. In order to embrace the monastic life I would willingly abandon the art by which from

Soissons to Beauvais I am well known in upward of six hundred towns and villages."

The monk was touched by the juggler's simplicity, and as he was not lacking in discernment, he at once recognized in Barnaby one of those men of whom it is said in the Scriptures: Peace on earth to men of good will. And for this reason he replied—

"Friend Barnaby, come with me, and I will have you admitted into the monastery of which I am prior. He who guided St. Mary of Egypt in the desert set me upon your path to lead you into the way of salvation."

It was in this manner, then, that Barnaby became a monk. In the monastery into which he was received the religious vied with one another in the praise of the Blessed Virgin, and in her honor each employed all the knowledge and all the skill which God had given him.

The prior on his part wrote books dealing according to the rules of scholarship with the virtues of the Mother of God.

Brother Maurice, with a deft hand, copied out these treatises upon sheets of vellum.

Brother Alexander adorned the leaves with delicate miniature paintings. Here were displayed the Queen of Heaven seated upon Solomon's throne, and while four lions were on guard at her feet, around the nimbus which encircled her head hovered seven doves, which are the seven gifts of the Holy Spirit, the gifts, namely, of Fear, Piety, Knowledge, Strength, Counsel, Understanding, and Wisdom. For her companions she had six virgins with hair of gold, namely, Humility, Prudence, Seclusion, Submission, Virginity, and Obedience.

At her feet were two little naked figures, perfectly white,

in an attitude of supplication. These were souls imploring her all-powerful intercession for their soul's health, and we may be sure not imploring in vain.

Upon another page facing this, Brother Alexander represented Eve, so that the Fall and the Redemption could be perceived at one and the same time—Eve the Wife abased, and Mary the Virgin exalted.

Furthermore, to the marvel of the beholder, this book contained presentments of the Well of Living Waters, the Fountain, the Lily, the Moon, the Sun, and the Garden Enclosed of which the Song of Songs tells us, the Gate of Heaven and the City of God, and all these things were symbols of the Blessed Virgin.

Brother Marbode was likewise one of the most loving children of Mary.

He spent all his days carving images in stone, so that his beard, his eyebrows, and his hair were white with dust, and his eyes continually swollen and weeping; but his strength and cheerfulness were not diminished, although he was now well gone in years, and it was clear that the Queen of Paradise still cherished her servant in his old age. Marbode represented her seated upon a throne, her brow encircled with an orb-shaped nimbus set with pearls. And he took care that the folds of her dress should cover the feet of her, concerning whom the prophet declared: My beloved is as a garden enclosed.

Sometimes, too, he depicted her in the semblance of a child full of grace, and appearing to say, "Thou art my God, even from my mother's womb."

In the priory, moreover, were poets who composed hymns in Latin, both in prose and verse, in honor of the Blessed Virgin Mary, and amongst the company was even a brother from Picardy who sang the miracles of Our Lady in rhymed verse and in the vulgar tongue.

Being a witness of this emulation in praise and the glorious harvest of their labors, Barnaby mourned his own ignorance and simplicity.

"Alas!" he sighed, as he took his solitary walk in the little shelterless garden of the monastery, "wretched wight that I am, to be unable, like my brothers, worthily to praise the Holy Mother of God, to whom I have vowed my whole heart's affection. Alas! alas! I am but a rough man and unskilled in the arts, and I can render you in service, blessed Lady, neither edifying sermons, nor treatises set out in order according to rule, nor ingenious paintings, nor statues truthfully sculptured, nor verses whose march is measured to the beat of feet. No gift have I, alas!"

After this fashion he groaned and gave himself up to sorrow. But one evening, when the monks were spending their hour of liberty in conversation, he heard one of them tell the tale of a religious man who could repeat nothing other than the Ave Maria. This poor man was despised for his ignorance; but after his death there issued forth from his mouth five roses in honor of the five letters of the name Maria, and thus his sanctity was made manifest.

Whilst he listened to this narrative Barnaby marveled yet once again at the loving kindness of the Virgin; but the lesson of that blessed death did not avail to console him, for his heart overflowed with zeal, and he longed to advance the glory of his Lady, who is in heaven.

How to compass this he sought but could find no way, and day by day he became the more cast down, when one morning he awakened filled full with joy, hastened to the chapel, and remained there alone for more than an hour.

After dinner he returned to the chapel once more.

And, starting from that moment, he repaired daily to the chapel at such hours as it was deserted, and spent within it a good part of the time which the other monks devoted to the liberal and mechanical arts. His sadness vanished, nor did he any longer groan.

A demeanor so strange awakened the curiosity of the monks.

These began to ask one another for what purpose Brother Barnaby could be indulging so persistently in retreat.

The prior, whose duty it is to let nothing escape him in the behavior of his children in religion, resolved to keep a watch over Barnaby during his withdrawals to the chapel. One day, then, when he was shut up there after his custom, the prior, accompanied by two of the older monks, went to discover through the chinks in the door what was going on within the chapel.

They saw Barnaby before the altar of the Blessed Virgin, head downward, with his feet in the air, and he was juggling with six balls of copper and a dozen knives. In honor of the Holy Mother of God he was performing those feats, which aforetime had won him most renown. Not recognizing that the simple fellow was thus placing at the service of the Blessed Virgin his knowledge and skill, the two old monks exclaimed against the sacrilege.

The prior was aware how stainless was Barnaby's soul, but he concluded that he had been seized with madness. They were all three preparing to lead him swiftly from the chapel, when they saw the Blessed Virgin descend the steps of the altar and advance to wipe away with a fold of her azure robe the sweat which was dropping from her juggler's forehead.

Then the prior, falling upon his face upon the pavement, uttered these words—

"Blessed are the simplehearted, for they shall see God."

"Amen!" responded the old brethren, and kissed the ground.

⮿ The 23rd Psalm

The book of Psalms was the ancient hymnal of the Jewish people. Most of the psalms were probably written for use in worship; one finds among them songs of praise, thanksgiving, adoration, devotion, doubt, and complaint. Martin Luther called the Psalter "a Bible in miniature." Psalm 23, a hymn of trust in God, is probably the most widely loved.

The Lord is my shepherd; I shall not want.

He maketh me to lie down in green pastures: he leadeth me beside the still waters.

He restoreth my soul: he leadeth me in the paths of righteousness for his name's sake.

Yea, though I walk through the valley of the shadow of death, I will fear no evil; for thou art with me; thy rod and thy staff they comfort me.

Thou preparest a table before me in the presence of mine enemies: thou anointest my head with oil; my cup runneth over.

Surely goodness and mercy shall follow me all the days of my life: and I will dwell in the house of the Lord forever.

The Fiery Furnace

RETOLD BY JESSE LYMAN HURLBUT

The book of Daniel in the Bible is about the Jewish hero Daniel, who is taken captive to Babylon and, along with his friends Shadrach, Meshach, and Abednego, brought up in the court of King Nebuchadnezzar. The literal trial by fire we read about here is one of our most memorable examples of steadfastness in one's faith.

At one time King Nebuchadnezzar caused a great image to be made to be covered with gold. This image he set up as an idol to be worshipped, on the plain of Dura, near the city of Babylon. When it was finished, it stood upon its base or foundation almost a hundred feet high, so that upon the plain it could be seen far away. Then the king sent out a command for all the princes, and rulers, and nobles in the land to come to a great gathering, when the image was to be set apart for worship.

The great men of the kingdom came from far and near, and stood around the image. Among them, by command of the king, were Daniel's three friends, the young Jews named Shadrach, Meshach, and Abednego. For some reason Daniel himself was not there. He may have been busy with the work of the kingdom in some other place.

At one moment in the service all the trumpets sounded, the drums were beaten, and music was made upon musical instruments of all kinds, as a signal for all the people to kneel down and worship the great golden image. But while the people were kneeling there were three men who stood up and would not bow down. These were the three young

Jews named Shadrach, Meshach, and Abednego. They knelt down before the Lord God only.

Many of the nobles had been jealous of these young men because they had been lifted to high places in the rule of the kingdom. These men who hated Daniel and his friends, were glad to find that these three men had not obeyed the command of King Nebuchadnezzar. The king had said that if anyone did not worship the golden image he should be thrown into a furnace of fire.

These men who hated the Jews came to the king and said, "O king, may you live forever! You gave orders that when the music sounded everyone should bow down and worship the golden image; and that if any man did not worship he should be thrown into a furnace of fire. There are some Jews whom you have made rulers in the land, and they have not done as you commanded. Their names are Shadrach, Meshach, and Abednego. They do not serve your gods, nor worship the golden image that you have set up."

Then Nebuchadnezzar was filled with rage and fury at knowing that anyone should dare to disobey his words. He sent for these three men and said to them, "O Shadrach, Meshach, and Abednego, was it by purpose that you did not fall down and worship the image of gold? The music shall sound once more, and if you then will worship the image, it shall be well. But if you will not, then you shall be thrown into the furnace of fire to die."

These three young men were not afraid of the king. They said, "O King Nebuchadnezzar, we are ready to answer you at once. The God whom we serve is able to save us from the fiery furnace and we know that he will save us. But if it is God's will that we should die, even then, you may understand, O king, that we will not serve your gods, nor worship the golden image that you have set up."

The answer made the king more furious than before. He said to his servants, "Make a fire in the furnace hotter than ever it has been before, as hot as fire can be made, and throw these three men into it."

Then the soldiers of the king's army seized the three young Jews as they stood in their loose robes, with their turbans or hats on their heads. They tied them with ropes, dragged them to the mouth of the furnace, and threw them into the fire. The flames rushed from the open door with such fury that they burned even to death the soldiers who were holding these men; and the men themselves fell down bound into the middle of the fiery furnace.

King Nebuchadnezzar stood in front of the furnace and looked into the open door. As he looked he was filled with wonder at what he saw; and he said to the nobles around him:

"Did we not throw three men bound into the fire? How is it then that I see four men loose, walking in the furnace, and the fourth man looks as though he were a son of the gods?"

The king came near to the door of the furnace as the fire became lower, and he called out to the three men within it:

"Shadrach, Meshach, and Abednego, ye who serve the Most High God, come out of the fire and come to me."

They came out and stood before the king, in the sight of all the princes and nobles, and rulers; and everyone could see that they were alive. Their garments had not been scorched nor their hair singed, nor was there even the smell of fire upon them. The king, Nebuchadnezzar, said before all his rulers:

"Blessed be the God of these men, who has sent his

angel and has saved their lives. I make a law that no man in all my kingdoms shall say a word against their God, for there is no other god who can save in this manner. And if any man speaks a word against their God, the Most High God, that man shall be cut in pieces, and his house shall be torn down." And after this the king lifted up these three young men to still higher places in the land of Babylon.

❧ The Healing of the Paralytic
RETOLD BY JESSE LYMAN HURLBUT

This story from the New Testament is a miracle story of a physical healing brought about through tremendous faith.

After a time Jesus came again to Capernaum, which was now his home. As soon as the people heard that he was there they came in great crowds to see him and to hear him. They filled the house, and the courtyard inside its walls, and even the streets around it, while Jesus sat in the open court of the house and taught them. It was the springtime and warm, and a roof had been placed over the court as a shelter from the sun.

While Jesus was teaching, the roof was suddenly taken away above their heads. They looked up and saw that a man was being let down in a bed by four men on the walls above.

This man was paralyzed, so that he could neither walk nor stand. He was so eager to come to Jesus that these men, finding that they could not carry him through the crowd, had lifted him up to the top of the house and had opened the roof and were now letting him down in his bed before Jesus.

This showed that they believed in Jesus, without any doubt whether he could cure this man. Jesus said to the man, "My son, be of good cheer; your sins are forgiven!"

The enemies of Jesus who were sitting near heard these words, and they thought in their own minds, though they did not speak it aloud, "What wicked things this man speaks! He claims to forgive sins! Who except God himself has power to say, 'Your sins are forgiven'?"

Jesus knew their thoughts, for he knew all things, and he said, "Why do you think evil in your hearts? Which is the easier to say, 'Your sins are forgiven,' or 'Rise up and walk'? But I will show you that while I am on earth as the Son of Man, I have the power to forgive sins."

Then he spoke to the paralyzed man on his couch before them, "Rise up, take up your bed, and go to your house!"

At once a new life and power came to the man. He stood upon his feet, rolled up the bed on which he had been lying helpless, placed it on his shoulders and walked out through the crowd, which opened to make a way for him. The man went, strong and well, to his own house, praising God as he walked.

ᕈ The Coming Of Maize

ADAPTED FROM A RETELLING
BY LEWIS SPENCE

In this beautiful Native American story, a young man's prayers for his family and his people are answered.

A boy of fourteen or fifteen lived with his parents, brothers and sisters in a little lodge by the side of a wide river. The family, though happy, was very poor. The father was a hunter who was not lacking in courage and skill, but there were times when he could scarcely supply the needs of his family, and so they often suffered hardship.

The time came for the boy to observe the fast prescribed by tradition for all young men his age, and his mother made him a little fasting-lodge in a remote spot where he might not suffer interruption during his ordeal. There the boy retired, meditating on the goodness of the Great Spirit, who had made all things beautiful in the fields and forests for the enjoyment of everyone. The desire to help his family was strong upon him, and he prayed hard that some means might be revealed to him in a dream.

On the third day of his fast he was too weak to ramble through the forest, and as he lay in a state between sleeping and waking there came toward him a beautiful youth, rich-ly dressed in green robes and wearing on his head wonder-ful green plumes.

"The Great Spirit has heard your prayers," said the youth, and his voice was like the sound of the wind sighing through the grass. "Listen to me, and you shall have your desire fulfilled. Rise and wrestle with me."

The boy obeyed. Though his limbs were weak, his mind was not clear and active, and he felt he must heed the words of the soft-voiced stranger. After a long, silent struggle the latter said . . . "That will do for today. Tomorrow I will come again."

The boy lay back exhausted, but the next day the green-clad stranger reappeared, and the conflict was renewed. As the struggle went on, the boy felt himself grow stronger and more confident, and before leaving him for the second time, the supernatural visitor offered him some words of praise and encouragement.

On the third day the youth, pale and feeble, was again summoned to the contest. As he grasped his opponent, the very contact seemed to give him new strength, and he fought more and more bravely, till his lithe companion was forced to cry out that he had had enough. Before he took his departure, the visitor told the boy that the following day would bring an end to his trials.

"Tomorrow evening I will come and wrestle with you one last time," he said. "I know you are destined to win and obtain your heart's desire. When you have thrown me, strip off my garments and plumes, bury me where I fall, and keep the earth above me moist and clean. Once a month let my remains be covered with fresh earth, and you shall see me again, clothed in my green garments and plumes." So saying, he vanished.

The next day the boy's father brought him food. The youth, however, begged that it might be set aside until evening. Once again the stranger appeared. Though the boy had eaten nothing, his strength, as before, seemed to increase as he struggled, and at length he threw his opponent. Then he stripped off the stranger's garments and plumes and buried him in the earth, not without sorrow in his heart for the slaying of such a beautiful youth.

His task done he returned to his parents, and soon recovered his full strength. But he never forgot the grave of his friend. Not a weed was allowed to grow on it, and finally he was rewarded by seeing the green plumes rise from the earth and broaden into graceful leaves.

When the autumn came, he asked his father to accompany him to the place. By this time the plant was at its full height, tall and beautiful, with waving leaves and golden tassels. The elder man was filled with surprise and admiration.

"It is my friend," murmured the youth, "the friend of my dreams."

"It is Mondamin," said his father, "the spirit's grain, the gift of the Great Spirit."

And in this manner was the maize given to the boy's people.

ᨒ The Bramblebush

Many religions teach that the struggle with evil is constant. They also teach that one's faith can give strength to win that struggle. But as this Muslim parable reminds us, the longer one waits to fight a wrongdoing, the harder it is to defeat it.

A man once planted a bramblebush in the middle of the road. The passersby reproached him and repeatedly told him to dig it up, but he did not do so.

And every moment that bramblebush was getting larger. Its thorns tore the people's clothes and wounded their feet.

The governor told the man to dig the bush up, and he answered, "Yes, I will dig it up someday."

For a long while he promised to do it tomorrow and tomorrow, and meanwhile his bramblebush grew firm and robust.

The governor said to him one day, "O promise-breaker, come do what you said you would do."

But the man replied, "The bush is too large now, and I no longer have the strength."

The governor said, "You who say 'Tomorrow,' learn you this, that in every day which time brings, that evil tree grows younger, and he who should dig it up grows older. The bramblebush every moment grows green and fresh, while the proposed digger becomes more helpless and withered. Be quick, therefore, and do not waste your time."

Consider the bramblebush as any bad habit of yours. Its thorns at last will wound your feet.

🐌 Acknowledgments

For permission to reprint copyrighted material, grateful acknowledgment is made to the following publishers, authors, and agents:

"The Rich Man's Feast" reprinted from *Cold Mountain,* by Han-shan, translated by Burton Watson, 1962, 1970, © Columbia University Press, New York. Reprinted with permission of the publisher.

"F. Scott Fitzgerald to His Daughter" reprinted from *F. Scott Fitzgerald: The Crackup.* Copyright 1945 by New Directions Publishing Corp. Reprinted by permission of New Directions Publishing Corp.

"Childhood and Poetry" by Pablo Neruda reprinted from *Neruda and Vallejo: Selected Poems,* edited by Robert Bly, Beacon Press, Boston, 1971, copyright 1971 by Robert Bly. Reprinted with his permission.

"Kill Devil Hill" reprinted from *Kill Devil Hill: Discovering the Secret of the Wright Brothers* by Harry Combs (Houghton Mifflin Company/TernStyle Press, Ltd.). Courtesy of the author.

"Excerpt from the Diary of Anne Frank" reprinted from *Anne Frank: The Diary of a Young Girl,* by Anne Frank. Copyright 1952 by Otto H. Frank. Used by permission of Doubleday, a division of Bantam Doubleday Dell Publishing Group, Inc.

♊ Index